S0-DQY-018

Conan drew back as far as the hall would allow. When he plunged forward, he was like an avalanche on a steep slope. The bolt was made to resist common men, not Cimmerians of Conan's size and strength. The bolt snapped like a twig and the door crashed open.

Conan flew into the room, nearly stumbling over Illyana, who knelt at the foot of the bed. She clutched the bedclothes with both hands and had a corner of the blanket stuffed into her mouth.

She wore only the Jewel of Khurag in its ring on her left arm. The Jewel seared Conan's eyes with emerald flame.

"Don't touch her!" Raihna cried.

"She needs help!"

"You will hurt, not help, if you touch her now!"

Conan hesitated, torn between desire to help someone clearly suffering and trust in Raihna's judgment. Illyana settled the question by slumping into a faint. As she fell senseless, the flame in the Jewel died.

The Adventures of Conan
published by Tor Books

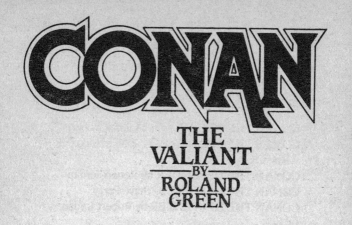

CONAN

THE VALIANT

BY

ROLAND
GREEN

A TOM DOHERTY ASSOCIATES BOOK
NEW YORK

CONAN THE VALIANT

Copyright © 1988 by Conan Properties, Inc.

A TOR Book
Published by Tom Doherty Associates, Inc.
49 West 24 Street
New York, NY 10010

Cover art by Ken Kelly

ISBN: 0-812- 50082-2   Can. ISBN: 0-812-50083-0

Library of Congress Catalog Card Number: 88-50472

First edition: October 1988
First mass market edition: August 1989

Printed in the United States of America

0 9 8 7 6 5 4 3 2 1

To L. Sprague and Catherine de Camp, with respect and gratitude, and with special thanks to the Guild of Exotic Dancers of the Middle Kingdom of the Society for Creative Anachronism, Incorporated.

Prologue

SUNSET TINTED GOLD and crimson the snows of the Lord of the Winds, monarch of the Ibars Mountains. Twilight had already swallowed its lower slopes, while night shrouded the valleys.

Bora, son of Rhafi, lay behind a boulder and studied the valleys before him. Three stretched away from the foot of the Lord, like the spokes of a cartwheel. Mist rose from all. Had he been citybred, given to such fancies, Bora might have discerned monstrous shapes already forming out of the mist.

Instead, Bora's family had been shepherds and wolf-hunters in the village of Crimson Springs, when the forebears of King Yildiz of Turan were petty lordlings. These mountains held no strangeness for him.

Or rather, they had not, until two moons before. Then the tales began. In one valley, the mists turned green each night. Those who ventured into the valley to see why did not return, except for one who returned mad, babbling of demons unleashed.

1

Then people began to disappear. Children at first—a girl filling water jugs by a lonely stream, a shepherd boy taking food to his father in the pasture, a baby snatched while his mother bathed. Never was there any trace of the reavers, save for a foul stench that made the dogs turn away howling and sometimes a footprint that might have been human, if humans had claws a finger long.

Then grown men and women began to vanish. No village was spared, until people dared not leave their houses after dark and went about even in daylight in stout, armed bands. It was said that caravans struggling over the passes and even patrols of Yildiz's soldiers had lost men.

Mughra Khan, Yildiz's military governor, heard the tales but doubted them, at least where the villages were concerned. He saw nothing but rebellion looming and his duty clear: to put it down.

He was not such a fool as to arrest men at random and try to persuade the Seventeen Attendants that they were rebels. The Seventeen were not fools either. Mughra Khan strengthened his outposts, arrested the few men who protested, and waited for the rebels to either strike or skulk back into their lairs.

Neither rebels nor anything else human did either. But entire outposts began to disappear. Sometimes a few bodies remained behind, gutted like sheep, beheaded, dismembered by more than human strength. Once, two men reached safety—one dying, both mad and babbling of demons.

This time, the tales of demons were believed.

Of course Mughra Khan continued to believe in rebels as well. He saw no reason why both could not be menacing the peace and order of Turan. Messengers rode posthaste to Aghrapur, with requests for advice and aid.

What fate those messengers might meet, Bora did not know, and hardly cared. He was more concerned about the fate of his father, Rahfi. Rahfi accused some soldiers of stealing his sheep. The next day the soldiers' comrades arrested him as "a suspected rebel."

What fate suspected rebels might meet, Bora knew too well. He also knew that pardons often came to those whose kin had well served Turan. If he learned the secret of the demon reavers, might that not procure his father's release?

It would be good if Rahfi could be home in time to attend his daughter Arima's wedding. Though not as fair as her younger sister Caraya, Arima would bear the carpenter of Last Tree many fine sons, with Mitra's favor.

Bora shifted slightly, without dislodging so much as a pebble. It might be a long wait, studying these nighted valleys.

Master Eremius made a peremptory gesture. The servant scurried forward, holding the ornately-shaped chased silver vials of blood in either hand. Thos hands were filthy, Eremius noted.

Eremius snatched the vials from the servant and plunged them into the silk pouch hanging from his belt of crimson leather. Then he struck the rock at his feet with his staff and threw up his left hand, palm outward. The rock opened. Water gushed, lifting the servant off his feet, then casting him down, gasping and whimpering for mercy. Eremius let the water flow until the servant was as clean in person and garments as was possible without flaying him.

"Let that be a lesson to you," Eremius said.

"It is a lesson, Master," the man gasped, and departed faster than he had come.

The wet rock slowed Eremius not at all as he descended into the valley. His long-toed feet were bare and hard as leather, seeking and finding safe holds without the least spell bringing light. At the foot of the path two more servants stood holding torches. The torches were of common rushes, but burned with a rubicund light and a hissing like angry serpents.

"All is well, Master."

"So be it."

They followed him as he climbed the other side of the valley to the Altar of Transformation. He wished to arrive in time to correct whatever was not indeed well. The assurances of his servants told him little, except that the Altar had not been carried away by vultures or any of tonight's Transformations escaped.

Ah, would that Illyana was still friend and ally, or that he had snatched the other Jewel of Kurag from her before she fled! Then it would have mattered little whether she escaped or not. Before she found any way to oppose him, the twin Jewels would have given him irresistible power, both in his own right and through human allies.

Eremius nearly thought a curse upon Illyana. He quickly banished the impulse. The magic he used in a Transformation was unforgiving of anything less than total concentration. Once, he had sneezed in the middle of a Transformation and found its subject leaping from the Altar, partly transformed and wholly beyond his control. He had to summon other Transformations to slay it.

The Altar seemed part of the hillside itself, as in truth it was. Eremius had conjured it into being out of the very rock, a seamless slab as high as a man's waist and twelve paces on a side. Around the edge of the slab ran in high relief the runes of a powerful warding spell.

Like the runes on the great golden ring on Eremius's left forearm, these runes were an ancient Vanir translation of a still more ancient Atlantean text. Even among sorcerers, few knew of these or any of the other spells concerning the Jewels of Kurag. Many doubted the very existence of the spells.

Eremius found this to his advantage. What few believe in, fewer still will seek.

He stepped up to the Altar and contemplated the Transformation. She was a young village woman, fully of marriageable age and exceedingly comely, had Eremius been concerned about such things. The whole of her clothing was a silver ring about her roughly-cropped dark hair and silver chains about her wrists and ankles. The chains held her spread-eagled on the slab, but not so tightly that she could not writhe from side to side in an obscene parody of passion. In spite of the night chill, sweat glazed her upthrust breasts and trickled down her thighs. Her eyes held shifting tints that made them look now ebony dark, now silver gray, then the fiery tint of a cat's eyes seen by firelight.

Indeed, all seemed well. Certainly there was nothing to be gained by waiting. Eight more Transformations awaited him tonight, nine more recruits for his army.

Soon he could bargain from strength, with the ambitious or the discontented at the court of Turan. No court ever lacked for such, and the court of Turan had more than most. Once they were his allies, he could set them in search of the other Jewel. Illyana could not hide forever.

Then the twin Jewels would be his, and bargaining at

an end. It would be time for him to command and for the world to obey.

He raised his left hand and began to chant. As he chanted, the Jewel began to glow. Above the Altar the mists took on an emerald hue.

Bora's breath hissed between his teeth. The mist in the westernmost valley was turning green. It was also the nearest valley. In daylight he could have reached it in an hour, for he was as keen-sighted by night as by day. Tonight, speed was not his goal. Stealth was what he needed, for he was a wolf seeking prey—an odd fate for a shepherd, but Mitra would send what Mitra chose.

Bora sat up and unwrapped the sling from around his waist. In the dry mountain air, the cords and leather cup had not stretched. In the mist-shrouded valley, it might have been otherwise; still, he could face anything but heavy rain. He had practiced almost daily with the sling, ever since he was no taller than it was long.

From a goatskin pouch he drew a piece of dry cheese and five stones. Since he was fourteen, Bora could tell the weight and balance of a stone by tossing it thrice in either hand. He had studied and chosen these five stones as carefully as if he were going to wed them.

His fingers told him that none of the stones were chipped. One by one he eased them back into the pouch, along with the last crumb of cheese. Then he tied the pouch back at his waist, picked up his staff, and started down the mountain.

It was no marvel that the mist turned the color of emeralds. The light pouring from the great stone in the ring was of such a hue. The stone itself might have been taken for an emerald the size of a baby's fist. Some men had done so. Two had been thieves; both would have preferred King Yildiz's executioners to what actually befell them.

Whether the Jewels of Kurag were natural or creations of sorcery, no living man knew. That secret lay beneath the waves, among the coral-armored ruins of Atlantis. For Master Eremius, it was enough to know the secrets of the Jewels' powers.

He chanted the first spell in a high-pitched singsong that might have been mistaken for the tongue of Khitai. As he chanted, he felt the vials of blood grow warm against his skin, then cool again. Their preservation spells were set aside. Now to make them his instruments of Transformation.

He set the first vial on the Altar beside the young woman. The herb-steeped cloth forced into her mouth had sapped her will but not destroyed it. Her eyes rolled back, wide with terror, as she saw the blood in the vial begin to glow. A faint moan forced its way through the cloth.

Eremius chanted three guttural monosyllables, and the lid of the vial flew into the air. He struck the Altar, five times with his staff, and chanted the same syllables twice more.

The vial floated into the air and drifted over the girl. Eremius' staff rose like an asp ready to strike. The light from the Jewel became a single beam, bright enough to dazzle any mortal eye unshielded by magic.

With a flick of his wrist, Eremius directed the beam straight at the vial. It quivered, then overturned. The blood rained down on the girl, weaving a pattern like silver lace across her skin. Her eyes were now wider than ever, but no thought now lay behind them.

Holding his staff level, Eremius passed it and the beam of light over the girl's body, from head to toe. Then he stepped back, licked his dry lips, and watched the Transformation.

The girl's skin turned dark and thick, then changed into scales, overlapping like plates of fine armor. Great pads of muscle and bone grew across her joints. Her feet and hands grew hard edges, then ridged backs, and claws a finger long.

The spell did not alter the structure of the face as much as the rest of the body. Scaly skin, pointed ears, pointed teeth, and eyes like a cat's still turned it into a grotesque parody of humanity.

At last, only the eyes moved in what had been a woman. Eremius made another pass with his staff alone, and the chains fell from wrists and ankles. The creature rose uncertainly to its hands and knees, then bowed its head to Eremius. Without hesitation or revulsion, he laid his hand upon the head. The hair fell away like dust, and the silver ring clattered upon the stone.

Another Transformation was accomplished.

From the darkness beyond the Altar stalked three more of the Transformed. Two had been purchased as slaves, one a captured caravan guard; all had been men. It was Eremius's experience that women fit for a Transformation were seldom found unguarded. Girls to yield up their blood for the Transformation of others were easier to come by.

The three Transformed lifted their new comrade to her feet. With a wordless snarl she shook off their hands. One of them cuffed her sharply across the cheek. She bared her teeth. For a moment Eremius feared he might have to intervene.

Then a familiar recognition filled the new

Transformed's eyes. She knew that for better or for worse, these beings were her chosen comrades in the service of Master Eremius. She could not deny them. Whatever she had worshipped before, she now worshipped only Eremius, Lord of the Jewel.

Eyes much less keen than Bora's could have made out the sentries at the head of the valley. Although no soldier, he still knew that they would bar entry that way. Nor was he surprised. The master of the demon light in the valley would not be hospitable to visitors.

With sure, steady paces, Bora passed along the ridge to the south of the valley. He reached a point halfway between the mouth and the source of the light. It seemed to lie in the open, not within one of the caves that honeycombed the valley's walls.

Below Bora's feet now lay a cliff two hundred paces high and steep enough to daunt the boldest of goats. It was not enough to daunt Bora. "You have eyes in your fingers and toes," they said of him in the village, for he could climb where no one else could.

To be sure, he had never climbed such a cliff in the dark, but never had he hoped to win so much or had so little to lose. The family of a convicted rebel would be fortunate indeed if Mughra Khan did no worse than to exile them.

Bora studied the cliff as far as he could see, picking out the first part of his route. Then he lowered himself over the edge and began his descent.

By the time he was halfway down, his hands were sweating and all his limbs had begun to tremble. He knew he should not be so tired so soon. Was the sorcery of the light-maker sapping his strength?

He drove the thought away. It could only bring fear, which would sap his strength and wits alike. He found a foothold, shifting first his right and then his left foot to it, then sought the next.

Below, the emerald light came and went. It now seemed to be a beam, like a lantern's. When it shone, he thought he saw dim figures in a ragged circle. Their form seemed other than human, but that might be the mist.

At last he reached a ledge of rock wide enough for sitting. To the right, toward the light, the cliff plunged straight to the valley floor, and the ledge vanished. Only a bird could find its way down there.

To the left, the slope was much easier. A carrion reek hinted of a lion's den, but lions were hard to rouse at night. Halfway down the slope, a sentry paced back and forth, a short bow on his shoulder and a tulwar in his hand.

Bora unwound the sling from inside his shirt: That sentry had to die. Unless he were deaf, he would hear Bora climbing down behind him. Even if Bora passed him going down, he would be well-placed to cut off retreat.

A stone dropped into the cup. The sling rose and whirred into motion, until no human eye could have seen it. Nor could any human ear more than fifty paces away have heard its sound.

The sentry was thrice that far. He died between one heartbeat and the next, never knowing what flew out of the night to crush his skull. His tulwar flew out of his hand and clattered down the slope.

Bora stiffened, waiting for some sign that the sentry's comrades might have heard the clatter. Nothing moved but the mist and the emerald light. He crept along the ledge, half-crouching, the loaded sling in one hand.

The carrion reek grew, clawing at his nose and

chest. He took shallow breaths, which helped little. There was more than carrion in that reek. Ordure and filth he dared not name lay behind it. No lion laired here. The thought of sorcery returned, this time not to depart.

Perhaps that thought saved his life by sharpening his ears. He heard the clawed feet on the rocks while their owners were still inside their cave. He was already recoiling when they burst into the open.

There was nothing dim about those shapes, for they shone with their own light. It was the same emerald demon-light that had drawn Bora into the valley. Now it showed monstrous travesties of men—taller, broader, scaled and clawed, their eyes blazing and fanged mouths gaping wide.

They neither spoke nor made any sound as they rushed toward Bora. They did something far worse, reaching into his very thoughts.

Stay a while, lad. Stay a while, and have the honor of serving us who serve the Master. Stay, stay.

Bora knew that if he obeyed for even a moment, he would lose the will to leave. Then he would indeed serve the servants of the Master, as the lamb serves the wolf.

His sling moved as if his arm had its own will. The being's skull was of more than human thickness, but then, the range was short. The stone drove in deep above the right eye, flinging the being into the arms of the one behind it. They toppled together.

The rearmost leaped over his fallen comrades. Bora felt his will attacked once more:

Obey me, or lose pleasures and treasures undreamed of by those who do not serve the Master.

In truth, Bora had never dreamed that being eaten alive could be a pleasure. He saw no cause to think otherwise now. His feet and hands carried him up the cliff as if they were wings.

The being hissed like a snake. Raw rage tore at Bora's mind. Almost, his fingers abandoned their search for holds.

The being leaped high, its clawed hands searching for Bora's ankles, its clawed feet scrabbling for a hold. It found neither. The being slid down, overbalanced, and toppled backward off the ledge. A final desperate hiss ended in a thud and the sliding of a body on stone.

Bora did not stop, and barely breathed until he reached level ground. Even then, he only stopped long enough to reload his sling. He had heard in tales the words "as if demons were after him." Now he knew their meaning far too well.

If he lived to return home and find anyone to believe his tale, he would have the secret of the mountain demons.

Unseen behind him, the beam of emerald light abruptly died.

When Eremius stood at the Altar, he closed his ears. He remained deaf to the falling tulwar. Only the call of the Transformed reached him, appealing to whomever they saw before them. Their appeal, then the death cries of first one, then the second.

Eremius shivered as if he were standing naked in the wind from a glacier. The syllables of the Transformation Spell grew muddled. On the slab, the nearly-complete Transformed writhed. Muscles writhed and heaved, strengthened by magic and driven by madness.

The ankle chains snapped first. Flying links scattered like sling stones. The Transformed rolled, freeing first one wrist, and then the other. It was on its hands and knees when Eremius launched his staff like a spear, smiting the Transformed across the forehead.

Eremius flinched at the cry in his mind. The Transformed sprang to its feet in one convulsion, then toppled off the Altar. It rolled over on its back, kicking and writhing. Then its outlines softened, as scales and claws, muscle and bone sagged into red- and green-streaked jelly. The jelly turned to liquid, and the liquid sank into the rock, leaving a greenish-black stain. Even with his human senses dulled, Eremius gagged at the stench.

He turned from the Altar, letting his arms fall to his sides. His concentration was broken, his spells uncontrolled, the night's Transformations ended.

A captain of sentries hurried forward and knelt. "Revered Master, Kuris has been found slain. A stone fell from the cliff and struck him on the head. Two of the Transformed are also slain, one by another stone and the other by a fall."

"A stone—?" Rage and contempt drove Eremius beyond speech. Those dead Transformed were pursuing some intruder when they died. One now probably beyond reach, thanks to this witling's blindness.

The staff came down on the captain's shoulders, twice on each side. He only flinched. Unless Eremius willed it so, the staff held no magic. The captain would still have bruises.

"Go!"

Alone, Eremius raised both hands to the sky and shrieked curses. He cursed the sorcerers of ancient Atlantis, who found or made the Jewels of Kurag so strong together and so weak apart. He cursed the weakness of his Jewel, that forced him to use such human servants. If they were not witlings by nature, they had to be made such lest they escape his control.

Above and beyond all else, he cursed Illyana. Had she been more loyal to him, or less shrewd in her escape—

Such thoughts were as futile now as ever. Bossonia was ten years gone and as unchangeable as the Ibars Mountains. It was the future that held hope—hope of human allies, who might still crown his quest with victory.

Bora stalked out of the gray dawn and into Crimson Springs before anyone was awake to see him. Before his own house, he stopped. Did he hear the sound of lamentation from within?

He knocked. The door opened a crack. His sister Caraya appeared. Red eyes and a puffy, tear-streaked face marred her beauty.

"Bora! Where have you been?"

"In the mountains. Caraya, what is it? Have they executed—?"

"No, no! It is not Father. It is Arima. The demons took her!"

"The demons—"

"Bora, have you been out all night? I said, the demons took Arima!" Suddenly she was pressing her face into his shoulder, weeping again.

He patted her hair awkwardly and tried to urge her inside. It finally took both him and Yakoub: Bora helped her to a chair, while Yakoub shut the door. From the other room, the sound of lamentation began again.

"Your mother mourns," Yakoub said. "The other children—the neighbors have taken them in."

"Who are you, to play host in this house?" Bora asked. He had never quite trusted Yakoub, who was too handsome and too clearly city-bred, although a good man with the stock. He had come to Crimson Springs two years before, speaking of enemies in Aghrapur. His skill with the animals had made him welcome enough, and not only in Crimson Springs. Nor had he gone against the customs of his hosts.

"Who are you, to turn away help?" Caraya snapped. "Will you play master in this house, if it takes bread from the mouths of your kin?"

Bora raised his hands, feeling more helpless than usual in the face of his sister's tongue. It was not the first time he agreed with Iskop the Smith, who said that Caraya's tongue was deadlier than any weapon he had ever forged.

"Forgive me, Cara. I—I have not slept this night, and my wits are dulled."

"You look weary," Yakoub said. He grinned. "I hope she was worth it."

"If you spent the night with—" began Caraya, her voice tight with rage.

"I spent the night learning the secret of the demons," Bora snarled.

After that he lacked no attention. Caraya heated water and wiped his face, hands, and feet while Yakoub listened intently.

"This is not easy to believe," Yakoub said finally.

Bora nearly choked on a mouthful of bread. "Are you calling me a liar?"

"Nothing of the kind. I but state an important truth. What good does it do you to have seen this, if no one believes you?"

Bora felt ready to weep. He had thought of that as he left the valley, but had somehow forgotten it during the long walk home.

"Do not fear. I—I do not know if I have friends in Aghrapur, after two years. I am sure that my enemies will have enemies, who may listen to me. May I bear word of this to the city?"

Bora gathered his wits. He still did not wholly trust Yakoub. Yet who with the power to send the army into that demon-haunted valley would believe the son of a suspected rebel? A city–bred man with knowledge of Aghrapur the Mighty's mightier intrigues might be heard.

"By the bread and the salt I have eaten in this house," Yakoub said, "by Erlik and Mitra, and by my love for your sister Caraya—"

Again Bora nearly choked. He stared at Caraya. She smiled defiantly. Bora groaned.

"Forgive me," Yakoub said. "I could not make an offer for Caraya until Arima was wed. Now you are a troubled house, in mourning. I will wait until I return from—wherever I must go, to find those who will believe. I swear to do nothing to dishonor the name of the House of Rahfi, and to do everything to secure his release and your reward. Has it struck you, Bora, that you are blessedly lucky to be alive and sane?"

The only reply was a snore. Bora had fallen asleep on the rug, with his back pressed against the wall.

One

AGHRAPUR BEARS MANY names. Some are fit to be written down. Among these are "Aghrapur the Mighty," "Aghrapur the Splendid," and "Aghrapur the Wealthy." None is a lie, but none is the whole truth, either.

Among men who know this royal city well, one name is thought the most truthful. It is a translation from the tongue of Khitai, for the man who first uttered it was a Khitan. He called Aghrapur "The City Where Anything That Cannot Be Found Does Not Exist Under Heaven."

An unwieldy name, as even its inventor admitted. But also the most truthful name ever given to Aghrapur.

The sun was long down, although the warmth of the day still clung to the stones and tiles. Those who could strolled in their courtyards or opened shutters to catch the breeze from the Vilayet Sea. Few were on the streets, save for the watch or those who had urgent business.

Much of that urgent business was less than lawful. Anything that could be found in Aghrapur could be found by day or by night, but if it was unlawful, it was easier to find it by night.

The captain of mercenaries, known as Conan the Cimmerian, sought nothing unlawful as he loped through the dark streets. He sought only a tavern called the Red Falcon, some of its best wine, a meal, and a wench for the night. Among them, they should take away the sour taste of the day's work.

To himself, Conan admitted that High Captain Khadjar had the right of it, when he said, "Just because you travel to Khitai and escort royal ladies doesn't mean your stones are rubies. You've a company to train. That means taking your share of the new recruits."

"Is a full score of witlings, ploughboys, and thieves really my share, Captain?"

"If you think yours are witlings, talk to Itzhak." Khadjar pushed the wine jug across the table to Conan. "By Black Erlik's beard, Conan, I show my trust in you! I know no captain twice your age who could knock more sense into recruits in less time. You owe it to those poor wretches to teach them what will keep them alive in the face of a Kozaki charge or an Iranistani ambush! Now drink up, hold your tongue, and go pay your debt."

Conan obeyed. He owed Khadjar not only obedience but respect, even when the Captain spoke as if Conan himself were but a recruit. It was Khadjar who had urged his promotion, put him forward for the secret journeys that made his name, and taught him much of what he knew about civilized warfare.

Cimmeria did not breed men who gave their loyalty easily. Its chiefs led by their own prowess and by the consent of the warriors who chose to follow them. Only the valor of those warriors and the remoteness and harsh climate of Cimmeria had kept it free of the rule of some more disciplined race. Cimmeria also did not breed fools who refused loyalty where it was deserved and earned. Khadjar had earned Conan's loyalty, but there was an end to it—for all that, Conan took as much pleasure in drilling recruits as he did in cleaning stables.

The Red Falcon stood near the top of the Street of the Twelve Steps, on the Hill of Madan. Conan climbed the hill with the ease of a hillman on a slope and the sinewy grace of a panther on the prowl. His eyes never ceased to roam from shadowed doorway to alley to rooftop, seeking lurkers. Twice he saw them; each time they let him pass. Robbers might take their chances with the watch; only fools challenged a man they could neither slay nor flee.

Conan's rank would have entitled him to a palanquin, but he never used them, save for when duty required it. He trusted neither the legs nor the tongues of slaves. Besides, he had been a slave himself on the winding road that brought him to Aghrapur.

A patrol of the watch trotted out of the shadows.

"Evening, Captain. Have you seen any trouble abroad?"

"None."

Another profession Conan had followed was that of thief. Thief-catchers, he believed, should do their own searching.

The patrol tramped off. Conan took the stairs at the Eleventh Step in two bounds, splashed water from a fountain on his hands and face, then turned in at the door of the Red Falcon.

"Ho, Conan! You look like a man who lost gold and found brass!"

"Moti, you've drunk too much of your own camel sweat to see anything clearly. Have you never spent a day breaking in new recruits?"

The scarred former sergeant of cavalry grinned. "Enough so that I pray to be an officer in my next life as a soldier."

Conan crossed the room, skirting the center where a pale-skinned Iranistani girl danced to tambourine and drum. She wore only a black silk loinguard, a belt of copper coins, and a shimmering coat of jasmine-scented oil. The rythmic swirling of her hips seemed about to divest her of even these scant garments. Watching her appreciatively, Conan noticed that the nipples of her firm young breasts were rouged. She also seemed able to move those breasts independently of one another.

Moti thrust a massive silver cup in the Vanir style at Conan. It came to the Red Falcon as a pledge for its owner's debt, which he never returned to pay. He was bones bleaching on the Hyrkanian shore, and the cup was Conan's when he drank at the Red Falcon.

"To worthy opponents," Conan said, lifting the cup. Then he pointed at the girl. "New, isn't she?"

"What of our Pyla, Conan?"

"Well, if she's free—"

"I am *never* free," came a cheerful voice from the stairs. "You know my price, and stop trying to beat it down, you son of a Cimmerian bog-troll!"

"Ah, the beautiful Pyla, as gracious as ever," Conan said. He raised his cup to the raven-haired woman swaying down the stairs. She wore crimson silk pantaloons and carved mother-of-pearl plates over her breasts. Only the ripe curves of those breasts hinted that she was any older than the girl.

"I hardly know why I am gracious, either," Pyla said, with a mock pout. "Everyone insults me, claiming that I am worth no more than a wharfside trull."

"You are worth more, of course," Moti said. "But not as much as you think. Indeed, you would be far richer if you charged much less. I doubt not that thinking of your price unmans half of those who would otherwise knock on your door—"

Moti broke off as five men entered from the street. Four wore leather tunics and trousers, with mail glinting at throats and wrists. Their heavy bronze-studded belts carried swords and short clubs.

The fifth man also wore tunic and trousers, but his were dark green silk, richly embroidered in gold. Gold likewise covered the hilt of his sword. Conan dismissed the party as some young nobleman and his bodyguards, wandering the city in search of pleasure. He doubted they would spoil an honest soldier's drinking if they did not overstay their welcome.

Moti and Pyla seemed to think otherwise. Pyla vanished like smoke, and when Conan turned around it seemed she had taken the dancing girl with her. Moti pulled out his own cure for unruly customers, a shipyard maul that even Conan needed two hands to swing easily. Then he poured wine into Conan's cup until it slopped over the edge.

Very surely the five were not what they seemed to Conan. Just as surely, nothing short of torture would loosen Moti's tongue. Conan moved until he could see the whole room while he spoke to Moti, then drank until the cup no longer overflowed.

"You said you hoped to be an officer the next time?," he prompted the innkeeper.

"If I remember what I learned this time, yes. Otherwise, small honor in being like him." Moti made a silent and subtle gesture at the silk-clad man.

"Best hope you serve under High Captain Khadjar in *his* next life," Conan said. "He could teach a shark or a hyena."

"I thought he was the one who had you sweating the recruits."

"So he is. He says it's a compliment. Perhaps it is." Conan drank again. "Is there food to be had tonight? Or has your cook been carried off by demons? I'll not take kindly to gnawing oats with your horses—"

As if in answer, Pyla and the Iranistani appeared with loaded trays for the newcomers. Conan saw that both wore loose, nearly opaque robes covering them from throat to ankles, and did not take their eyes off the five men. Neither did Moti, until they were served. Without moving more than his hand, Conan made sure that his sword rested lightly in its scabbard.

"There is no 'perhaps' about it," Moti said. "Conan, if Khadjar thinks you worth teaching, the gods have been generous. Too generous to an outlander, by my way of thinking."

"Yes, yes, O son of a Vendhyan dancing girl," Conan replied. Moti's voice was as brittle as an ill-tempered sword. A sense of danger crept up the Cimmerian's spine like a spider.

"My mother was the greatest dancer of her day," Moti said, "as Khadjar is the greatest soldier of ours." He looked at Conan. "You are—how old?"

"By the Turanian reckoning, twenty-two."

"Ha. The same age as Khadjar's bastard son. Or the age he would have been, had he not died two years ago.

Perhaps Khadjar seeks another son in you. He had no other kin and few friends, save for the boy. It was said, too, that the boy—"

The door opened and a woman entered. She could hardly have drawn more eyes had she risen from the floor in a cloud of crimson smoke, to the blare of trumpets.

She was tall and of a northern fairness, with wide gray eyes and scattered freckles under a tan. In age she was clearly a woman rather than a girl, and her figure could contest honors with Pyla's. Conan's eyes followed the line of her thigh up to the slender waist, then marched across the breasts that strained the brown woolen tunic and rested on the long fine neck.

When he had done this, he saw that the eyes of every other man in the room had marched with his.

The woman took no notice. She strode across the room with a grace that few dancers could have equalled. The men's eyes followed her, but they might have been the eyes of mice for all she seemed to care. Conan doubted that this woman would have broken stride crossing the room even if she had been as bare as a babe.

She reached the bar and said, in accented Turanian, "Honorable Motilal, I would have business with you." Bawdy laughter rippled around the room. She went on, as if blushing was beneath her. "I would buy a jug of wine, bread, cheese, and smoked meat. Any you have ready will do, even horse—"

"Do not insult Moti by thinking he serves horsemeat, good lady," Conan said. "If your purse is somewhat scant . . ."

The woman's smile did not reach her eyes. "And how am I to repay you?"

"By drinking some of that wine with me, no more."

This woman looked like a goddess in disguise, and could hardly be given to sporting with Cimmerian mercenary officers. She would give no pleasure save to his eyes, but that would be enough.

"If your purse is empty, girl, we can fill it before dawn," a bodyguard said. His comrades joined in the bawdy laughter. Few others did, least of all Conan. They saw the ice in the woman's eyes.

Moti struck the bar with the handle of his maul. The drummer pulled his drums into his lap and began pounding out a sensuous Zamoran beat. "Pyla! Zaria!" Moti shouted. "To work!"

The women whirled onto the floor. The shouting and clapping rose, until the drummer was sweating to make himself heard. First Pyla, then Zaria, threw off their robes. The man in green silk drew his sword and caught Zaria's on the point, without taking his eyes off the northern woman.

Conan considered the man anew. A fop he might be, but likely enough a dangerous one.

A kitchen girl appeared with a rush basket of food and a jug of fine Aquilonian wine. Moti handed them to the woman, counted the coins she drew from inside her belt, then slapped the girl on the rump.

"No more cooking tonight, Thebia. Dancers are what we need!"

In spite of the din, Conan heard in Moti's voice the tone of a man ordering a rearguard to stand and die. The tickling spider-legs of danger on Conan's spine became sharp hooves. Two years ago he would have drawn his sword.

Pyla cast aside her breast plates. They clattered to the floor amid cheers, as the northern woman turned for the door. Conan followed her with his eyes, and saw that the silk-clad man was doing the same. Pyla, Zaria,

and Thebia might have been carrion birds pecking at
ox bones for all he saw of them.

The woman could avoid the dancers only by passing
close to her watcher and his guards. The man saw that
in the same moment as Conan. His fingers did a dance
of their own. Conan had taken two steps when one of
the guards thrust a thick leg into the woman's path.

In the next moment Conan knew she was a warrior.
She dropped both jug and basket to free her hands and
save her balance. When she knew that her balance was
lost, she twisted in midair and crashed down with both
hands free. Rolling, she drew a dagger from one boot
and uncoiled like a snake.

The lordling leaped from his chair, one hand on his
sword hilt and the other held out in what Conan much
doubted was friendship. As his guards also rose, the
woman gripped the lordling's hand, then held on as
she twisted again. The man's pearl-sewn shoes were no
aid on the wine-slick floor. He sat down with a thump.

Conan was now close enough to hear the woman
say, "Forgive me, my lord. I only wished—" Two of the
guards turned toward him. Conan's instinct to draw
his sword seethed and bubbled beneath a skin of
civilization.

The lordling contemplated the ruby stains on his
clothes, then he contemplated the woman. His voice
rose to a screech. "She attacked me! My clothes are
ruined! Do your duty!"

The woman had her back to one of the guards. As his
comrades drew swords, he drew a club. It came down
to meet the flat of Conan's out-thrust sword. Conan's
massive right arm easily held the sword, as the club
slid down to strike the woman a glancing blow to her
shoulder, instead of a stunning one to her head.

The woman rolled again, giving Conan fighting

room. For a moment he had no need of it. The lordling
and his guards seemed bemused at being opposed.
Conan shot a quick glance at Moti. Sweat streamed
from the innkeeper, and his white–knuckled hands
gripped the handle of the maul.

Conan much doubted that he would drink again at
the Red Falcon. The lordling had put Moti in such fear
that he would see an honest customer attacked. Conan
would call no man a coward without proof, but neither
would he be bound by his host's fears.

"This woman no more attacked you than a she-
mouse," Conan growled. "If we're to talk of attacks,
what about that great barge of a foot I saw thrust at
her?"

The woman unwisely turned to smile at Conan. One
guard had recovered his wits. His sword rasped free,
thrusting clumsily but hard at the woman. She
whirled, enough so that steel intended to pierce her
belly only raked her ribs. A red stain spread across the
side of her tunic.

The guard nearest to Conan owed his life to the
Cimmerian's scruples about cutting down a man who
had not yet drawn. A stool, flung like a stone from a
catapult, took the guard's legs out from under him.
Conan's boot crashed into his ribs, then into his belly.
The guard doubled up, trying to spew and breathe and
scream all at the same time with precious little success.

By now, more than half of Moti's customers had
recalled urgent business elsewhere. One guard retreated among the empty tables and benches. Two
others and their master charged Conan, staying close
together rather than spreading out. They also took
their eyes off the woman.

Bloody ribs and all, the woman sprang onto a vacant

table. The closest guard turned on her, his sword snaking toward her thigh.

"Don't kill her, you fool!" the lordling screamed.

The guard's reply was hardly respectful. Conan knew a moment's sympathy for the man. No order could be harder to obey than to take a she-lion alive. No man but a fool gave it, save for better cause than wounded vanity.

The woman drew a second dagger from her boot, then sprang down. She landed so close to the guard that he lacked room to use his sword. Before he could open the distance she locked his sword arm with one dagger, then thrust the point of the other up under his chin. His outraged scream turned into a gurgle as blood sprayed from his nose and mouth.

"Look out, woman! Behind you!"

The guard who had retreated was advancing as his dead comrade took all the woman's attention. Conan could only shout a warning. The lordling and one guard were coming at him. Both seemed to know the curved Turanian sword well enough to demand the Cimmerian's full attention. Greater speed and longer reach could too easily be set at naught by ill-luck.

His warning to the woman might still have been too late. By the gods' favor, the guard tried to obey his lord's orders to take the woman alive. He closed and grappled her from behind, one arm around her throat, one gripping her right arm. She wriggled like an eel, trying to stab backward. His mail turned away one dagger, and he hammered her wrist against the edge of a table until she dropped the other.

Conan's own fight of two against one would have been easier if the three women of the Red Falcon hadn't gone on dancing. They had no one to dance for now, or at least none with eyes to spare for them save

for Moti behind the bar and the drummer on his stool.
Pyla and Zaria were now wholly nude. The kitchen girl
Thebia was bare to the waist. Her skirt slid farther
down her thighs with each wriggle of her hips. They
had been commanded to dance, and would do so until
the command came to stop.

"Crom, women! Either give me room or give me
help!"

Suddenly the girl's skirt slipped its moorings, slid to
the floor, and tangled around her feet. She stumbled
and would have fallen, save that she stumbled against
the lordling. He thrust her back savagely, forgetting
that his free hand now held a dagger. The keen edge
scored a long, bloody furrow across her thigh.

She gave a high, shrill wail, clapping one hand to the
wound while she cast the skirt wholly aside with the
other. This drew the lordling's attention again, a
mistake for which his guards paid dearly.

Conan closed with the first and slashed his arm off at
the elbow. The second had the woman disarmed and
was discovering that was only half the victory when
Moti charged out from behind the bar. His maul
swung, striking the guard with a glancing blow on the
hip. That broke the guard's grip on the woman, freeing
her to ram an elbow into his throat. The guard reeled
back, clear of another swing of the maul, fell backward
over a chair, and crashed to the floor at the feet
of the drummer. The drummer lifted one of his
drums—Kushite ebony bound with brass—and
slammed it down on the fallen man's head. He lay
still.

"Now, son of more fathers than you could count
with your shoes on—" Conan began.

The lordling looked at Conan as he might have at a
horde of demons, dropped his dagger, and bolted out

the door. The northern woman stayed just long enough to retrieve her daggers, then also vanished into the night. Still nude, Pyla and Zaria set themselves to binding Thebia's wounds, then turned to the guards.

"No doubt the watch will catch him, if she does not," Conan said.

Moti shook his head. He was now as pale as the Iranistani. The maul thudded to the floor, his hands suddenly unable to grip it.

Conan frowned. The expression had made new recruits tremble. Moti turned paler, if such was possible. "Or is our departed friend in the green silk a royal prince or some such?"

"He—he is not far from that," Moti stammered. "He is the son of Lord Houma."

That name was not altogether unknown to Conan. Houma was one of the Seventeen Attendants, a proven soldier and a great partisan of a larger army and an expanded Turanian empire.

"Then he needs to thrash some manners into that little cockerel. That, or else geld him and sell him for a eunuch, to get some profit from him."

"Conan, I had to be sure the matter was past settling peacefully. It—"

"It was past settling peacefully the moment they laid hands on that woman!" Conan growled. "I'll say so to the watch and anyone else who'll listen, up to King Yildiz himself! If Thebia hadn't been attacked, I might be chasing Houma's pretty pimp of a son through the streets now, hoping to finish him off before the woman did!"

Moti drew in breath like a frog. "That was no attack," he said slowly. "She deliberately drew that stroke, so that I would have to fight.

"By Hanuman's stones, girl, I'll have you out on the streets with a name to make you stay there! And you, Pyla! She'd never have thought of it without you. You're no longer—*gkkkhhhh!*"

Conan lifted Moti to the top of the bar, picked up the maul, and held the handle in front of the innkeeper's nose.

"Moti, my former friend and host, you have two choices. I can ram this up your arse sideways and leave you that way to explain tonight's matters to the watch. I can also leave you intact and help explain them, in return for a few favors."

Moti licked his lips. "Favors?"

"Your best room free whenever I want it, with food and wine as well. Not the best wine, I'll allow, but enough for me and any company I keep. Oh, yes—and any woman I entertain doesn't have to pay *you* a single brass piece!"

Moti squalled as if he were already being impaled. Conan's frown and the women's giggles silenced him. He tried to throw up his hands in disgust, but they were shaking too hard to make the gesture convincing.

"Well?"

"As you wish, ruiner of my name and destroyer of my house. May you have much joy in it, before Lord Houma's men burn it over your head."

"Lord Houma may have fewer but wiser men if he tries that," Conan said. "Now, I want a room tonight, and food and wine for—" He looked at the women.

"One," with a nod to Pyla.

"Two," smiling at Zaria.

Thebia grinned and put her hands behind her back. Her young breasts rose, quivering. Conan pointed at her bandaged thigh. "You want to be the third, with that? Oh, very well. I'm no great hand at arguing with women."

"Just as well, then, that our northern friend took herself off," Pyla said. "Otherwise, she might be joining us. I much doubt that even a Cimmerian can do justice to *four!*"

Two

"THAT'S A BOW in your hands, you son of a cull!" Conan snapped. "It's not a snake. It won't bite you. Even if it did, that's not half of what I'll do to you if you don't string it *now*!"

The gangling youth turned the color of the dust underfoot. He looked at the cerulean sky overhead, as if imploring the gods for mercy. Conan drew breath for more advice. The youth swallowed, gripped the bow, and managed to string it, gracelessly but without dropping it again.

One by one, Conan took his recruits through the art of stringing the powerful curved Turanian horsebow. Certainly, some were destined to be midden-sweepers. Others already knew everything that Conan proposed to teach them.

He would not ask how they had learned the bow. Among the mercenaries of Turan, the life of a soldier began the day he took the copper coin of enlistment. What he had been before, no one asked. It was a custom that Conan thought wise, and not only because his own past would not have borne the weight of too much curiosity.

At last Conan spat into the dust and scowled at the men. "Why the gods addled your wits, making you think you could be soldiers, they only know. I don't. So I have to do what King Yildiz pays me for. That's turning you into soldiers, whether you like it or not. Sergeant Garsim! Take them on a run, ten times around the range!"

"You heard the Captain," shouted Garsim, in a voice that could have been heard in King Yildiz's palace. "Run!" He flourished his stick until it whistled, then fell in behind the recruits with a wink to Conan. Although Garsim could have been grandfather to some of the recruits, he could easily outrun any of them.

As the recruits vanished through the gate, Conan sensed someone behind him. Before he could turn, he heard Khadjar's voice.

"You talk to those men as though you have heard your own words from others."

"I have, Captain. Sergeant Nikar said much the same when he was teaching me archery."

"So old Nikar was your instructor? I thought I saw his touch in your draw. What happened to him, by the way?"

"He went home on leave, and never reached it. A band of robbers disappeared that same month. I'd wager Nikar won a fine escort."

"Would you wager on your archery against mine? Five arrows a turn, three turns?"

"Well, Captain—"

"Come, come, oh defender of dancing girls. Did I not hear of your winning free hospitality at the Red Falcon two nights ago? Your purse should be ready to burst with the weight of unspent coin!"

Conan was ready to burst with curiosity, as to how the Captain had learned so much so soon. He only said, "It was no dancing girl I defended, at least at the start. It was a northern woman, and a fine fighter if a trifle overmatched against four."

Khadjar laughed. "Most would be, save yourself. I trust the lady was grateful?"

"Not so a man would notice it," Conan said. He grinned. "The dancing girls were, though. So grateful that I much doubt I am fit to shoot against you."

"Conan, you say a mere three dancing girls have drained your strength? Go back to your hills, then, for Turan is making you old before your time!"

"Take a bow, Captain. Then we shall see who may call whom 'old'."

"As you—Mitra! Who let *her* in?"

Conan whirled at Khadjar's words. The woman from the Red Falcon was striding toward them from the gate. She walked as she had that night, although the gate guards were openly stripping her with their eyes. If her wound hurt, none could have told it from her gait.

She wore the same cut of tunic and trousers, in fine blue linen with vines and trees embroidered in red at the wrists and throat. She also wore a well-sheathed broadsword and a dagger just too short to be called a second sword. A headdress of white silk in the Turanian manner shielded her northern fairness from the sun.

"You look as if you know the wench, Conan," Khadjar said.

"No wench she, Captain. That's the woman from the Red Falcon."

"Oho! Well and good. You learn what brought her

here. *I* shall learn why those camels' bastards at the gate let her in!"

Conan unstrung his bow and waited impassively for the woman's arrival. By the time she was within speaking distance, Khadjar was shouting at the guards.

"He will learn that I showed them this," the woman said calmly. Dark against her freckled palm and long fingers lay an ancient gold coin, cast in the reign of King Ibram two centuries ago. Over Ibram's fork-bearded face were stamped three letters in the Zamoran script.

Such stamped coins were the mark of Mishrak, lord of King Yildiz's spies, and those who went about his business. It did not occur to Conan to doubt the sign, curious as it might be for this woman to be carrying it. Those who disobeyed the command of Mishrak were wise to be far from Aghrapur by sunrise of the next day.

"So Mishrak sent you. Why?"

"To bring you, Captain Conan."

"To bring me where?"

"To Mishrak, of course."

"I see your tongue is as well guarded as ever."

"Give me one reason why it should be otherwise."

Perhaps this woman knew little, which would be much like Mishrak. The spy lord never told any of his servants enough to let them piece together any of his secrets. Whether she knew much or little, she would clearly tell Conan nothing.

At this moment Khadjar returned, in an evil temper. A look at the coin did nothing to soothe him. He growled like a winter-waked bear and jerked a hand toward the gate.

"Go, Conan. Neither of us is the kind of fool to

quarrel with Mishrak. I'll have Garsim finish the day's drill."

"As you wish, Captain. Now, woman, if you'll let me wash and arm myself—"

"Arm yourself as you wish, Captain Conan. Otherwise, Mishrak says that you will lack nothing if you make haste."

"Nothing?" Conan said with a laugh. His eyes ran lightly over a figure that lacked only garb fit to display it properly. Or perhaps lacking all garb would display it best?

The woman blushed. "Nothing that his hospitality can supply."

"I will not be long." No longer than it would take to don mail under his clothes and secrete a few daggers in unexpected places, at any rate.

"Mishrak lies in the Saddlemakers' Quarter," the woman said, as she led Conan out the gate. The Cimmerian was a head and more taller, but found the pace she set no child's play to match. Hillfolk blood in her, perhaps?

In the Coopers' Square Conan started to turn south. The woman planted herself by the fountain, ignoring a cartload of staves that all but ran her down.

"Captain, the Saddlemakers lie to the north."

"Anyone would think you were no stranger to Aghrapur."

"Anyone who thinks would know that a stranger can learn if she meets those willing to teach."

"Then teach me what you learned," Conan growled. The Saddlemakers' Quarter did in truth lie to the north. He'd hoped to lead the woman some distance by devious routes, where none could easily follow or lay ambushes.

If she would not follow where he led, though, there was nothing to do but follow where she led. Otherwise he'd earn her wrath, lose her guidance, fail Mishrak, and thereby earn a wrath more to be feared than any in Turan save perhaps that of King Yildiz.

Besides, any ambush was most likely to come within the rat's warren of the quarter itself. Conan trusted to his sword and mail to make that ambush a most unhappy affair for any who took part, beginning with the woman herself.

"One moment," the woman said. She lifted her headdress, drank from the fountain, then darted into the nearest alley.

Alleys and byways and reeking dark flights of stairs where Conan had to stoop were their road deeper and deeper into the quarter. Conan followed three paces behind and to the right, hand on the hilt of his sword. Eyes and ears searched for signs of danger, meeting only the din of fifty saddlemakers' shops hard at work. Turning leather and wood and metal into saddles made one din. Masters roaring at their apprentices made a second.

Another turn. Conan had a good view now of the woman's dagger. The pommel was a silver-washed iron apple, and the quillions were double, set at right angles to each other. He resolved to ask the woman to show him the dagger's use, if the laws and customs of steel ever allowed.

They came forty paces from the last turn when the attackers swarmed out of an alley to the left and a window to the right.

Conan counted six opponents as his sword leaped into his hand. One was the guard who'd fled the Red Falcon. Odds enough to make the best careful, unless the woman was better than she'd been that night.

Right now she seemed struck witless by fear as the three from the alley closed.

At least she was no foe, if a poor friend. Conan cut down the odds a trifle by hamstringing the last man out of the window. The man dropped farther and harder than he'd planned, going to hands and knees. A Cimmerian boot in the belly lifted him like a dog, hurling him against a comrade. The second man was rising when a Cimmerian broadsword split his skull from crown to the bridge of his nose.

A scream danced off the stones. The guard reeled back, blood streaming from blinded eyes. The same blood dripped from the woman's dagger. Conan grinned as he realized the woman's craft. She'd feigned fear, to draw the three men close. There she had two blades against their three, one more agile than any of theirs.

Two more men darted from the alley. The woman had the wall to guard her left and two opponents at her front. The newcomers ran to take her from the right. Conan faced the last man from the window.

Taking his opponent's measure, Conan feinted high. He took the man's riposte on his mail, then followed the same line again. The second cut tore into the side of the man's neck. His half-severed head lolled on his shoulders. He reeled backwards into his comrades, drenching them in his blood.

They were men of stout nerve, casting the dying man aside without breaking stride. This took just long enough for Conan's sword to fall like an executioner's ax. The righthand man gaped as his swordarm dangled ruined and bloody. Conan freed his sword and gave ground with a backward leap that took him clean over the fallen men behind him.

He landed in a half-crouch. The cut aimed by an upright opponent whistled over his head. His own cut took the man's right leg off just below the knee. The man contrived one more desperate slash, then toppled.

With time at last to think of the woman, Conan saw she needed little thought and hardly more help. She'd thrust one opponent through the throat. He sat against the wall, fingers laced around his neck. As Conan watched, the fingers unlaced and the eyes rolled up in the pale face.

The woman no longer used her dagger as a weapon. Instead she'd made it into invisible, swift-moving armor, catching every cut on the quillions. Her opponent wore mail, so her own slashes had shredded his coat but not his flesh.

"Mine!" she shouted, as fierce as if Conan were another foe.

"Yours," Conan replied. That pride demanded more than a nod. So did those sharp, ready, deadly-swift blades.

The woman stepped back, freeing her dagger and her opponent's sword. Doubtless she expected an attack. Instead he turned and plunged into the alley. In a moment he was only the fading sound of pounding feet.

"Gods, woman! Why did you do that? You think he'd have done as much for you?"

"I suppose not. There's still time to remedy matters, if you choose."

"Chase a man through this maze when he may have been born here? Every time you open your mouth, more of your wits seem to fly out of it!"

"If you're afraid—" She blanched at Conan's face, as she had not at the ambush. "Forgive me. Truly. I merely thought to give him an honorable end, not butcher him like a hog."

"Shake off your whims about honor, woman, if you want to live long in Turan. Mishrak will tell you that, if you won't listen to me."

"He did. But—Master Barathres taught me well. Gratitude to him, old habit—they will make me think of honor when perhaps I should not." For the first time a smile lit her whole face. "You are not so free of honor yourself. Else why did you take my part at the Red Falcon?"

"I hate to have a quiet night's drinking spoiled. Besides, I took your part only after I saw that Moti was too afraid of that lordling's kin to lift a finger for you. That's the first time I had to brawl at the Red Falcon. If it isn't the last, Moti will pay more than he did that night!"

"What did he pay, if you think it fit to tell me?"

No woman likes to hear of a man's exploits in bedding others. Learning that lesson had nearly cost Conan his manhood. "He paid dearly enough, but I'd rather tell you when we've put a few streets between us and our late friends. The man you let flee may be summoning help."

"I pray not."

"Pray all you wish, but the sooner Mishrak's door closes behind us, the better."

The woman nodded, grimaced at the nicks in her dagger, then sheathed it. Conan knelt, to examine the bodies, frowning as he recognized another. The man whose leg he'd slashed off was a soldier in Captain Itzhak's company. He'd seen the man at the Red Falcon once or twice, gambling and losing. Had he hired out his sword to pay his debts, or did his secret lie deeper than that?

Well, the woman was leading him to the man in all Turan most likely to know, if least likely to tell. She was already turning down the alley, sword in hand. Conan followed, considering that this was twice he'd fought shoulder to shoulder with the woman without knowing her name.

Three

"WHO SEEKS ENTRANCE to this House?" said a soft voice. It seemed to come from the air above the great iron gate in the whitewashed stone wall.

"Captain Conan and she who was sent for him," the woman replied.

They waited, while the owner of that voice studied them. At last Conan heard a series of clangs like a blacksmith at work, then a faint scrape of metal on metal as the gate slid open.

"You may enter this house," came the voice again.

Entry was through a gateway more deserving of the name of tunnel. The walls of Mishrak's house were two men thick and solid stone every finger of the way. Conan counted four arrow slits and two dropholes in the walls and ceiling. At the far end lay another gate, this one of Vendhyan teak, lavishly carved with dragons and tigers in the Khitan style.

Beyond the second gate they entered a guardroom. Two of the guards were black, one of Vanaheim, and the last clearly a native of Shem. None but the Shemite was as small as Conan, and that one wore enough knives to let out the blood of six men before his own flowed.

The four exchanged looks, then elaborate gestures. Conan judged them all to be mutes. At last one of the blacks nodded and pointed to a door in the far wall, plated in mirror-bright silver. It swung open, as if the black had cast a spell on it.

A distaste for sorcery lay deep within all Cimmerians, and Conan was no exception. Moreover, his experience with the breed of magic-wielders had taught him that magic ate at a man's honor and judgment faster than gold. Most of that breed he'd met had ended in seeking to rule all who would obey them and ruin all who would not. Being little inclined to be ruled or ruined at another's whims, Conan could hardly be other than a foe of such wizards.

Reason told him that if Mishrak had magic at his command, he would hardly need the guards. The lord of spies clearly had other resources, beginning with a house built like a fortress.

How like a fortress, Conan began to learn as he and the woman penetrated deeper into it. Their route seemed to have as many turns and windings as the Saddlemakers' Quarter. At every turn was some display of splendor—Aquilonian tapestries, Vendhyan statues of dancing gods, rich ebony carvings of asps. Conan's danger-sharpened senses picked out spy holes in the tapestries, the sharpened daggers held ready in the hands of the gods, the live asps nesting among the carved ones.

From time to time they passed iron-bound doors set in deep recesses. Conan pitied any man foolish enough to think they offered a safer way to the heart of Mishrak's kingdom. They would lead any stranger nowhere except to death—and probably not a quick one.

At last the way grew straight. No longer was the floor alone tiled. Walls and ceiling shone with gilded mosaic work or dripped with tapestries done in cloth of silver and the finest silk. They ended in another guardroom, with an open arch beyond it and the sounds of splashing water and a flute.

"Who comes?" demanded the chief guard.

This room held six instead of four, one another Shemite and the rest with an Iranistani cast to their features. Neither mutes nor giants, the six all wore silvered mail and helmets and the plainest and most-used swords Conan had seen in Turan.

"Captain Conan of the King's mercenaries and a lady sent to bring him to Mishrak," Conan said before the woman could speak. She started.

"I am no mute, like our friends at the first gate," Conan went on. "I am a Cimmerian and a soldier, and both have a certain quaint custom. When we have twice fought side by side with someone and they owe us their lives, we enjoy knowing their names. I know not what barbarous land you call home, but—"

The woman's nostrils flared and she had the grace to flush. "I am Raihna of the Stone Hill in the Marches of Bossonia. I serve the Mistress Illyana."

Which, Conan reflected, answered his question without telling him much.

He set his wits to devising a new question. Before he found words, a voice like a bull's bellow filled the room.

"Come and let us be about our business. We do not have the whole day!"

Conan took Raihna firmly by the arm and led the way into Mishrak's innermost refuge.

From the splendor of the way in, Conan expected more of the same beyond the arch. Instead everything was bare, whitewashed stone walls and ceiling. Only on the floor did rich Iranistani carpets and dyed Hyrkanian fleeces offer softness to both the eye and the foot. On the floor—and around the pool in the middle of the room.

Five women and a man sat on benches around the pool. Four of the women were a pleasure to any man's eye, the more so as they wore only sandals, gilded loinguards, and silver collars set with topazes. It took nothing from Conan's pleasure in the women to detect small daggers hidden in the sandals and loinguards. He wondered what weapon might lurk in the collars. Like much else in Mishrak's house, the women were both a delight to the senses and a menace to unsuspecting enemies.

The fifth woman had the air of a guest rather than a guard. She wore a white robe, held a wine cup, and seemed older than the others.

Before Conan saw more, the bull's bellow came again. "Well, Captain Conan? Will you be once more a thief, and of women this time?"

The bellow came from the man on the bench. Conan doubted that he could rise from it unaided; below the knees his legs were shrunken nightmares, seamed and ravaged with scars. Above the waist, he was as thick as the mast of a galley, with arms like tree-roots. The hair of arms and chest was gray shot with white. So were the few strands of beard and hair that escaped the black leather mask covering Mishrak from crown to chin.

Conan grinned. "Keeping stolen gold is hard enough. Keeping what has legs to run with, if it likes not your company or your manner in bed . . . Do I look so great a fool?"

"You've been gaping about you like one, I must say."

"Call it gaping if you will, Lord Mishrak. I call it admiring fine work. I know now why you have so many enemies, yet live to serve King Yildiz so well."

"Oh? And what magic do I have to perform this miracle?"

"It's neither magic nor miracle. It's making ready to kill your enemies faster than their courage can endure. Most men can be brave if they have some hope of life or victory. Losing all hope of either would turn most into cowards."

"Save yourself, no doubt, Cimmerian?"

"I have not tested the defenses of your house, Mishrak. Nor do I have any cause to do so. I am not yet your enemy, and I doubt you plan to make me so. Killing me here might do injury to your rugs and ladies."

"So it would. Yet I would suggest that you learn why I have summoned you, before you call me friend."

"It will be a rare pleasure to be told something, for once," Conan said.

"I predict the pleasure will be brief," Mishrak said, in a tone that told of a grim smile under the mask. "Yet your life might be even more so, if you do not accept what I offer you."

"No man lives as long as he wants to," Conan said. "That's the way of the world, just as no man can have every woman he desires," he added, grinning at Raihna. She flushed again. "What is going to shorten my days this time?"

"Lord Houma. Ah, I see I have finally driven a dart

deep enough in that thick Cimmerian skull to gain your attention."

Conan wasted no breath denying it. "I understand he's rather fonder of his son than the young witling deserves. You should understand that Raihna and I met his first band of hired swords on our way here. Only one of them left alive, and he only because he fled." Conan would have sworn Raihna threw him a grateful look for not mentioning her mistake.

"As you say, they were the first band sent against you. They will not be the last. Your eye is keen, but can it stay open forever? Who will guard your back when you sleep?"

Almost imperceptibly, Raihna shook her head. Conan shrugged. "I could take leave for a time. Or are you going to tell me that Lord Houma is one of those men with short tempers and long memories? Such have sought my life before, with what success you can see."

"You could not be away from Aghrapur long enough to foil Lord Houma without breaking your oath of service. Are you ready to give up your captaincy?"

"Out of fear of Houma? Lord Mishrak, you can make your offer or not, as you choose. Do not insult me in the bargain."

"I would insult you more by implying that you are too stupid to be afraid. Houma has not the strength he once had, but he is still more than a match for you."

Conan did not doubt the first part of that statement. Houma had owed some of his former strength to his friendship with the Cult of Doom. Conan himself had cast the Cult down to utter and final destruction the best part of two years ago.

As for the rest—

"Granting that Houma might be my match, how would you change that?"

"If you will leave Aghrapur on—a task—for me, I will find ways to change Lord Houma's mind. The task should not take you more than a month. By then you can return to Aghrapur and sleep in peace."

"And this task?"

"In a moment. While you are traveling, I will also protect those you leave behind, who might also feel Houma's vengeance. I do not imagine that you care much what happens to Sergeant Motilal, but—would you see Pyla's face turned into something like my legs?"

Conan cursed himself for a witling. Houma was clearly the kind of coward who would hurt a foe however he could, whether honorably or not. He should *not* have forgotten the women.

"I would not like that at all," Conan said, then grinned at the look in Raihna's eyes. So let the swordwench be jealous! He owed Pyla and her friends more than he owed Raihna of Bossonia! "If you can protect them, it would indeed make your offer worth hearing."

"Although," Conan added more calmly than he felt, "I imagine you have plans for Lord Houma whether I'm part of them or not. You might be keeping him too busy to worry about taverns and their girls anyway. He has more in hand than letting his son misbehave, doesn't he?"

In the silence that followed, Conan clearly heard the *snik* of a crossbow being cocked. He laughed. "Best tell that archer to cock his bow while people are still talking. When everyone's gaping like dead fish, it's too easy to hear—"

The white-robed woman broke the silence with

warm if high-pitched laughter. "Mishrak, I told you several times. I have heard Raihna speak of this man and I have studied his aura. He is not one to be led by the nose, or by any other part of his body. Lead him by his sense of honor, and he will go where you will. Otherwise do not waste your breath."

A choking noise crept from under the leather hood. Conan suspected that if Mishrak could have strangled anyone, he would have started with Conan and gone on to the woman. Beside Conan, Raihna was pressing her face into a pillar to hide her blush and what looked remarkably like laughter.

"May I deserve your praise, lady," Conan said. "Would I be speaking to Mistress Illyana?"

"You would."

The woman also seemed to have northern blood in her, but her hair was brown with tints of auburn. She wore a simple flowing gown of white silk with saffron borders and silver-decorated sandals. The gown was too loose to show much of her body, but from the lines in the long face Conan judged her to be upwards of thirty. A trifle thin-flanked for his tastes, but not unhandsome.

Illyana accepted Conan's scrutiny in silence for a moment, then smiled. "With Lord Mishrak's permission, I will tell you what is asked of you. But first I will thank you for saving Raihna from death or shame. She began as a hired sword, but the years have made us spirit-sisters."

Conan frowned. "Auras" and "spirit-kin" were things of priestcraft if not wizardry. What was this woman?

"I ask your aid in a search for the missing Jewel of Kurag. It is a thing of ancient Atlantean magic, set in an arm–ring of Vanir work—"

She went on to describe the history of the Jewels, as much as was known of it, from their mysterious origins in Atlantis to the present day. It seemed they had a long and bloody history, for the spells needed to use them safely were hard to learn even for the most accomplished sorcerers.

"Then why bother with the Jewels at all?" Conan asked.

"Even separately, they confer great power on a skilled user. Together, no one knows what limits there might be on the magic of their possessor."

Conan reflected that he had learned nothing about sorcerers he had not long since known.

Illyana continued with the possession of the Jewels by her master Eremius, his growing ambition to use the powers of the Jewels to rule the world, their quarrel, her flight with one of the Jewels, and much else. She ended by saying that the tales of demons coming out of the Ibars Mountains hinted of Eremius's presence.

"With all in fear of him, his strength will grow steadily. Soon it will make him a valuable ally to ambitious men like Lord Houma. They will aid him, thinking to use his powers against their enemies. They will only be buying themselves the strongest chains of all, forged by the most ancient and evil magic."

"Ancient and evil magic . . ." Conan heard those words with icy clarity, although he had heard most of what went before with only half an ear.

Mishrak was not only asking him to flee like a thief from Aghrapur and Lord Houma's vengeance. He was asking a Cimmerian to guard the back of a sorceress on a quest for a menace no honest steel could face. He would also have wagered his sword that Illyana was telling less than the whole truth about the Jewels.

No honor in any of this. But even less in leaving Pyla and Zaria and young Thebia (who might grow no older) to the mercy of those who had none, either.

Curse all women and whatever god created them as a joke on men! They might be a mystery themselves, but they certainly knew how to bring a man to them, like a trainer with a half-grown hunting dog!

"By Hanuman's stones!" Conan growled. "I never thought listening could be as dry work as talking. Bring me and Raihna some wine, and I'll promise to fly to the moon and bring back its queen's loinguard!"

Two of the guardswomen sprang up without an order and vanished like hares fleeing the wolf. Conan sat down cross-legged and drew his sword. Sighting along the blade for nicks, he concluded he'd best put it in the hands of a smith before setting out on serious business.

When he knew he had everyone's attention, he laughed. "You want me to run off to the Ibars Mountains, with a half-mad swordwench and a more than half-mad sorceress. Then we hunt for a magic jewel and steal it from a completely mad wizard, fighting our way through whatever magic-spawned monsters we find. If we snatch the jewel, you'll win, whether we live or die."

Mishrak laughed for the first time since Conan mentioned Houma. "Conan, you should be one of my spies. I have none who could say half as much in twice as many words."

"I'd rather be gelded!"

"Why not do both? A fighting eunuch would be a valuable ear and eye in Vendhya. I'm sure you would rise high in my service."

Raihna gave up trying to stifle her laughter and buried her face in Conan's shoulder. He put an arm around her and she did not resist, only shaking the harder until tears streamed down her face.

By the time she was sober, the guardswomen had returned with the wine. Mishrak poured out the first cup, drank from it, and then watched in silence until the others were served.

"Well, Conan?" he said at last.

"Well, Mishrak. It's not to my taste, running like a thief because I didn't want my drinking spoiled by seeing a woman mishandled. It's less to my taste going anywhere in the company of a wizard.

"But you don't have the name of a fool, Mishrak. If you want me for this nonsense, I suppose you can have me."

Raihna threw her arms around Conan. From the look on Illyana's face, she would have liked to do the same. From under the black leather hood came only a harsh laugh.

Four

"NOW HERE'S A finer mount than I'll wager you thought I had," the horse dealer said exuberantly. "Look at those legs. Look at that depth of chest. Look at that noble—"

"How is his wind?" Raihna said.

"He's no colt, I'll not deny that. He's better. A seasoned, trained mount fit to carry either of you wherever you might want to go. Begging your pardon, Captain, my lady, but neither of you has the look of dwarfs to these old eyes. To be sure, I'm a better judge of horses than of men, but—"

Raihna ignored the dealer and stepped up to the horse. He gave her what seemed to Conan a wary look, but showed no obvious skittishness or signs of mistreatment. He stood patiently for Raihna's examination, then tossed his head and whinnied when she patted his neck.

"No colt indeed," Raihna said. "Were he a man, I'd say he was most fit to sit in the sun until his days were finished."

"My lady!" The dealer could hardly have seemed more outraged if Raihna had questioned his lawful birth. "This fine, long-striding beast has many more years—"

"A few more years, perhaps. Not enough to be worth half what you ask for him."

"Lady, you insult both my honor and this horse. What horse so insulted will bear you willingly? If I reduce the price by a single brass piece, *I* will be insulting him. Mitra strike me dead if I wouldn't!"

"I'm surprised that someone you sold a vulture's dinner disguised as a horse hasn't saved Mitra the trouble!" Conan said. He was far from sure why Raihna was spending so much time bargaining for a huge gelding clearly at home only on level ground. He did know that if the dealer thought he could appeal to Conan, he would do so and all would waste more time.

The bargaining waxed hot and eager. Conan was reminded of a game he had seen among the Iranistani, where men on ponies batted a dead calf about with long-handled mallets. (He had heard tales that sometimes a dead enemy's head took the place of the calf.)

At last the dealer cast up his hands and looked much as if he would gladly go and hang himself. "When you see me begging for alms in the Great Square, remember that it was you who made me a beggar. You will offer no more?"

Raihna licked dusty lips. "By the Four Springs! I will have precious little to put in your begging bowl if I pay more! Would you have me selling myself in the streets because you know not the true value of a horse?"

The dealer grinned. "You are too fine a lady for the likes of those you would meet in the streets. The watch would also demand their share. Now, if you wished some time to come privily to me, I am sure—"

"Your wife would notice what was missing, the next time she bedded you," Conan growled. "Shape more respectful words on your tongue, or carry it home in your purse!"

"There will be little else in that purse," the dealer grunted. "Oh, well and good. For what you're offering, I can hardly throw in much beyond the bridle and bit."

That was no loss. Mishrak had ordered Conan and Raihna to scatter his gold widely about Aghrapur. They would purchase their remaining horses from other dealers, their saddles and tack from still others, and so on.

Conan was prepared to obey. Reluctantly, because he knew little of Mishrak's reasons and those he suspected he much disliked. But he would obey. To make an enemy of both Mishrak and Houma would mean leaving Aghrapur with more haste than dignity.

Conan was footloose enough not to mourn if that was his fate. He was proud enough to want a worthier foe than Houma to drive him forth.

The dealer was still calling on the gods to witness his imminent ruin when Conan and Raihna led the horse out the gate. In the street beyond, she stopped, gripped the bridle with one hand and the mane with the other, and swung herself on to the horse's back.

"So you can mount unaided and ride bareback," the Cimmerian growled. Raihna had managed no small feat, but he'd be cursed if she'd know it from him! "Small help that will be, when we take this great lump into the mountains. He'll starve in a week, if he doesn't break a leg or maybe his rider's neck sooner."

"I know that, Conan."

"Then why take him at all?"

"There's a good long ride across open country before we reach the mountains. If we took mountain horses all the way, it would take longer. Time is something we may not have.

"Also, mountain horses would tell thóse watching us too much about where we are going. We would be followed and perhaps run dówn, because those who followed would surely ride heavy mounts! Do you deny that we are being watched?"

"I think that fruitseller over there—and don't look, for Erlik's sake!—is the same man as the painter who followed us yesterday."

"You told me of neither."

"Crom! I didn't think you needed telling!"

Raihna flushed. "You were hiding nothing from me?"

"I'm not that big a fool. You may not know Aghrapur, but you'll be fighting beside me until this witling's errand is done!"

"I am grateful, Conan."

"How grateful, may I ask?" he grinned.

The flush deepened, but she smiled. "You may ask. I do not swear to answer." She sobered. "The next time, remember that what I know of Aghrapur, I know from Mishrak. Anything you can teach me about this city will be something I need not learn from the lord of spies!"

"Now I'll listen to that. I'd teach a serpent or a spider to spare him needing to learn from Mishrak!"

Raihna reached down and gripped Conan's massive shoulder. Her grip was as strong as many a man's, but no man could have doubted that those fingers were a woman's.

They passed on down the street in silence for another hundred paces. At last Conan lifted his water bottle, drank, then spat the dust from his mouth into the street.

"I'd lay a year's pay on Mishrak having it in mind to use us as bait," he said. "What think you?"

"Much the same," Raihna replied. "I would be less easy if Illyana were not so determined to come to grips with Eremius. It is not just ending the danger of the Jewels of Kurag that she seeks. It is vengeance for what she suffered at his hands." Her tone made it plain she would not speak of those sufferings.

"If your mistress is going to join us on Mishrak's hook, she'd best be able to ride anything we put under her. This is no stroll in a country garden!"

"My mistress is a better rider than I am. Remember that Bossonia is in great part hill country." That explained her stride, so familiar and so pleasing to Conan's eye.

Raihna's voice hardened. "Also, her father was a great landowner. He kept more horses than I saw before I left home." Her voice hinted of a tale Conan would have gladly heard, if he'd dreamed she would tell him a word of it.

Conan sought a subject more pleasing to both of them. "Will bringing the Jewels together end the danger? Perhaps they'll be safer apart."

"There is no corruption in Illyana!" Raihna snapped.

"I didn't say it was her I doubted," Conan replied. At least he doubted her no more than any other wizard, and perhaps less than some. "I was thinking of other wizards, or even common thieves. Oh well, once we have the Jewels they'll be a boil on Mishrak's arse and not ours!"

* * *

"Hssst! Ranis!" Yakoub whispered.

"Tamur!" The guard called him by the name under which Yakoub had dealt with him.

"Softly, please. Are you alone?"

Ranis shrugged. "One man only. I could hardly travel alone to this quarter without arousing suspicion."

"True enough." Yakoub covertly studied Ranis's companion. Given no time to flee or call for help, he would be even less trouble than his master.

"So, Ranis. What brings you here? I already know that you failed."

Ranis could not altogether hide his surprise. He had the sense not to ask how Yakoub knew this. Indeed, he suspected Yakoub would not have needed Houma's aid to hear of a fight that left seven men dead or maimed in an alley of the Saddlemakers' Quarter.

"I want to try again. My honor demands that I try again."

Yakoub swallowed blistering words about the honor of those who flee and leave comrades dead behind them. Instead he smiled his most charming smile. "That speaks well of you. What think you will be needed, to once more face the Cimmerian? Remember, the tale in the streets runs that any man who faces him is cursed for self-destruction!"

"I can believe that. I've seen him fight twice. But by all the gods, no barbarian is invincible! Even if he were, he's insulted my lord and me twice over!"

So Ranis had enough honor to recognize an insult when it was given? A pity he had not enough to recognize the need of dying with his men, thereby saving Yakoub a trifle of work. Not that the work would be dangerous, save for the odd chance, but there was always that.

Part of Yakoub's disguise as a crippled veteran was a staff nearly his own height. A single thrust crushed the throat of Ranis's companion before he knew that he faced an armed foe.

The staff whirled, then swept in a low arc as Yakoub sought to take Ranis's legs out from under him. Ranis leaped high and came down on Yakoub's unguarded left side. Or at least, the side he thought unguarded. The staff seemed to leap into his path and that of his sword. The blade sank into wood, met steel, and rebounded. Before Ranis could recover, one end of the staff smashed against his temple. He staggered, sword hand loosening its grip but desperation raising his arm once more to guard.

He was too slow to stop the lead-shod end of the staff from driving into his skull squarely between his eyes. Ranis flew backward as if kicked by a mule, striking the wall and sliding down to slump lifeless in the filth of the tavern's rear yard.

Yakoub saw that Ranis's companion had died of his crushed throat and would need no mercy steel. Kneeling beside each body in succession, he closed their eyes and placed their weapons in their hands. Such was honorable treatment. Also, to any who did not look too closely at the wounds, it would seem that they had slain each other in some petty quarrel.

Doubtless Mishrak would be suspicious, when word reached him. By that time, however, the bodies would be too far gone to tell anyone without magic at his command very much. Not less important to Yakoub, he himself would be some distance on the road back to the mountains and his work there. His saving Bora's father Rhafi should assure him, if not a hero's welcome, at least freedom from awkward questions.

"You know what to do," Conan said to the four tribesmen. "Have you any questions, besides when you will be paid?"

The men grinned. The eldest shrugged. "This is no matter for pay, as you well know. But—we cannot *kill* those who would steal what is yours?"

"He whom I now serve wishes live prisoners, who may tell him what he needs to know."

"Ah," the man said. He sounded much relieved. "Then you have not grown weak, Conan. Those who live may yet be killed afterward. Do you think your master will let us do the work for him?"

"I will tell him all that the gods will permit me to say," Conan replied. "Now, is anything else lacking?"

"This food of the city folk is hardly food for men," the youngest man said. "But I do not suppose it will turn us into weaklings or women in a few days."

"It will not. And if you are needed for longer than that, I shall see that you have proper food. By what is known but may not be talked of, I swear it!"

The tribesmen made their gesture of respect as Conan turned and led a mystified Raihna out of the stable. In the courtyard between the stable and the inn, she turned to him with a bemused expression.

"Those were Hyrkanians, were they not?"

"Your eye improves each day, Raihna."

"They look as likely to steal our goods as to guard them."

"Not those, nor any of their tribe. We owe each other blood debts."

"The Hyrkanians honor those, or so I have heard."

"You have heard the truth."

Much to Conan's relief, Raihna did not seem disposed to pursue the matter further. His battle against the Cult of Doom in company with the tribesmen was not for the ears of anyone who might tell Mishrak.

Raihna strode across the courtyard and into the inn with her back even straighter than usual. As they climbed the stairs, Conan heard the jingle of her purse.

"How much have you left?" She told him. "I'd be happier with more, if we're going to buy horses for the mountains."

"Mishrak expects us to find them at the army outposts."

"Meaning he has his own men in the outposts? Likely enough. I'd still much rather have a second choice, one that won't take us close to the outposts. If Mishrak can put his men into them, why can't Houma do the same?"

"You see clearly, Conan."

"I'm still alive, Raihna. I've always thought being alive has it over being dead. If Mishrak will spend a little more of his gold, we may not have to spend our blood. Tell that to your mistress, since she seems to have his ear!"

They were at the door of her room. Mishrak's gold had bought them not only horses and gear, but separate rooms at one of Aghrapur's best inns. Of a certainty their enemies would hear of their presence, but could hope to do nothing. Between the watch and the inn's own guards, nothing could be attempted without a pitched battle.

Why attack a bear in his den, when you knew he would soon have to leave it?

"Sleep well, Raihna." She turned to unlock her door. As always, Conan's blood stirred at the swell of breasts and hips, the long graceful lines of back and leg. Well, the inn did not ask a man to sleep alone—

Raihna gripped his hand and led him through the door. She kicked the door shut, and before he could speak had lifted her tunic over her head. The upper slopes of her breasts were lightly freckled; their firm fullness seemed to cry out for a man's hand.

Conan's blood no longer stirred. It seethed, on the verge of boiling over.

"You wished me a sound sleep, Conan. Well, come here and let us both find it. Or must I disrobe you as well as myself? I warn you, if I must do that I may be too weary for bedsport—"

"Hah!" Conan said. His arms went around her, lifting her off her feet. Desire thundered in him, and he felt the same in her. "If it's weary you want to be, Raihna, then I can give you the soundest sleep of your life!"

Five

"ENTER IN MITRA'S name," Ivram said. Hinges long unoiled screamed as the priest opened the door for Bora. Bora followed Ivram inside. In the center of the chamber a hearth of bricks was at work on Ivram's dinner. Pungent smoke tickled Bora's nostrils, as did the more appetizing odors of baking bread and bubbling stew. They reminded Bora that he had eaten not a bite since morning.

Around the hearth lay dyed fleeces and rugs of simple design but exquisite workmanship. More rugs hung on the wall above a richly-carved chest. The figure of Mitra on the lid had eyes of amber and coral.

From beyond the door to an inner chamber floated the soft murmur of a flute. The priest's "niece" Maryam was playing for the night's devotions and for whatever else might be expected of her during this night. Few in Crimson Springs could name her "niece" without smiling, at least when Ivram was elsewhere. Most suspected that she had learned the art of the flute in the taverns of Aghrapur.

"Sit, son of Rhafi," Ivram said. He clapped his hands and the flute was silent. "Maryam, we have a guest."

The woman who emerged from the inner room was barely half the priest's size or age. She bore a brass tray covered with a piece of embroidered linen. On the linen rested honeycakes and bits of smoked lamb. She knelt gracefully before Bora, contriving to let her robe fall away from her neck and throat. The neck was slender and the dark-rose throat firm and unlined. Bora knew other sensations than hunger.

"Wine?" Maryam asked. Her voice was rich and soothing. Bora wondered if this was another art of pleasing she had learned in taverns. If so, she had learned it well.

"Forgive me if I seem ungrateful for your hospitality," Bora said uneasily. "I need wise counsel more than anything else."

"My ears are open and my heart at your service," Ivram said. In another priest's mouth the ritual words might have rung hollow. In Ivram's, they could hardly be doubted. The villages around his shrine forgave him gluttony and a "niece" and would have forgiven him far more, because he listened. Sometimes he also gave wise counsel, but as often, the mere knowledge that he listened eased those who came to him.

"I know the secret of the mountain demons," Bora said. "Yet none will believe me. Some call me mad, some a liar. A few have sworn to have my blood if I do not cease to put them in fear.

"They say it is their women and children they do not wish frightened, but I have seen their faces. They think that if they do not know what the danger is, it will not come near them!"

"They are fools," Ivram said. He laughed, so that his

jowls danced. "They also do not care to have a boy be
more of a man than they are."

"Do you believe me, then?"

"*Something* stalks these mountains, something reeking of uncleanness and evil magic. Any knowledge of
that is more than we have had before." He took a
honeycake between thumb and forefinger. It vanished
in two bites.

Bora looked at the plate, to discover it half-empty
already. "Maryam, I will be grateful for that wine."

"It is our pleasure," she replied. Her smile made
Bora's head spin as though he had already emptied a
cup.

Now that he had found someone of the hills ready to
believe him, Bora could hardly credit his good fortune.
Nor could he muster the courage to speak, without
strengthening himself with drink.

Ivram scanted neither his guests nor himself in the
matter of wine. By the time the second cup was
half-empty, Bora had done more than tell his story. He
had begun to wonder why he had ever been reluctant
to tell it. Maryam was looking at him with wide,
worshipful eyes. He had never dreamed of having such
a woman look at him so.

"If you saw half what you describe, we are in more
peril than I had dared imagine," Ivram said at last. "I
almost understand those who did not care to hear you.
Have you told anyone outside the village? This is not
our secret, I think."

"I—well, there is one. Not quite outside the village,
although he has gone to Aghrapur—" The wine now
tangled Bora's tongue rather than freeing it. Also, he
did not much care to talk of his sister Caraya's unmaid-
enly passion for Yakoub.

"It is Yakoub the herdsman, is it not?" Ivram said gently. Bora nodded without raising his eyes from the floor.

"You do not trust him?" Bora shook his head. "Who else do you know who would both listen to you and bear your tale to Aghrapur? Mughra Khan's soldiers have arrested your father. They will be slow to listen to you.

"The friends of Yakoub may not be in high places. Yet they will not be the men of Mughra Khan. Yakoub is your best hope."

"He may be our only one!" Bora almost shouted. The wine on a nearly empty stomach was making him light-headed. "Besides the gods, of course," he added hastily, as he remembered that he was guest to a priest of Mitra.

"The gods will not thank us for sitting like stones upon the hillside and waiting for them to rescue us," Ivram said. "Yakoub seems a better man than those who seek only rebels when they should seek wizardry. Perhaps he will not be good enough, but—"

"Ivram! Quickly! To the south! The demon fire burns!"

Maryam's voice was half a scream and wholly filled with terror. She stood in the outer doorway, staring into the night. Bora took his place beside her, seeing that her dark-rose face was now pale as goat's milk.

Emerald fire climbed the slopes of the Lord of the Winds. The whole mighty peak might have been sinking in a lake of that fire. At any moment Bora expected to see the snowcap melt and waft away into the night as green-hued steam.

Ivram embraced Maryam and murmured to her. At last she rested her head on his shoulder in silence. He looked beyond her, to the demon light. To Bora he seemed to be looking even farther, into another world.

When he spoke, his voice had the ring of prophecy. In spite of his wine-given courage, Bora shuddered at the priest's words.

"That is the light of our doom. Bora, I will join my words to yours. We must prepare ourselves, for what is about to come upon us."

"I cannot lead the villages!"

"Cannot, or will not?"

"I would if they listened to me. But I am a boy!"

"You are more of a man than those who will not hear you. Remember that, speak as you have spoken to me tonight, and the wise will listen."

A witling's thought passed through Bora's mind. Did Ivram mean that he should stay drunk until the demons had passed? The idea tempted him, but he doubted that there was so much wine in all the villages!

Eremius flung his arms toward the night sky, as if seeking to conjure the stars down from the heavens. No stars were to be seen from the valley, not through the emerald mist around the Lord of the Winds.

Again and again his arms leaped high. Again and again he felt the power of the Jewel pour from them like flames. Ah, if he could unleash such power with one Jewel, what might he do with both?

Tonight he would take a step toward possessing both. A long step, for tonight the Transformed would pour out of the mountains to strike far and wide.

Thunder rolled down the sky and echoed from the valley walls. The ground shuddered beneath Eremius's feet.

He took a deep breath and with the utmost reluctance reined in the power he had conjured. With his senses enhanced by the Jewel, he had seen the flaws and faults in the walls of the valley. One day he would cast it all down in rubble and ruin to show the world his power, but not tonight.

"Master! Master! Hear me!" It was the captain of the sentries.

"Silence!" A peremptory gesture held menace.

"Master! You put the men in fear! If they are to follow the Transformed—"

"Fear? Fear? I will show you fear!" Another gesture. Eremius's staff leaped into his hand. He raised it, to smite the captain to the ground in a pile of ashes.

Again he took a deep breath. Again he reined in the power he would have gloried in unleashing. Near witless as they were, his human fighters had their part in everything he did until he regained the second Jewel.

The Transformed could be unleashed only when Eremius was awake to command them. When he slept, so did they. Then the spellbound humans must do the work of guarding and foraging, however badly.

With both Jewels, one like Eremius could command the loyalty of the finest soldiers while leaving their wits intact. With only one, he could command only those he had made near-kin to simpletons.

The thousandth curse on Illyana shrieked through his mind. His staff danced in the air, painting a picture between him and the captain. Illyana appeared, naked, with nothing of the sorceress about her. Rather, it was her younger self, ready to receive a man as the real Illyana never had (though not for want of effort by Eremius).

The staff twitched. Illyana's image opened its mouth

and closed its eyes. Its hands curved into claws, and those claws began to twist in search of the man who had to be near.

At Eremius's command, the image did all that he had ever seen or imagined a woman doing in the grip of lust. Then the image surpassed lust, entering realms of blood and obscenity beyond the powers of most men even to imagine.

They were also beyond the powers of the captain to endure. He began by licking his lips at the display of lust. Then sweat glazed his face, except for dry lips. Under the sweat the face turned pale.

At last his eyes rolled up in his head and he crashed to the ground. He lay as senseless as if Eremius truly had smitten him with the staff. Eremius waved the staff, now to conjure sense back into the captain instead of out of him. The man lurched to his knees, vomited, looked wildly about him for the image, then knelt and kissed the ground at Eremius's feet.

For the moment, it seemed to Eremius that the man had learned enough of fear.

"Go and send your men up to the valley mouth," Eremius said. "They are to hold it until the last of the Transformed are past. Then they are to fall in with the pack animals."

The human fighters were not as the Transformed, able to endure for days between their meals of flesh. They would need rations until the raiders reached inhabited farms. Pack horses would serve, their scents altered by magic so that they would not rouse the hunger of the Transformed.

"I go in obedience to the Master of the Jewel," the captain said. In spite of his fear, he vanished swiftly into the darkness. Or perhaps his fear gave wings to his feet. Eremius hardly cared, as long as he was obeyed.

Oh, for the day when he would hear "I go in obedience to the Master of the Jewels" from a soldier worthy of the name! A soldier such as High Captain Khadjar or even his obedient son Yakoub.

The thought that this day drew closer hardly consoled Eremius. To punish only an image of Illyana instead of the real woman reminded him of how far he had to go.

So be it. Only a fool feared to unroll the parchment, lest he miscast the spell!

Eremius cast his thoughts up and down the valley, in a silence more complete than the tomb's.

Come forth. Come forth at your Master's command. Come forth and seek prey.

The Transformed came forth. A carrion reek rode the wind ahead of them, thickening until the stench seemed a living, palpable entity. Eremius conjured a bubble of clean air around himself. As an afterthought he added the scent of Illyana's favorite bath oil to the air.

The Transformed filed past. They shambled, lurched, and seemed perpetually about to stumble. This was as Eremius wished it, when they were close to him. Unleashed and ranging free, the Transformed could overtake a galloping horse.

Emerald light glowed on scales and red eyes. Here and there it shone on the spikes of a club slung from a crude rope belt or on a brass-bound cestus encasing a clawed hand. Even after the Transformation, the Transformed were not wholly alike. Some had the wits to chose and wield weapons. Others lacked the wits, or perhaps were too proud of their vast new strength.

At last the Transformed were gone into the night. Eremius chanted the words that would bind the spell of control into the staff. For some days to come, he would need no other magic, unless matters went awry.

Even if they did, a single Jewel of Kurag was no mean weapon in the hands of a sorcerer such as Eremius. Those who doubted this might find themselves learning otherwise before long, although they would hardly live to profit by this lesson.

Six

To THE EAST, the foothills of the Ibars Mountains crept upward toward the blue sky. Somewhere among them the Shimak River had its birth. In those hills it swelled from a freshet to a stream. Flowing onward, it turned from a stream to a river before it reached the plains of Turan. Here it was halfway to its junction with the Ilbars River. Already its width and depth demanded a ferry rather than a ford.

The ferry herald blew the signal on a brass-bound ivory horn the length of Conan's arm. Three times the harsh blast rolled across the turbid waters. Three times the pack animals rolled their eyes and pecked uneasily.

Raihna dismounted to gentle them, leaving Conan to tend to her mount. Illyana remained mounted, eyes cast on something only she could see. Without looking closely, a man might have thought her half-witted. After looking closely, no man would care to do so again.

She rode as well as Raihna had promised and made

little extra work, for all that she did less than her share of what there was. No one called sorcerer was easy company for Conan, but Illyana was more endurable than most.

It did not hurt that she was comelier than most sorcerers Conan had met! She dressed as though unaware of it, but a handsome woman lay under those baggy traveling gowns and embroidered trousers.

A handsome woman, whose magic required that she remain a maiden even though of an age to have marriageable daughters. It was wisdom for her to be companioned by another woman—who was no maiden.

Indeed, Raihna was enough woman for any man. After a single night with Raihna, Conan could hardly think of Illyana as a woman without some effort. Doubtless this was Raihna's intent, but Conan hardly cared.

Three hundred paces away, the ferry left the far bank and began its return across the Shimak. To describe the craft as bargelike would have insulted any barge Conan had ever seen in Aghrapur's teeming port. Amidships a platform allowed human passengers to stand clear of their beasts and baggage. On either side slaves manned long sweeps, two on each.

Behind Conan other travelers assembled—a peasant family loaded with baskets, a solitary peddler with his mule and slave boy, a half-dozen soldiers under a scar-faced sergeant. The peasants hardly looked able to buy a loaf of bread, let alone ferry passage, but perhaps they would trade some of their baskets.

The ferry crept across the river until what passed for its bow scrunched into the gravel by the pier. Conan sprang on to the pier, which creaked under his weight.

"Come along, ladies. We were first at the landing,

but that won't count for much if we're slow off the mark!"

Raihna needed little urging. She helped her mistress dismount, then led the three riding mounts on to the ferry. It had two gangplanks, and the one for beasts was stout enough to support elephants, let alone horses.

Conan stood on the pier until Raihna had loaded and tethered all five animals. No one sought to push past him, nor did he need to draw his sword to accomplish this. The thickness of the arms crossed on the broad chest and the unblinking stare of the ice-blue eyes under the black brows were enough to daunt even the soldiers.

Illyana sat down on the platform under the canopy. Conan and Raihna stood in the open. The soldiers and the peddler watched Raihna appreciatively.

Conan hoped they would confine themselves to watching. He and the women were traveling in the guise of a merchant's widow, her younger sister, and the merchant's former captain of caravan guards. That deception would hardly survive Raihna's shedding the blood of even the most importunate fellow-traveler.

The peasants and the peddler joined Conan's party aboard the ferry. Two deckhands heaved the animals' gangplank aboard. Then the soldiers tramped onto the pier, leading their mounts. The ferrymaster gasped in horror and turned paler than the muddy river.

"By the gods, no! Not all of you! The ferry cannot bear the weight. The gangplank still less. Sergeant, I beg you!"

"I give no ear to beggars," the sergeant growled. "Forward, men!"

Conan sprang off the platform. The planks of the deck groaned as if a catapult stone had struck. He strode to the edge of the deck and put his foot on one end of the passenger gangplank. The sergeant put his foot on the other end. He was only a trifle shorter than Conan, and quite as broad.

"Sergeant, the ferrymaster knows what he can carry and what he can't."

"Well and good. You can get off. Just you and the livestock, though. Not the ladies. My men and I will take care of them. Won't we, lads?"

A robust, lewd chorus of agreement drowned out sulphurous Cimmerian curses. Conan spread his arms wide.

"Sergeant, how well can you swim?"

"Eh?"

"Perhaps you should take a swimming lesson or two, before you try overloading a ferry."

Conan leaped, soaring half his own height into the air. He came down on the gangplank. He was out of swordreach of the sergeant, but that mattered not at all.

The gangplank writhed like a serpent. The sergeant staggered, fighting for balance, then lost the fight. With a mighty splash he plunged headfirst into the river. It was shallow enough that he landed with his legs waving frantically in the air.

Conan pushed the passenger gangplank clear of the ferry, to discourage the soldiers from taking a hand. Then he bent, grasped the sergeant by both ankles, and swung him back and forth until he coughed up all the water he had swallowed.

When the coughs gave way to curses, Conan set the sergeant down. "You need more lessons, sergeant. No doubt of that. My lady's younger sister will be glad to teach you, if you've a mind to be polite to her. Swimming only, mind you, and nothing else—"

More curses, this time on "the lady's younger sister" as well as Conan. The Cimmerian frowned.

"Sergeant, if I can't mend your manners with water, I'll try steel the next time. Meanwhile, do you want to cross with us or do your men need you to change their smallclothes—?"

The sergeant threw out a final curse, then lurched off the deck into the water. This time he managed to land on his feet. Finally too breathless to curse, he splashed to the pier. His soldiers helped him up, glaring at Conan all the while.

"Ferrymaster, I think we'd best push off," Conan said.

The ferrymaster, even paler than before, nodded vigorously. He waved to the drummer amidships, who raised his mallet and began pounding out a beat for the slaves. Gravel scraped and growled under the ferry, then she was once more afloat and underway.

Compared to the ferry, a snail had wings. In the time needed to reach the middle of the river, Conan could have eaten dinner and washed it down with ale worth savoring.

The ferrymaster stood on the platform, eyes roaming between the slaves and the receding bank with its cursing soldiers. Instead of fading, his pallor seemed to be growing on him. Had he taken a fever?

"Hi, ha, ho, hey!"

Frantic shouts erupted from aft. Conan whirled, to see half of one of the steering oars vanish over the side. A deckhand made to strip and swim after it, but it vanished before he could leap.

"Vendhyan teak," the ferrymaster said, as if the words were a curse. "Heavy as iron and sinks like it too. An ill-favored day, this one. We must turn about in midstream and make our bow our stern. I hope you are in no great haste, you and your ladies."

Nothing in those words made other than good sense. They still rang strangely on the Cimmerian's ears. Since he could put no name to that strangeness, he watched the ferrymaster hurry aft, calling to the hands.

"How long do we spend out here because some sailor was fumble-fingered?" Illyana snapped.

"As long as it takes to turn this drunken sow of a ferry," Conan said. "How long that will be, the gods know. Maybe the ferrymaster, too. Best not look at me. I'm no sailor."

"Perhaps. But can you at least ask the master?"

"As you wish, my lady."

Conan turned to head aft, where the master and two hands were now wrestling with the ferry's light skiff. Raihna put a hand on his arm in what to all eyes would seem a gesture of affection. Her whisper was fierce but unheard by anyone else, including her mistress.

"Be careful, Conan. I would go with you, but Illyana's back needs guarding more than yours."

"That's the truth. But who from?"

"I don't know. But what the master said—I've seldom heard a speech that smelled more of long practice. He spoke like an old beggar who's been asking for alms on the same temple steps for twenty years."

"Maybe this happens every third crossing," Conan grunted. "With this floating lumberpile, anything's possible."

"I need no reassurance!" Raihna's whisper was fiercer yet. "I need to know that you're not a fool."

"Woman, you can warn me without insult. If the master's plotting anything, he's outnumbered."

"How so?"

"You're worth two of him, and as for me—". He shrugged. "You be the judge."

"You great Cimmerian oaf—" Raihna began. Then she laughed softly. "The gods be with you."

"With all of us, if the master has any friends aboard," Conan said. He was ruefully aware of the help the soldiers might have given. Well, only the gods had foreknowledge, and they only if the priests told the truth, which likely as not meant that *no one* knew what lay before him!

Loosening his sword in its scabbard, Conan strode aft to join the master.

By the time Conan reached the stern, the two hands were lowering the skiff into the water. The master, paler than ever, stood watching them. Watching the master, Conan saw that his hand did not stray far from his dagger. Nor did his eyes stray far from the peasant family. In their turn the peasants had their eyes on the master, with the attention of a cat watching a bird's nest. Gone were the dull-witted stares with which they had come aboard.

Conan felt more than sweat creeping down his spine. Raihna had most likely seen clearly. Something was afoot.

The skiff splashed into the river. One of the hands set the oars into their locks, while the other held the line. The master turned to Conan.

"With two stout fellows at the oars, the skiff will turn us about in good time. Then we can steer again, and seek a landing."

In the shallows by either bank the Shimak had

hardly more current than a millpond. Here in midstream matters were otherwise. The ferry was already well downstream from the pier on the far side.

Not far downstream, Conan saw that the banks rose steep and high on either side. A man landing there would have a fine scramble before he reached open ground. In that time he would be an easy target for archers on the river. Farther downstream still, if Conan remembered rightly, lay rapids, their fangs mostly drawn at this season of low water but not harmless to this ferry . . .

The second hand climbed into the skiff and took his oar. The master reached into the shadows beneath the platform. He came out with a stout purse in one hand. A hooded peasant woman stepped forward, hands raised as if to beg for alms.

Conan drew his sword and raised it hilt-first. He and Raihna had agreed on that signal to be ready for a fight but let others begin it. The master scurried for the edge of the deck, thrusting his purse into the bosom of his shirt as he ran. At the edge of the deck he drew his dagger and leaped.

As he leaped, so did the peasant woman. The hood flew back, revealing a gap-toothed, hook-nosed brown face whose curling black beard no woman had ever grown. A long knife leaped from under the robes to slash at Conan.

It reached only where Conan would have been. A backward leap took him clear of danger. He tossed his sword. It came down with hilt cleaving to his hand as if it had grown there.

From over the side came the crunch of wood and shrill curses. Eager to escape, the master had leaped too swiftly and come down too heavily. One foot had gone straight through the bottom of the skiff.

"I hope you swim better than the sergeant," Conan shouted. Then it was time to think of his own opponents, three "peasants" advancing with the air of trained fighting men.

Not only trained but trained to fight together. Conan saw this in their movements and in that saw danger. Three men were not enough to overcome him swiftly, or indeed at all. They were doomed. They could also well take long enough dying to let their comrades reach Illyana and Raihna.

First of all, let us make this one and not two. Again Conan leaped backward, his sword cleaving the air to discourage too close a pursuit. He hoped for no more; a swordsman could hardly strike accurately without his feet firmly planted.

The arcing gray steel did its work. The three let Conan open the distance. One tried to close, drawing a second dagger. A desperate parry brought the dagger up as Conan's sword descended. The dagger flew with a clang and a clatter. A moment later the man sagged to his knees, clutching at his useless arm. Clear sight left his eyes as the blood left his body.

One of the man's comrades used his death well. He slipped past Conan to block the Cimmerian's passage forward. Another "peasant" joined the remaining man. If Conan tried to pass the first man, the other two would have time to come up behind him.

A sound stratagem, against any other man than Conan. *They should have learned more about hillfolk before they tried to fight one*, was his thought.

Conan leaped to the edge of the deck, then dropped onto the first sweep. The slaves' eyes grew round and their hands loosened their grip. The sweep slanted down and trailed, but Conan had already shifted his weight to the next one.

The man who'd thought to block Conan waited too long to believe what the Cimmerian had done. Raihna came leaping aft, like a she-lion upon prey. Her sword split the man's skull and her dagger drove into his bowels. He collapsed without a sound, dead too swiftly even to foul himself. Conan heaved himself back aboard, to stand beside Raihna.

"Leave these to me," she cried. "Look to Illyana!"

Frantic braying and the drumming of hooves sounded on the far side of the ferry. Hard on their heels came curses, then a shrill scream from Illyana.

Another cry hammered at Conan's ears as he pushed through the baggage and animals underneath the platform. He reached the open in time to see a "peasant" leap overboard, frantic to flee the peddler's mule. The beast was thrashing about madly, panic-stricken out of what wits he had. In another moment the panic would spread through all the animals aboard. Then Conan and his ladies would have more than Lord Houma's hired swords to concern them.

Illyana was backed against one of the platform's supporting posts, facing three foes. In his mind Conan both cursed her for coming down from comparative safety and praised her courage. She held a long dagger, the twin of Raihna's, with a trained grip. Her slow movements would still have done little against even one opponent, had they been free to come at her. For Illyana, the mule was as good as another guard. The men feared to come within reach of its hooves and teeth.

That fear gave Conan time he put to good use. One man died with his skull split before he knew a foe stood behind him. The second whirled, sword leaping up to guard. He was both subtle and strong. Conan knew that he had the edge on the man, but would have to take care.

The meeting of two expert swordsmen drove the maddened mule back. The last man found a gap and slipped through it. He had no sword, but his two knives danced with swift assurance against Illyana's clumsy parries. He might have been playing with her, seeking to put her in fear and see her cringe and sweat before taking her life.

Conan cursed and shouted for Raihna, neither of which he expected to do much good. Something that Illyana could do, on the other hand—

"Put a spell on him, can't you?" he roared. "Or what good is your magic?"

"Better than you would dare to believe, Cimmerian!" Illyana shouted. A lucky parry held one knife away from her left breast. She gripped the man's other arm and held on with desperate strength.

Conan knew that neither her strength nor her desperation would be enough for long. If either failed before he could deal with this opponent—

"Then if it's so cursed good!—"

"It—is—not swifter—than—*uhhh*!" as the man tore his arm free. Illyana drove her knee up toward his groin but he shifted his footing so that she only struck his hip. A moment later one hand was wound in her hair while the other raised a knife toward her throat.

In that same moment Conan's sword found his opponent's life. Shoulder and chest poured blood onto already-stained robes. The man neither cried out nor fell. Instead he lurched toward Conan, still a barrier between him and Illyana, who had only a few heartbeats of life left to her.

As the knife blade touched Illyana's throat, a loop of iron chain tightened around the knife wielder's foot.

He kicked to clear his foot, sending himself off balance. The chain tightened again, pulling him away from Illyana. He threw out an arm to save himself—and Conan's sword came down on that arm. Severed arm and knife wielder fell to the deck at the same time.

Illyana stood, gripping the post with one hand. The other she held to her throat, stroking it as if she could scarcely believe it was not gaping from ear to ear. Her dagger lay unheeded on the deck. Conan picked it up and handed it to her.

"Don't ever let loose of your steel until the last enemy's dead!"

She swallowed and licked full lips. Her face would have made fresh milk look brightly colored, and a vein pulsed in the side of her long neck. She swallowed again, then sagged forward into Conan's arms.

It was not fainting. She babbled words that would have made no sense even in a language Conan understood and gripped him with arms seemingly turned to iron. Conan freed his sword arm and put the other around her, holding her as he might have held a puppy or a kitten.

Under the sorceress was enough woman to crave a man's touch when she needed assurance. Conan would leave matters there. To steal her maidenhood would be the kind of theft he had always disdained even as a new-fledged thief in Zamora. It was still not unpleasant to find in Illyana more kinship with ordinary folk than he'd ever expected to find in a sorceress.

"Come," he said at last. "Embracing men is like dropping your steel. Best save it until we've heard from our last enemy." Gently he pushed her away, then followed the chain around the dead man's leg to the edge of the deck and looked down.

One of the slaves stood on tiptoe, staring over the

edge of the deck. There had been just enough slack in the chain that held him to his sweep to let him use it as a weapon.

"My friend," Conan said. "I don't know if you've earned yourself freedom or impalement." From the slave's gaunt face and lash-marked back, it seemed unlikely that he cared greatly.

The eyes in the gaunt face were still steady. So was the voice. "The master was plotting, and I owed him nothing. You be the judge of your debt to me, you and your woman."

"I'm not—" Illyana began indignantly, then found the strength to laugh. She was still laughing when Raihna appeared, wiping blood from her sword.

"The two you left me are both down, Conan. One may live to answer questions if you have any. Oh, our friend speaks the truth about the master. He was to join the fight, too, but lost his courage at the last moment."

"Where is he?"

"Clinging for his life to the end of the skiff's line," Raihna said with a wicked grin. "The two hands threw him overboard and cut it loose. They were still well short of the bank when it sank under them. One of them could swim. I saw him clambering up the bank."

Conan wished sunstroke, snakebite, and thirst upon the treacherous hand and strode aft. The master was no longer pale, but red as if scalded with the effort of hanging to the line.

"For the love of the gods, don't let me drown!" he wheezed. "I can't swim."

"The gods don't love traitors and neither do I," Conan said. "Nor does Lord Mishrak."

The master nearly lost his grip on the line. "You serve Mishrak!"

"I can make him interested in you or not, as I choose. It lies in your hands."

"Then have mercy! To name me to Mishrak—would you slay me and all my kin?"

"I'd see you drown without blinking," Conan said brusquely. "Your kin may be worth more. Tell me what you know about these knifemen and I may hold my tongue."

For a man nearly at his last gasp, the master managed to tell a great deal in a short time. It appeared that the knifemen were indeed Lord Houma's. The master had never heard of Master Eremius or the Jewels of Kurag, nor did Conan choose to inform him.

At last the master began to repeat himself. Conan decided that there was little more to be heard worth the danger of losing the man to the river.

He reached down, heaved the man aboard, then shook him over the side like a wet dog. When he finally set the master down, the man's knees buckled. Conan tied his hands behind his back with his own belt.

"You swore—" the master began.

"I didn't swear a thing. You don't need hands to give orders. All you need is a tongue you had best shape to something like respect. Or I may kick you overboard and not trouble Mishrak with the work of learning any more from you."

The master turned pale again and sat mute as a stone, watching Conan turn forward and stride away.

It was a while before they could bring the ferry to a safe landing on the far bank of the Shimak. The master could barely speak at all. The peddler and his boy seemed concerned only that their mule was unhurt.

"Demons take you!" Conan swore at their fifth refusal to help handle the ferry. "Will it help your precious pet if he dies of thirst or drowns in the rapids?"

"When we know Lotus is well, then you can call on us," the peddler said. "Until then, leave us."

"Please, lady," the boy added, addressing Illyana. "If you can do magic, can you do a healing on Lotus? We couldn't pay very much, but we'd miss him a lot."

Conan wrestled notions of spanking the boy or throwing the mule overboard. It helped that Illyana was smiling at the boy.

"My magic isn't the kind that can help animals," she said. "But my sister was raised around horses. Perhaps she can help you."

Conan strode away with a curse, as Raihna knelt to take the mule's left hind foot in both hands.

It was Massouf, the slave who'd saved Illyana, who finally brought them to safety. Freed from his chains with a key Conan found in the master's purse (along with a good sum in gold that he decided the master had no further use for), Massouf put his comrades to some sort of regular stroke. With Conan to lend strength if not skill to the steering oar, they eventually crunched ashore some ways downstream.

"We're in your debt once more," Illyana said, as she emerged from behind a boulder in clean garb. "You already have your freedom. Is there more we can give? We are not ill-provided with gold—"

"Best not say that too loudly, my lady," Massouf said. "Even the rocks may have ears. But if you have gold to spare—" For the first time he seemed to lose his self-assurance, so unlike a slave's.

"If you have gold, I beg you to take it to the house of Kimon in Gala and buy the slave girl Dessa. They will ask much for her, comely as she is. But if you free her, I will be *your* slave if I can repay you no other way."

"What was she to you?" Raihna said. "We are not unwilling—"

"We were betrothed, when—what made us both slaves came about. It was ordered that we be sold separately, and each serve as hostage for the other. Otherwise, we would long since have fled or died together."

Conan heard an echo of his own thoughts as a slave in the young man's words. "What made you turn against your master this time? If Dessa is still a slave—"

"If you perished, Captain, I would not long outlive you. All the slaves would have been impaled as rebels. That is the law. With no hold over Dessa, Kimon might have sold her to Vendhya, or slain her outright." He straightened. "I had nothing to lose by aiding you."

"Mishrak didn't send us out here to rescue slave girls," Conan growled.

"He didn't send you out here to be rescued by slaves, either," Massouf said cheerfully. "But that's been your fate. Take it as a sign from the gods, Captain."

"You may take this as a sign to hold your tongue," Conan said, raising one massive fist. "I'm a good deal closer than the gods, too. Never fear. We'll pay a visit to Gala and free your Dessa. We'll even pay for her out of your master's gold." Conan hefted the master's purse. "If Kimon thinks this isn't enough, I'll show him reason to change his mind.

"But don't think you can jaunt along with us beyond Gala! Or I'll send *your* name to Mishrak, for keeping us from going about his business!"

Seven

THEY RODE INTO Gala as sunset flamed in the west. The Three Coins, where Dessa had worked, lay shuttered and silent, its garden a rank tangle of weeds. Inquiries of passing villagers took them to the Horned Wolf at the far end of the village. Illyana's nostrils flared in distaste as she contemplated the second inn.

"Is that the best we can hope for?"

"That depends, mistress," Conan said. Tales of the battle at the ferry might well have reached Gala already. It still seemed best to continue their masquerade until they knew it was useless.

"On what?"

"On how comfortable you find sleeping in open fields among sheep turds. The Horned Wolf may offer only lice-ridden straw, but—"

"You lie! Not the smallest louse ever found a home in my inn!"

A broad, florid face topped by a haystack of gray hair thrust itself out the nearest window. The woman shook her fist at Conan and drew in breath for another accusation.

"Mistress," Conan said, in a chill voice. "Perhaps the sheep will offer better hospitality. Turds and all, they'll not call us liars."

Ruddiness turned to pallor at the prospect of losing a customer.

"Forgive me, my lord and ladies. I meant no insult. You'd have a cold hard bed with the sheep. I swear I can offer better than that."

"We're neither lords nor ladies," Raihna snapped. "We're honest merchants, who know what a thing's worth. We can also recognize lice when we see them. Now, what are your prices?"

Conan let Raihna do the bargaining, with accustomed skill. He used the time to study the village, with an eye to where the houses might let foes wait in ambush. He also took a moment to counsel Massouf to stop fidgeting.

"You'll make the whole village remember you without freeing Dessa a moment sooner. She'll not thank you if that keeps her captive."

From Massouf's horror-stricken gape, this was clearly a new idea. Conan's curses were silent; they owed Massouf too much.

At last Raihna struck a bargain that Conan suspected was nothing of the kind, from the glee on the old woman's face. Louse-ridden straw still offered more comfort than stones. Perhaps the woman also knew where Dessa was.

They ate their own food but drank the inn's wine, near kin to vinegar. Two women brought it, both looking old enough to be Pyla's mother.

At last Conan felt he could cease insulting his stomach without insulting their hostess.

"Goodwife," he called. "The last time I was here I stayed at the Three Coins. They had a fine dancing girl who went by the name of Dessa. She wore rose scent and precious little else. It would be worth much, to see her dance again."

"Ah, you'll have to guest with Lord Achmai. Not that he's much of a lord, but he does have the Hold. He'd long had his eye on Dessa too. When Master Kimon died, he left so many debts that his kin were glad to sell all they could. Dessa went up to the Hold, and Mitra only knows what happened to her then."

Conan ignored strangled noises from Massouf. "What's this 'Hold'? I saw no such thing, the last time."

"Oh, perhaps you did. But it was only a ruin then. Achmai's put it to rights. Even in the old days it couldn't have been half so fine. Lord Achmai struts around now, like he was one of the Seventeen Attendants."

Conan made some ill-natured sounds of his own. This part of Turan was dotted with the old forts of the robber lords who'd infested the countryside before the early kings put them down. From time to time some lordling would bribe a governor to let him move back into one of them.

Doubtless Achmai would overreach himself one day. Then Mughra Khan would descend on the Hold with an army and an executioner. That would help neither Dessa nor those who wished to rescue her tonight.

"Well, I shall see if Lord Achmai's hospitality is worth having," Conan said, feigning doubts. "Who knows? If he's open-handed, perhaps I'll come back to serve him when my mistress and her sister are safe with their kin."

"Oh, he'll not refuse a fine stout young soldier like yourself," the innkeeper said. She giggled lewdly.

"Nor will the women he keeps, I'll wager. Half the men in his service are old enough to be father to such as you."

"How can you stand here talking, when Mitra only knows what Dessa may be suffering?" Massouf shouted. "Mistress, you owe me—*ukkkh*!"

A massive Cimmerian hand closed on the neck of Massouf's tunic. An equally massive arm lifted him until his feet were kicking futilely in the air two hands above the floor.

With a harsh ripping, the filthy tunic gave way. Massouf thumped in a heap on the floor. He glared at Conan but the look on the Cimmerian's face froze the words on his lips.

"Outside!" Conan snarled. Massouf regained his feet and bolted as if the inn had caught fire. The women followed at a more dignified pace.

Conan said only the smallest part of what he wanted to say, nor did he raise his voice. He still left Massouf looking much like a recruit caught stealing. At last the young man fell to his knees, not to beg mercy but because his legs would no longer support him.

Illyana turned her gaze from the sable sky above to Conan. "I wonder now about the wisdom of trying to rescue Dessa."

Massouf leaped up, with a choking cry. "Lady, for the love of all the gods—!"

"Leave the gods in peace, and us as well," Illyana snapped. "Because I say I wonder about something, does not mean I will not do it. *I* use my wits before I use my tongue. Do not think that I have as little honor as you have discretion!"

"What will you do if I think otherwise?" Massouf said uneasily. "Turn me into a frog?"

"Turn you into something useless to Dessa or any other woman, more likely," Illyana said. Her smile grew wicked. "If you spend less of your few wits on women, you will have more to spend on other matters.

"Now be silent. You can hardly help us rescue your Dessa. Have the goodness not to hinder us. Now, I must seek something in my baggage. I shall return as swiftly as I can."

Conan much doubted that anything short of stuffing Massouf into a sack would silence him. Nonetheless, he and Raihna took places where they could see each other, Massouf, and all approaches to Horned Wolf. They would also have a quick and safe way to the stables.

The last glimmers of light died in the village and the west. Even the cries of the night birds fell silent, as one by one they found their nests. In the stables a horse stamped restlessly; another whickered softly.

"Raihna?"

"You fear for Illyana?"

"She's been inside a good while. Our innkeeper may have decided to settle matters herself."

"Her and what army, Conan? I've seen only lads and women inside. Illyana's no fool. If she's to be taken, it will need more than our hostess—"

The inn door creaked open and a woman appeared. She moved with the gliding step of an accomplished dancer and the sway of a woman who knows everything about exciting men. She was of Illyana's height but a trifle less slender in those places where it mattered, fairer of skin and with hair that fell in a crimson cascade over freckled shoulders. Conan could see all the freckles, for the woman wore only a brief silk garment that covered her from breasts to loins.

Massouf stared as if he had indeed become a frog. At last he closed his mouth and stepped forward, reaching for the woman. Her hand leaped toward his, then batted it playfully aside.

"Come, come, Massouf. Have you forgotten Dessa so swiftly?"

Massouf swallowed. "I have not. But if she is in the Hold, perhaps I should. Will you help me forget her? I have—"

"Massouf, my friend," the woman said again. "I will do better than that. I will help her escape from Lord Achmai and all his old soldiers. She deserves a—"

"By Crom!" Conan growled. He'd finally recognized the voice and set aside the evidence of his eyes. "Mistress Illyana, or have my ears been spelled as well as my eyes?"

"Ah, Conan, I thought you would not be long in seeing through the glamouring. I do not imagine that Lord Achmai or his men will be as keen of ear or wits."

"Very likely not," Conan said. "But what good is that going to do us?"

"Conan, we do not know what we face in the Hold. I much doubt that even you could snatch Dessa from within it unaided."

"That doesn't mean your help will be better than none. If I had Raihna's—"

"Oh, we both will. I will go with you and use this glamouring. When Achmai and his men are thoroughly bemused, you will seek and rescue Dessa. Raihna and Massouf will await us outside, to help us if we need it and cover our retreat."

Raihna had her mouth open to protest, but Massouf silenced her by falling on his knees before Illyana. He threw his arms around her waist and pressed his face into her supple belly.

"Mistress, oh, mistress, forgive me that I doubted you! Forgive me—"

"I will forgive you much and that swiftly if you stop blubbering and stand like a man. Dessa will need one when she is free, not a whimpering child." Slowly Massouf obeyed.

"I've heard worse schemes," Conan said. "I'll go as a soldier looking for work. You can enter the Hold disguised as a man. Or will that glamouring hold for a whole day?"

"Not without more effort than I could make and still be fit for other work," Illyana admitted. "I am not using the Jewel for this. Not unless all else fails. Together, the Jewels build each other's strength. Apart, each Jewel must be rested between spells."

"I'll leave the magic to you," Conan said, resting a hand on his sword hilt. "Now I'd best find out where the Hold lies. If it's close enough, I can spy it out tonight and return before dawn. If we know beforehand—"

"Oh, you have no need to trouble yourself, Conan." Illyana's smile held a sensuousness that Conan much doubted was all the glamouring.

"How is that? Did you read our hostess's thoughts?"

"Just so. She came by and asked what I wanted in our chambers. While she was close, I read in her thoughts that she would send warning and where she would send it. Then I altered her thoughts. She will send warning only of those who will come to the Hold tomorrow night—you and I."

"Well and good." That sounded grudging and mean, even to Conan's ears. By Crom, good work was good work, even if a sorceress did it! Why complain about your sword because the smith was loose-living?

"I'm grateful, Mistress Illyana. Now, let's agree on a

place to meet if you must flee this inn. Then I'll be off to the Hold—"

"You have little need to roam this nighted land, Conan. The innkeeper has been at the Hold. What I took from her mind, I can show you."

Ice filled Conan's bowels. Put himself at the mercy of a spell reaching into his mind?

"It is *my* spell, Conan. Surely you can trust me? And no, I did not read your thoughts. You spoke aloud without knowing it."

"Captain Conan, if I might speak—" began Massouf.

"Would you care if I said no?"

Massouf laughed. "It is only that you do not know what you may face there. I am sure Mistress Illyana will do all that she can. But unless she can conjure up dragons and trolls, you will have much hard work. Why not save your strength for it?"

"I suppose your first post as a free man will be advising King Yildiz on strategy," Conan growled. "There may be some sense in what you say, if our hostess can tell a gate tower from a privy!"

"Trust her, Conan," Raihna said. "Everything the innkeeper has ever seen, you will see as clearly as if you were there yourself. You can learn enough and still sleep tonight."

All three of them were right, much as Conan disliked admitting it. Rescuing Dessa at all was crackbrained enough; why make matters worse?

His eyes met Raihna's, and she smiled. Conan had no art of reading thoughts, but hers were plain on her face. She was not saving his strength entirely for fighting, and as for sleep, she did not intend to allow him much.

Eight

GRAVEL RATTLED UNDER the hooves of the hired horses as Conan and Illyana reined in before the frowning gate of Achmai's Hold. The stout timbers were yet unweathered and the massive iron hinges showed only a faint tinge of rust.

Otherwise the ruddy stone walls stood much as they had for centuries. Conan had seen a few of these old bandit-lords' strongholds and heard tales of many. This seemed larger than most. When it rose on the hill, the looting must have been good.

From a tower to the right of the gate, a voice hailed them.

"Who comes?"

"Two soldiers, seeking speech with Lord Achmai."

"Why should he speak with soldiers?"

"Does he then hire men unseen and unheard?"

"You wish to enter his service?"

"If his service seems fit for us, yes."

Two heads thrust out of the tower. One was shaven, the other wore an old cavalry helmet. Under the

96

scrutiny, Conan saw unease in Illyana's eyes. He could see nothing else, so thoroughly did her man's garb conceal her. Had he not known she was a woman, he himself would have taken her for a youth.

"Is this wise?" she whispered. "Speaking as though we do Achmai a favor by seeking his service?"

"No soldier with pride in his sword does otherwise," Conan assured her. "If I spoke otherwise, they grow suspicious."

Before Illyana could reply, the voice hailed them again.

"Enter, and be welcome."

The size of the courtyard within the walls told Conan that indeed this had once been a mighty fortress. Now the courtyard was half-filled with out-buildings, stout but roughly-built stables, sheds, and barracks. Only the keep had been restored to its original strength, and the Great Hall to at least some of its original splendor.

Six men met them in the center of the courtyard. Their arms were well-kept and their clothes clean, if ragged. Their features bore the stamp of more different races than Conan could have numbered on the fingers of both hands.

"We'll take your horses," one said. He seemed to be mostly a Shemite, with a hint of Vanir in the fairness of his beard.

"Show us the stable, and we'll lead them there ourselves," Conan said. Like the horses, the saddles were hired. The saddlebags bore certain items best not closely examined.

The fair-bearded Shemite seemed to hesitate, then shrugged. "As you wish."

The quick yielding made Conan more suspicious

than a long argument. He signed Illyana to stay mounted. The gate was still open. If the worst came, she'd have a hope of flight.

The Cimmerian swung lithely from his saddle and strode to the head of the horses. As he took the reins, he felt a hand on the hilt of his sword.

The reins flew from Conan's hands as he whirled. One hand seized the sword hilt and the intruder's hand, imprisoning it as if a boulder had fallen upon it. The other hand paused only long enough to clench into a fist. Then it crashed into a beardless jaw. The intruder flew backward to spread-eagle himself on the stones.

Conan glared down at him. "Learn to keep your hands off other men's swords, my young friend. The next lesson may cost more than a sore jaw."

Only then did the Cimmerian notice that Fairbeard and the rest were watching him with catlike attention. He almost drew his sword. Then Fairbeard laughed.

"Well done, my friend. It will be worth Lord Achmai's while to speak with you."

"That's as may be," Conan said. "Now, what test shall I set him, to be sure it's worth *my* speaking with *him*?"

Again the sky outside held only stars. The men gathered in the Great Hall had better light. Torches blazed in iron sconces along the walls, and lamps filled with scented oil glowed on the high table.

Lord Achmai grinned at Conan and arranged his oily black beard with a beringed hand.

"You should have come to me at once, after your old master's death. You'd have been high in my service long since."

"I had to see the widow and her sister safe to their

kin," Conan replied. His fingers were making short work of a fat quail, slow-roasted and stuffed with succulent fruit and herbs. "My oath would have bound me, if common sense had not."

"Ah yes. You Cimmerians put much stock in your oaths, when you bother to take them."

Conan knew a chill along his spine. To be recognized as a Cimmerian was not a common experience. Was Achmai playing with him again?

"Will you tell me that I was mistaken, in calling you Cimmerian?" the man added. "If that blood shames you—"

"Ha! I know my forefathers and kin as well as you do."

Probably better, in truth. The innkeeper said that Achmai's family had been lords for five generations. Perhaps they had, if one counted lordship of another's kitchen or stables.

"Doubtless. It is only that one seldom sees a man of your coloring who is not a Cimmerian. And one sees few Cimmerians in Turan."

"Most of us have the sense to stay at home, where we need not listen to insults," Conan growled, with a grim smile to set Achmai at ease.

"Well, if you have the greater sense to come to me, when you have no more duty to your ladies, there will be a place for you. Likewise for your comrade.

"As for Dessa, whom you sought—you need seek no further."

Once more Conan contemplated the serving girls, clad only in nearly transparent trousers with bells on wrists and ankles. Once more he saw none who could be the Dessa Massouf had described.

Then a drum began a swift, insistent beat, and a girl danced into the room. She wore only a short robe of transparent red silk, and that cut so that it flew out like wings as she whirled. Otherwise she wore only bells, not just at wrists and ankles but at her throat, in her ears, and on a silver chain at her waist. The torchlight played on her oiled skin, sometimes wreathing her in light, sometimes revealing her more clearly.

Back and forth across the room she wove a path of tinkling bells, light, and lush beauty. Conan had seen fairer women, but never one so likely to make a man forget them.

Her path wove closer to the high table. Closer still—and Achmai's arm shot out like a javelin. The beringed fingers snatched the robe from Dessa's shoulders, waving it like a trophy.

The men cheered. Dessa grinned and executed a somersault that slapped her feet down on either side of Conan's plate. Then she leaped up, flowed down, and flung her arms around Conan.

Two perfumed breasts enveloped his face, but his ears were free to hear the roars of laughter. He also caught a glimpse of Illyana. Again he could see only her eyes, but they told him clearly enough that she was in a cold rage. The Cimmerian contemplated what might happen if that rage turned hot.

Conan wondered if it would have been wiser to come here openly, invoking Mishrak's name to gain Dessa's release. Most likely, disguise had been the best course. Achmai had gold from somewhere far beyond this province, perhaps beyond Turan. He would not enjoy having Mishrak learn where, and he had two-score well-trained and well-armed men to guard his secrets.

Dessa turned a back somersault off the table, landing on the piled rugs, flaming scarlet and orange with threads of gold woven into their swirling patterns.

Almost as easily as if she'd risen to her feet, she stood on her hands, waved a foot at the drummer, and began once more to sway to his beat.

As Dessa's gleaming body blazed against the rugs, Conan felt as if he sat between two blazing hearths.

A strangled cry burst from Illyana. She leaped up from the table, knocking her plate to the floor. She clutched her wine cup as she fled, but dropped it as she vanished out the door of the Hall. The guards were too bedazzled by Dessa to stop her.

"What means this?" Achmai said. His voice was even, but his hand was close to his sword hilt. "Is your companion so young he cannot bear the sight of a woman?"

"Or would he prefer the sight of a man?" shouted someone. "No doubt Pahlos could oblige him—"

"Oh, bite your tongue out and your cods off," snarled someone else, likely enough Pahlos.

"Silence!" Achmai roared. His eyes drifted back to Conan.

"Oh, you will find little to complain of in my companion," Conan said. "Perhaps the flux he had last year is returning. We shall doubtless learn soon enough. If you have any potions—"

"Oh, we know how to ease the flux," Achmai said. His smile did not reach his eyes. "We also know how to cure liars and fools."

"You will not need those cures tonight," Conan said, with an ease he did not altogether feel. *Erlik take the woman, what* is *she planning? Or have the wits to plan deserted her now, of all times?*

"I hope not," Achmai said. "Dessa has given us all too much pleasure, to have the evening end in a quarrel."

Dessa had indeed given pleasure. Conan began to

doubt that returning the girl to her betrothed was going to be half as simple as he'd expected.

Dessa knew the power her dancing gave her over men. Knew it and savored it like fine wine. Conan could not imagine her putting all that behind her to settle down as the wife of a clerk and the mother of a pack of squalling brats.

Well, that was Massouf's problem. Conan had his own, a well-formed one named Illyana. Where had that magic-wielding wench taken herself, and how long would it take before Achmai sent his men in search of her?

At least Dessa was still dancing. If Achmai ordered his men out of the hall before she stopped, he'd have a mutiny on his hands!

Dessa's dancing now grew slower, as her strength at last began to flag. She knelt, swaying her torso back and forth until it was almost level and her breasts rose almost straight up. Her belly rippled, her arms curved and recurved, her bells made wicked music, and the light gleamed still brighter as sweat joined the oil on her skin.

At last she found the strength to execute a final somersault. She landed on her back, feet resting on the high table. Achmai pushed a cup of wine between them. The long toes curled, then gripped. Slowly, without spilling a drop, Dessa rocked back on her haunches. Still more slowly, using her hands only for balance, she brought the cup to her lips. Silence as thick as a fog on the Vilayet Sea filled the room.

Then the silence shattered, as the door guards sprang aside and Illyana returned.

She returned with the glamour upon her, so that she seemed as she had when first Conan saw it. He was proof against the surprise that stunned every man in the room.

He was not proof against the sensuality wafting like perfume from Illyana's magical image. No woman he had ever bedded had so heated his blood. He gulped wine, and found it odd that the wine did not boil in his throat!

All this, with Illyana only standing in the doorway. To be sure, she was clad only in a gilded loinguard and a silver ring about her red hair, from which flowed a long red veil. Firm young breasts with rouged nipples, a faintly curved belly, legs that seemed to go on without end—all lay bare to the eye, all glowed with oil or magic or both.

"You rogue!" Achmai growled. He seemed to be having difficulty breathing, for it was some moments before he could say more. Then he added, "Were you traveling with *that*?"

"Kindly refer to the woman as *her*," Conan said with a broad grin. "Or do you think she is some wizard's creation?"

"Ah—well, there's magic in her, more than in most women. But—to think of *hiding* her!"

"Does a wise man show a purse of gold to a band of robbers?"

Achmai was too bemused by Illyana to reply for a moment. Conan used that moment to study the room. If Illyana truly needed her maidenhood to work her magic, she'd best have ready to hand either mighty spells or a fleet pair of heels.

"Such a woman—it's an insult to compare her to gold," Achmai said at last. Something seemed to be stuck in his throat. He was trying to clear it with wine when Illyana began dancing.

Clearly there was only Illyana's own suppleness and

skill under the glamouring. She did not vie with Dessa in somersaults and other feats. Nor did any music follow her, except the beat of the drum when the drummer stopped gaping like a thirsty camel.

Instead she whirled across the floor, her feet moving too fast for even Conan's eye to follow. She wove a complex path among the rugs, over and around the piles, swaying from head to toe like a blade of grass in a spring breeze. Her head swung from side to side, tossing the veil. Not that it concealed anything even in those rare moments when it hung straight.

Conan felt his head pounding with more than the fire in his blood and the beat of the drum. He turned his wine cup mouth down and searched for Dessa. She stood by the doorway, ignoring one of the guards' arms resting lightly across her shoulders. She stared at Illyana with the look of a barely-fledged journeyman watching a master display her art.

Now Illyana bent down, one leg thrust out gracefully for balance, swaying as she gripped a rug. A howl of outrage rose as she lifted the rug and wrapped it around herself from neck to knees. Then it died as she whirled across the room again.

Far from concealing her movements, the thick rug seemed to make them more provocative. Crimson and wine patches leaped like flames under the thrust of hips and breasts.

A spearlike thrust of Illyana's head cast the veil aside. It floated across the hall as if a breeze blew it. Conan knew magic lifted it. No one else knew or cared. Tables tilted, spilling their loads, or toppled entirely as men leaped for the veil. A half-score reached it in the same moment. Without drawing steel, they rent it into a piece for each man.

Or had the veil rent itself, before the men reached it? Conan could not have sworn one way or the other.

Illyana now essayed a somersault. The rug stayed almost in place. Magic, of a certainty. Again Conan saw none who seemed to either understand or care.

The headring leaped free of Illyana's flame-hued hair. It rolled across the floor, chiming with an insistent, maddening music, avoiding all the rugs. It rolled almost to Achmai's feet before anyone thought to catch it.

Before any could move, Achmai's hand snatched up the ring. Conan noted the sureness and grace of the man's movement. He would still be clear of wit and swift of sword if matters came to a fight.

Then everyone surged to his feet as Illyana cast off the rug and the loinguard in the same movement. The rug rolled itself up as it crossed the floor. The loinguard flew like an arrow to Conan's outthrust hand.

"Cimmerian, my friend," Achmai said. "I offer you and your—friend—a place in my service. Now, next year, five years from now. What the gods allow me to give you, you shall have!

"Only—that woman. I want her for a night. Just one night. By all that either of us holds sacred, I will not force her or hurt her. No other shall so much as give her an unseemly look—"

"I call you friend too," Conan said, laughing. "But I also call you mad, if you think your men will cast no longing looks. Indeed, the lady would be much offended if they did otherwise. Only promise what the gods will allow you to do, and one thing more."

"Anything—if the gods allow it," Achmai said, without taking his eyes from Illyana's sinuous writhings.

She now lay on the rugs, describing a serpentine path toward the high table.

"Dessa, for tonight."

For a moment both wine and desire left Achmai's eyes and a shrewd bargainer looked out at Conan. Then the man nodded.

"As you wish." He clapped his hands. The guard removed his arm from Dessa's shoulder, patted her, and gave her a little shove. She strode across the room, head high, too proud to show that she knew every man's eye was on Illyana.

"Tonight, be a friend to this new friend of mine," Achmai said. "I did not think you found him unpleasing, and certainly no man ever found *you* so."

"As you wish, my lord," Dessa said, with a smile that widened as she saw Conan now had eyes only for her. "Since it is no secret that this is *my* wish too . . ."

She vaulted over the table and settled on Conan's lap. Illyana showed no sign of ending her dancing. Still less did she show any sign of telling Conan what her plans were—if any.

Conan had asked for Dessa with the notion that the closer she was to him, the easier their escape would be if matters went awry. Of course they might now go awry from Illyana's jealousy, but Conan knew no cure for jealous women and expected to find none tonight!

He shifted Dessa to a more comfortable position on one knee and picked up Illyana's discarded loinguard. As his fingers tightened on it, he felt a tingling. Surprised, he nearly dropped the garment. His fingers would not obey his will. The chilling presence of sorcery drove out both wine and pleasure in Dessa's company.

Then a familiar voice spoke in his mind:
Be at ease, Conan. I have other glamourings besides

this one. One of them will make Achmai think he has taken more pleasure from me than he could have imagined from six women. Neither of us will lose anything we yet need.

When I am done, I shall come to you. Be ready, and Dessa likewise.

The voice fell silent. The tingling ceased. Conan's fingers obeyed his will, and he stuffed the loinguard into his tunic.

Dessa ran her fingers up his arm and across his cheek. "Ah, you will soon forget her. That I swear."

Conan tightened his grip. Illyana seemed to have her wits about her, he had a willing bedmate for the night, and the rest could be left to chance.

Nine

DESSA LAY SNUGGLED on Conan's shoulder like a kitten. Had they been elsewhere, her gentle breathing might have lulled him as deeply asleep.

Instead he was as alert as if he had been standing sentry on the Hyrkanian frontier. Only a fool slept in the house of a man who might swiftly become an enemy, in spite of good wine and willing women.

A faint knocking sounded at the door. Conan listened for the rhythm until he heard three strokes, then one, then two. He pulled his sword out from under the blankets, padded catlike to the door, and drew the bolt.

Illyana stood in the doorway. She wore her man's clothing save for the headdress. Deep indigo circles beneath both eyes made them look twice as large as before, and her face was pale.

She stepped into the room, pushed the door shut, then slumped onto the chest beside the bed. Conan offered her wine. She shook her head.

"No. I am only a trifle weary. I would like to sleep,

but not as soundly as our friend Achmai. He will have sweet dreams of what he thinks happened between us, as sweet any man could wish."

"How does a maiden sorceress learn of men's dreams after bedding a woman?"

Illyana shivered, then bowed her head. Her throat worked. For a moment Conan thought she was about to spew.

The moment passed. She drew in a rasping breath and stared at him without seeing.

"I have learned. That is all I can tell you."

With that look on her face, Conan would not have asked her more for the Crown of Turan. After a moment he drank the wine himself, donned his clothes, and set about waking Dessa.

From the wall outside, a sentry called.

"The fifth hour, and all's well!"

The sentry could barely be heard over the drunken snores of the men in the Great Hall. He also sounded a trifle drunk himself. He was still on duty, though, ready to give the alarm.

Conan led the way to the outer door of the hall, to find the door locked from the inside. Illyana stepped forward, holding up the arm bearing the Jewel of Kurag.

The Cimmerian shook his head. He had never studied under the master thieves of Zamora, men to whom no lock held many secrets for long. He could still open a crude lock such as this in less time and with less uproar than any spell.

Outside, the courtyard was deserted and seemingly lifeless. Only the faint glow of a brazier outside the stables showed a human presence. Conan gave the ruddy glow a sour look. Well, it was a soldier's luck, to find that the only place guarded was the one he wanted.

The cool night air awoke Dessa from her near-sleepwalking. She looked about her, and her dark eyes widened.

"What—where are you taking me? This is not the way to Lord Achmai's—"

"You will not be going back to him," Conan said. "We have come to take you to Massouf, your betrothed. He is waiting for you."

"Massouf? I thought he was long dead!"

"You received no messages from him?" Illyana asked. "He sent all he could."

"Oh, some reached me. But how could I believe them?"

Illyana looked bewildered.

"Believe me," Conan said. "It's easy to believe everyone's lying to you when you're a slave. Most do."

Dessa smiled, as if he had praised her dancing or beauty. Then her face changed to a mask of determination. She opened her mouth and drew in breath for a scream.

None but the Cimmerian could have silenced Dessa without hurting her. His massive arms held her as gently as an eggshell, but she could make no more sound than a man entombed.

As Conan shifted his grip, Illyana stepped close. One hand rested on Dessa's forehead. Conan felt a tingling in his arms, his head swam, and Dessa slumped boneless and senseless against him.

"What—what did you do?" The effort to stand and speak made his voice grate harshly. As through a mist, he saw light fading from within the Jewel.

"A simple sleeping spell."

"Cast so quickly?"

"Against Dessa, yes. Against someone alert and strong–willed, it would not be so easy. I would not care to cast it against you at all."

"So you say."

"Conan, you still see evil in my magic? What can I do to persuade you otherwise?"

The Cimmerian smiled grimly. "If your magic made me King of Aquilonia, I wouldn't call it good. I wouldn't call *you* evil, though."

Illyana contrived a smile. "With such crumbs I must be content, I suppose."

The brazier still glowed before the stable door when Conan's party reached it. The stable guards were nowhere to be seen. Illyana vanished into the stable to retrieve their mounts, while Conan laid Dessa on a bale of straw and drew his sword.

He had begun to think of searching for Illyana when the stable guards returned. Neither was quite sober, and they supported between them a giggling girl, less than half-clad and rather more than half-drunk.

"Ho, Cimmerian," one man called. "Come to join our sport?"

"It will be better sport if there's some wine," Conan replied.

"In truth," the second man said. "Faroush, go and find that jug you—"

"You go and find *your* jug," the first man began indignantly.

"What, and leave you alone with Chira?" the second man growled.

Faroush was about to reply when Illyana emerged from the darkness, leading the horses.

"Ho, ha, sweet lady. Have you come to dance for us?" said Faroush.

"In truth, no," Illyana said. "I beg you to excuse me." Her voice was steady, but to Conan her eyes had the look of a trapped animal's.

"Beg all you want," the second man said. His voice was all at once level, and his hand on the hilt of his sword. Conan marked him as the more dangerous.

"Again, I must say no," Illyana went on. "I am far too weary for any dancing that would please you."

"That I much doubt," said the second man. "It's the kind of dancing best done lying down, and—"

The man had talked a moment too long and not drawn his sword fast enough. A Cimmerian fist hammered into his jaw like a boulder. He flew backward, crashing into the stable door and sliding down to sprawl senseless in the dung-laden straw.

Faroush drew his sword, apparently sobered by his comrade's fate. Conan saw fear in his eyes, but in his stance and grip a determination to fight even against such an opponent.

Mishrak will want to know how Lord Achmai commands such men, was Conan's thought. *For that matter, so do I.*

Meanwhile, the girl had been swaying as she pulled her clothes into order. At last she drew a deep breath, and Conan cursed. From where he stood, he could only silence the girl by cutting her down, and that he would not do.

A moment later, the girl let out all her breath in a wild shriek.

"Help! Help! Guards! Thieves in the stables! Help! Help!"

Then she turned and ran. Faroush seemed to consider the alarm given and did the same, sword in hand.

Conan turned to Illyana. "Do you have a spell to speed our way out of here, by chance?"

Illyana frowned. "I cannot fly us all. Not the horses, certainly, and we will need them to outstrip—"

"Curse you, woman! Is this a time for bantering? Yes or no?"

"Yes. If you can give me a trifle of time and find some way to slow the pursuit."

Conan looked at the stable door. It looked stout enough to defy anything short of a battering ram or fire. Achmai's men would hardly burn the stable over the heads of their own horses.

Conan bent to pick up Dessa and jerked his head toward the stable. "Inside, and be quick about it."

The door crashed shut. Darkness embraced them. Conan fumbled for the bar. As he slid it into place, fists began pounding on the outside.

A dim emerald glow swelled behind him. He turned, to see the Jewel glowing on Illyana's wrist. She was taking off her tunic.

"What in Erlik's name—?"

Illyana drew her tunic off and bared all her teeth in a grin. "Have you never heard that one must be unclothed to cast a spell?"

"I've seen a good many women who could indeed cast spells unclothed, but they weren't your kind."

"Well, Cimmerian, you learn something new of magic every day you are in my company."

"Whether I wish it or not!"

Conan listened to the din outside the door, the shouts, the curses, the rasp of drawn swords, and a few men trying to make their orders heard. By the time he knew they faced no immediate danger, Illyana was bare save for the Jewel on one wrist and a rune-carved ivory bracelet on the other.

The emerald light from the Jewel flowed over her fair skin, turning the hue of bronze long under the sea.

She might have been some Atlantean goddess, risen from the waves to strike at those who overthrew her city.

Conan drew his dagger and stalked down the line of horses, cutting their tethers or opening their stall doors. By the time all were free, Illyana was standing by her mount, wearing an impatient look as well as the Jewel and bracelet.

"All that I can do here has been done. It is time to ride."

Conan heaved Dessa over the neck of his horse and swung into the saddle. Illyana lifted the Jewel and chanted.

"Chaos, thrice-cursed, hear our blessing—" followed by something about twice as long in a tongue Conan neither knew nor wanted to know.

A whirlwind burst the straw and hay bales apart. The loose straw and hay rose above Conan's head, then fell back into a corner, piled as high as a man. As if kicked, the brazier toppled over, scattering burning coals into the straw and hay. Flames ran up the pile, touched the pitch-laden walls, and leaped toward the ceiling.

Then Illyana made a fist of the hand bearing the Jewel and brought it down like a blacksmith's hammer. The stable door burst apart as if a battering ram had indeed struck it.

"Hiyaaa!"

Conan screamed the war cries of half a dozen races as he spurred his horse into the ranks of Achmai's men. His broadsword leaped and flashed in the firelight, slashing to either side.

He still made poor practice. His mount was hardly war-trained, besides carrying double. It mattered little, since his foes were scattering even as he reached them. A good many had fallen to the scything timbers of the stable door. The rest might have fought against men, but not against magic. Illyana's appearance, nude and blazing with emerald light, finished them.

It was as well that the courtyard was swiftly clear. Illyana had to ride thrice in a circle, chanting more arcane words, before flame leaped once more from the Jewel. It struck once, twice, at each hinge and fastening of the gate. At each stroke of fire, metal smoked, then melted and ran. A final stroke pushed the gates down altogether, like a child pushing down a sand castle.

Over the smoldering ruins of the gates, Conan and Illyana rode into the night.

They stopped about halfway back to the meeting place with Raihna and Massouf, to rest the horses and listen for sounds of pursuit. Conan heard none, nor was Illyana much surprised.

"Few of the horses will take much harm, if the men lead them out of the stable in time. Fewer still will be fit for work tonight."

"They won't be coming after me?" Dessa sounded half-outraged, half-relieved.

"With no horses and their chief so sound asleep an earthquake couldn't wake him? Those are men, not wizards!" Conan growled.

"*She's* a wizard," Dessa said, pointing at Illyana. "And you're some kind of soldier. Why did you take me away from the Hold?"

"We told you. We are returning to your betrothed."

Illyana burrowed into her saddlebags and started pulling out clothes. She had ridden naked from the Hold, uncaring of the night chill.

Dessa was less enduring. She snatched the clothes from Illyana, then dropped them as if they were an armful of nettles.

"Now what?" Conan growled.

"I won't wear *her* clothes. They might be tainted with her magic."

"Then wear mine," Conan said. One of his tunics came down nearly to Dessa's knees, but it did more or less clothe her.

"I suppose I should thank you," Dessa said at last. "But—did you ever think I might have wanted to stay? I did, you know."

Conan's and Illyana's eyes met above Dessa's head. The sorceress was the first to find her tongue.

"Dessa, Massouf loves you. Or so he says," she added.

"What he says and what he does are two different things, lady. His real love is gold. That's why he was enslaved. Even if he'd succeeded at his schemes, he wouldn't have given me half as much as Achmai and his men. I was better off even at the Three Coins, for Mitra's sake!"

She looked beseechingly at Conan. "Captain, if I might have something for my feet, I'll trouble you no more. I can make my own way back to—"

"Crom!" The oath flew out of Conan's mouth like the flame from the Jewel. Both women flinched. Conan drew breath.

"Dessa, we swore an oath to bring you back to Massouf. We're somewhat in his debt. The gods do not love unpaid debts." Dessa opened her mouth but a glare from Conan pushed the words back into it unuttered.

"You won't find yourself welcome back at the Hold, either," Conan went on. "They can't be sure you didn't want to escape. You'll be scrubbing the pots and being scrubbed out by the potboys if you go back."

Dessa still looked obstinate. "If you don't fear the gods or Achmai's men, try fearing me," Conan finished. "Dessa, if you take one step toward the Hold, you'll have to meet Massouf standing. I'll leave you in no state to sit down!"

Silently consigning all women to a place as far as possible from him, Conan unhooked the water bottles and went in search of a spring.

Ten

THEY RODE OUT at dawn, as the Iranistanis measured it—when a man could tell a black horsehair from a white one.

For a while Conan and Raihna led their mounts, to ease their way across the broken ground. With the two hired horses for Dessa and Massouf, no one needed to ride double for lack of mounts.

Lack of riding skill was another matter. Dessa rode like a sack of grain and Massouf hardly better. If it came to swift flight, Conan and Raihna would be taking their saddle-shy charges up on their own mounts.

So far they had seen no sign of pursuit, and Conan aimed to put off that moment as long as possible. They kept away from the main roads and indeed from the greater part of the mountain byways. Sheep tracks or bare hillside saw them pass, and of men only an occasional herdsman and once a hermit.

"They are a close-mouthed breed, these mountain

folk," Conan said. "Oh, gold or torture can open their mouths like any man's. But it takes a while. Besides, torturing free Turanians is a fine way for Achmai to lose whatever good will he has in Aghrapur."

"Their flocks can see anything the herdsmen see," Illyana said.

"All the sheep and goats I've known were even more close-mouthed than the herdsmen," Conan replied, with a grin. It was a fine fair morning and although tired he was in high good humor. A battle fairly fought and splendidly won always left him so.

"There are ways to make even the dumb speak," Illyana said soberly.

"How?" Conan laughed. "I can just imagine Achmai shouting at a ram—'Who passed this way yesterday? Answer, or I'll roast you for our dinner!' I can't imagine him getting an answer."

"Not that way, no."

Conan's grin twisted. "Are there spells for making animals speak?"

"For learning what they have seen, yes."

"Does Achmai command them?" The upland morning suddenly seemed as cold as a Cimmerian autumn.

"Neither he nor anyone who serves him commands any magic. But if he wished vengeance enough and knew of Eremius—the Master of the other Jewel knows all the spells. He might even have learned to cast them over such a distance. It has been ten years since we met. I no longer can be sure I know everything he does."

She forced a smile. "At least there is one consolation. He can no longer be sure that *he* knows everything *I* know. And I have not spent those ten years in idleness or debauchery."

The smile widened. "Why, Conan, I truly begin to think you are curious about magic. Are you becoming willing to live with it?"

"Maybe, when I can't live without it," Conan growled. "Of course, I can live with the kind of magic you danced up, any day or night. I wonder if your whole scheme came from wanting to show yourself like that—"

The smile vanished and the fair skin flushed. Illyana dropped back to ride beside Dessa and Massouf. Conan spurred forward, to ride level with Raihna, muttering rude remarks about women who could be neither chaste nor unchaste.

"That was an ill-spoken jest," Raihna said, when the Cimmerian fell silent.

"Am I to learn why, or must I guess?"

"You will learn if Illyana chooses to tell you. Not otherwise. It is not my secret to tell."

"Not telling me all I need to know is sending me into this fight blind."

"Ah, Conan. Surely not that. One-eyed at worst."

"That's bad enough, against an opponent with two eyes. Or didn't Master Barathres teach you that? If he didn't, you should go back to Bossonia and get your fees back from him, at the point of a—"

Raihna's hand leaped at his cheek so swiftly he had no time to seize it. Instead he blocked the blow, then gripped Raihna's arm just above the elbow.

"Another ill-timed jest?"

"Let me go, curse you!"

"I've been cursed by a good many men and women, and I'm healthier than most of them."

Then he saw that tears were starting from her eyes. He released her and guided his horse to a safe distance, while she reined in and sat in silence, shaking and weeping silently.

At last she pushed her fists into her eyes, sighed, and faced Conan once more.

"Conan, forgive me. That was a cruel jest indeed, but you could not have known how much so. I am an exile from Bossonia. I have no home save where Illyana chooses to lead me. Illyana or someone worse.

"So I owe her silence about her secrets and perhaps a trifle more. Tell me, my Cimmerian friend. What would you say to a jest, that High Captain Khadjar was in the pay of Lord Houma?"

Conan felt the blood rush to his face. Raihna laughed, pointing at a fist he'd raised without realizing it.

"You see. I owe Illyana as much or more as you owe Khadjar. Let's follow an old Bossonian saying—'if you won't burn my haystacks, my cattle won't befoul your well.' Truce?"

Conan guided his horse close again and put an arm around her. She nestled into it for a moment.

"Truce."

From the ravine, the last frantic bellowings had died. So had the last of the herd of cattle. Even Master Eremius heard only the gobbling, tearing, and cracking as the Transformed dismembered the bodies. From time to time he heard growls and squeals as they quarreled over some particularly succulent piece.

He did not fear the quarrels would turn bloody. The Transformed were no disciplined army, but the elders among them had ways of keeping the peace. At times, Eremius suspected, those ways meant the disappearance of one or two of their number. A waste, but not a great one.

Today nothing of that nature would happen. The Transformed had a feast under their claws. They also had foreknowledge of a greater feast tonight, with human flesh to rend and human terror to savor.

Captain Nasro scrambled up to Eremius's perch and knelt.

"Master, the stream at the foot of the ravine grows foul. Blood and ordure make it unfit for drinking."

"It matters not at all to the Transformed. Or have you forgotten that?"

"I remember, Master." He swallowed, sweat breaking out on his face. "Yet—do you—I also remember —that our men, those not Transformed—they need clean water."

"Then let them go upstream from the ravine and drink there!" Eremius snarled. The force of his anger made his staff lift from the ground and whirl toward the captain's head. Eremius let the staff come so close that the man flinched, then made it tap him lightly on the cheek.

"Think, man. Would I have let your men go thirsty? I have left you and them alike enough wits to find food and water. Go use them, and leave me in peace!"

Nasro flinched again, bowed again, and retreated.

Alone save for his thoughts and the din of the Transformed feeding, Eremius sat down, staff across his knees. It was a pity he could not hope that Nasro and all his men would perish in tonight's battle among the villages. The villagers would hardly offer enough resistance.

Besides, he still needed Nasro and the rest of his witlings. Only when both Jewels were at his command could he amuse himself by disposing of them.

That promised to be a most agreeable day. So did

another, the day he made the Transformed able to breed and breed true. Transformed and commanded by the powers of a single Jewel, they were barren. When Eremius held both Jewels, matters would be otherwise. Then he would also command a regular tribute of women to be Transformed and bear more such.

It was said that the children of those Transformed by both Jewels reached their full growth in a single year. Eremius would most assuredly put that to the proof at the earliest moment. If it was true, he would have one more irresistible gift to offer his allies.

Of course, with Illyana's aid or at least her Jewel he could have proved the matter and offered the gift ten years ago! That thought no longer ruled his mind, as the day of open battle and victory drew closer. It still lurked in his spirit, snarling like a surly watchdog and able to darken the brightest day.

"The stream's turned all bloody!"

"The demons have cursed it!"

"Who brought their wrath upon us?"

"Find him!"

At those last words Bora broke into a run. He wanted to reach the stream before the crowd decided he was the one they should find and turned into a mob searching for him.

The shouting swelled. Bora had never run so fast in his life, save when fleeing the mountain demons. He burst out of the village and plunged through the crowd. He was on the bank of the stream before anyone saw him coming.

There he stopped, looking down into water commonly as cool and clear as his sister Caraya's eyes. Now it was turning an evil, pustulant scarlet. Bits of name-less filth floated on the surface and an evil reek smote Bora's nostrils.

Around him the villagers were giving way. Did they fear him or was it only the stink of the stream? He laughed, then swallowed hard. He feared that if he began laughing now, he would not easily stop.

Holding his breath, he knelt and scooped up a bit of floating filth. Then he smiled.

"Now we know what became of Perek's cattle!" he shouted. "They must have fallen into some ravine upstream. Hard luck for Perek."

"Hard luck for us, too!" someone shouted. "Can we all drink from the wells, until the stream runs clear again?"

"What else is there to do?" Bora asked, shrugging.

This reasonable question made some nod. Others frowned. "What if the cattle died—in a way against nature?" one of these said. None dared say the word "demons," as if their name might call them. "Will the water ever run clean again?"

"If—anything against nature—had a hand in this, it will show in the water," Bora said. He had to take a deep breath before he knew he could say the next words in a steady voice. "I will step into the water. If I step out unharmed, we need fear no more than rotting cattle."

This speech drew both cheers and protests. Several arguments and at least one fight broke out between the two factions. Bora ignored both and began stripping off his clothes. If he did not do this quickly, he might well lose the courage to do it at all.

The water was chill as always, biting with sharp, angry teeth that began on his toes and ended at his chest. He would *not* sink his face and head in that filthy water.

Bora stayed in the stream until numbness blunted the water's teeth. By then the crowd was silent as the mist in the demons' valley. He stayed a trifle longer, until he began to lose feeling in his toes and fingers. Then he turned toward the bank.

He needed help to climb out, but enough villagers rushed forward to help a dozen men. Others had brought towels. They surrounded him, to chafe and rub until his skin turned from blue to pink and his teeth stopped chattering.

Caraya came, with a steaming posset cup and a look he had seldom seen on her face. Her tongue was no more gentle than usual, however. "Bora, that was a foolish thing to do! What would have become of us if the demons took you?"

"I didn't think there were any demons. But I could hardly ask anyone to believe me, unless I proved it. If I hadn't—what would have become of you if they thought I'd brought the demons and stoned me to death!"

"They wouldn't dare!" If her eyes had been bows, half the crowd would have dropped dead with arrows in them.

"Caraya, men in fear will dare anything, if it lets them strike back at that fear." It was one of Ivram's pieces of wisdom. Now seemed a good time to bring it forth.

Another charitable soul brought a bucket of hot water and a sponge. Bora sponged himself into a semblance of cleanliness, then pulled on his clothes. The crowd still surrounded him, many gaping as if he were a god come to earth.

Anger sharpened his voice.

"Is there no work that needs doing? If nothing else, we must bring water from Winterhome if our wells cannot give enough. Doubtless they will share if we ask. Not if we stand about gaping until the birds build nests in our mouths!"

Bora half-feared that he had finally said too much. Who was he, at sixteen, to order men old enough to be his grandfather?

Instead he saw nods, and heard men offering to walk to the other village with a message. He refused to decide who should go. He took one of the towels, dipped it into the stream, then wrung it out and tied it around his left arm.

"I will take this to Ivram," he shouted, raising the arm. "The demons were too weak to harm me, so there is little to fear. There may be much to learn, and Ivram will know how to learn it."

Bora hoped that was true. The priest was said to know many odd bits of arcane lore, without being truly a sorcerer. Even so, Ivram might not be able to answer the most urgent question.

How close were the demons? To send men out to seek them would be murder. To wait and let them come at a time of their own choosing would be folly. What else could be done? Bora did not know, but Ivram could at least help him hide this ignorance.

Also, Ivram and Maryam were the two people in the whole village to whom Bora could admit that he was frightened.

By mid-afternoon Conan judged it safe to leave the hills and press on to the next town. He would have felt safer pressing all the way to the garrison at Fort Zheman, but that would have meant riding by night.

Also, Dessa and Massouf were near the end of their strength.

"They might go farther if they hadn't spent so much time quarreling," Conan told Raihna. "I won't turn that young lady over *my* knee, but I'll pray Massouf does and soon. For all our sakes, not just his!"

"I much doubt he'll find it in himself to do that," Raihna said. "He sounds like a man who isn't quite sure now he wanted his dream to come true."

"If he doesn't know what he wants, then he and Dessa will be well-matched," Conan growled. "I'll even pay for their wedding, if they have no kin left. *Anything*, just so we don't have to carry those witlings into the mountains!"

Unmoved by Conan's opinion, the reunited lovers were still quarreling when the party rode into Haruk. They fell silent while Conan found rooms at an inn with stout walls, a back door, and good wine. Then their quarreling began again, when Illyana announced that they would share a room to themselves.

"I won't!" Dessa said simply.

"I won't touch you, Dessa," Massouf said. He sounded genuinely contrite. "Don't be afraid."

"Afraid! Of *you*? A real man I'd fear, but—"

Glares from Illyana, Raihna, and Conan silenced her, but not soon enough. An angry flush crept up into Massouf's face and his voice shook as he spoke.

"I'm not man enough for you? What are you, Dessa? Did you find a trull's heart in—"

The slap Dessa aimed would have floored Massouf if Conan hadn't stepped between them. He held one hand over Dessa's mouth while he opened the door of her room with the other. Then he shifted his grip, to the collar and hem of her borrowed tunic, swung her back and forth a few times, and tossed her neatly on to the bed.

"Now, Massouf," Conan said with elaborate courtesy. "Would it be your pleasure to walk into the room? Or would you prefer to imitate a bird?"

Massouf cursed but walked. Conan kicked the couple's baggage in after them, then pulled the door shut and bolted it from the outside.

"Here," Illyana said. She held out a cup of wine. Conan emptied it without taking it from his lips.

"Bless you," he said, wiping his mouth. He stopped short of adding that she knew well what a man might need. Such jests clearly reached some old, deep wound. If he could give her no good memories, he could at least not prod the scabs and scars.

"I don't know if they'll have a peaceful night," Raihna said. "But I intend to." She put an arm around Conan's waist.

"If it's peace you want, Raihna, you may have to wait a while for it."

"Oh, I hope so. A long, *long* while." Her attempt to imitate a worshipful young girl was so ludicrous that even Illyana burst out laughing.

"If you're that hot, woman," Conan said, "then let's see what this inn has for dinner. Man or horse, you don't ride them far on an empty stomach!"

Eleven

SOMEWHERE NEARBY A woman was screaming. Pleasantly entangled with Raihna, Conan was slow to spare the woman a single thought. Even then, his thought was that Dessa and Massouf had finally come to blows. Dessa, in Conan's opinion, could well take care of herself without help from people who had more important matters at hand—

The screams grew louder. Raihna stiffened, but not in passion. She stared at the door.

"Woman—!" the Cimmerian muttered.

"No. That—it's Illyana. She is in pain or fears danger."

Raihna flung herself out of bed and dashed to the door. She stopped only to snatch up sword and dagger. Similarly clad, Conan followed.

In the hall, Dessa and Massouf stood before Illyana's door. Dessa was clad as Conan and Raihna, without the weapons. Massouf had a blanket wrapped around his waist. As Conan reached them, the screaming ceased.

"Don't just *stand* there!" Conan snarled.

"We tried the door," Massouf said. "It is bolted from within, or perhaps spell-bound." His voice was steady, although his eyes ran up and down Raihna.

Thank the gods the lad isn't so besotted with Dessa that he sees no other woman!

From behind Illyana's door came the mewling of someone in pain or fear, now fighting to hide it.

"Give me room!" Conan snapped. "And Massouf— find the innkeeper if he isn't already summoning the watch!"

Conan drew back as far as the hall would allow. When he plunged forward, he was like an avalanche on a steep slope. The bolt was made to resist common men, not Cimmerians of Conan's size and strength. The bolt snapped like a twig and the door crashed open.

Conan flew into the room, nearly stumbling over Illyana, who knelt at the foot of the bed. She clutched the bedclothes with both hands and had a corner of the blanket stuffed into her mouth.

She wore only the Jewel of Khurag in its ring on her left arm. The Jewel seared Conan's eyes with emerald flame.

"Don't touch her!" Raihna cried.

"She needs help!"

"You will hurt, not help, if you touch her now!"

Conan hesitated, torn between desire to help someone clearly suffering and trust in Raihna's judgment. Illyana settled the question by slumping into a faint. As she fell senseless, the flame in the Jewel died.

Raihna knelt beside her mistress, listening for a heartbeat and breath. Conan mounted guard at the door, while Dessa pulled blankets off the bed to improvise garb for everyone.

"You've your wits about you, girl," Raihna said grudgingly.

"You think a witling could have lived as I have?"

"No," Conan said, laughing harshly. If Dessa truly wanted to queen it over a tavern, best send her to Pyla. In Aghrapur, any friend of Pyla had few enemies. If that friend was a woman, she was off to a fine start in the taverns.

At this moment Massouf returned. The innkeeper and two stout-thewed manservants either followed or pursued him. Conan showed them steel and they halted, while Massouf darted into the room.

"What is this din?" the innkeeper bellowed. He contemplated everyone's improvised garments and Illyana's lack of any. "I'll have you know I keep a quiet house. If it's a woman you want—"

"Oh, go play with your women!" growled Conan. "If you're man enough, that is. My lady mistress has been having a nightmare. She's a widow, and her husband met a hard death."

The landlord seemed mollified. He was turning, when Illyana began to mutter, "The Transformed. No hope—stopping them—this far away. Try to—weaken —power over them. Try—everyone (something wordless) doomed—"

"Witchcraft!" one of the servants screamed. He clattered off down the stairs. His comrade followed. Raihna ran to her mistress's side, dropping her blanket in her haste. The innkeeper remained, his mouth agape, whether at Raihna or the witchcraft Conan didn't know.

"The watch!" the man finally gasped. "I'll call the

watch. If they won't come, I'll raise the town. There'll
be no witcheries done in my house. No, not by all the
gods—"

"Go raise the town and much good may it do you!"
Raihna shouted. Her sword nearly slit the innkeeper's
nose. He backed away, reached the top of the stairs,
and would have fallen backward down them if Conan
hadn't gripped his arm.

"Look you, my witless friend," the Cimmerian said.
He would have gladly flung the man after his servants,
but a small chance of peace remained. "My mistress
does have some magic at her command. That's true.
She can also sense others casting spells. The one she's
sensed is old and evil. Leave her be, and perhaps she
can protect you!"

The man frowned, but some of the panic left his
face. When Conan released him, he walked down the
stairs, instead of running.

"I may have won us time," Conan said. "Then again,
I may not. Those fools of servants will have the town
here before you can spell a pot of soup to boiling!"

"I must do what I can," Illyana said, shaking her
head. "Horror is on the march, and I must do what I
can to fight it."

"If it's not close—" Conan began.

"That matters not," Illyana said, drawing herself up
with a queen's dignity. "When I fled from Eremius, I
swore to fight Eremius whenever I had the slightest
hope of doing so. Now I have more than a hope, if you
will give me time, you and Raihna."

She clearly had her mind made up, and Raihna
would stay, fight, and if needs be die whether Conan
stayed or not. The matter was settled.

"As you wish," Conan said. "Get on with it, while
Raihna and I pack what can't be left behind. Dessa,

you and Massouf need not come with us. I much doubt they'll blame you—"

"Before this, perhaps not," Dessa said. "But as you said last night—now it's too late. I'll be accused whether I deserve it or not." She grinned wickedly, then stuck out her tongue at Conan.

The soft night wind carried the carrion reek, the growls, the shuffling feet of the Transformed to Eremius. Ears sharpened by magic judged that they were close to the village's sentries.

Those sentries had not long to live. Doubtless they would not die silently, but that would hardly matter. In fact, their dying would begin the sowing of fear in the village. Enough of that, and Eremius would hardly need to—

A horse's scream sundered the night. The Transformed howled in triumph. Raw with fear came a human cry.

"Demons! Demons! The demons are upon us! Fly, fly—*yaaaagggh!*" as claws and teeth tore the man's life from him.

Eremius allowed himself a frown of displeasure. Had the village contrived to mount their sentries? Or had the Transformed stumbled upon a man riding out on some entirely different matter? Yet once more, Eremius would have sworn to guard Illyana's maidenhood, to have the services of a good war captain at his command!

At least he needed no captain's advice to know that the village had been warned too soon. The villagers would have more time to flee. The Transformed could pursue them only so far before they escaped from Eremius's command.

A village hurled into panic-stricken flight would

send a powerful message to would-be allies. A village reduced to rubble and corpses would send one still more powerful.

Eremius raised his staff. For tonight, the Jewel flamed from its head, bound there by a silver ring and carefully-hoarded strands of Illyana's hair. Eremius had proven several times over that the Jewel was not bonded to the ring. He had long known the spells for removing it from the ring and returning it, but tonight was the first time he had removed it for serious work.

Eremius began to chant, calling on every craftsman of ancient Atlantis whose name was known. It was a long list. He then passed on to all the Atlantean gods and demons, a list nearly as long.

One day he would receive a clear sign of who had made or found the Jewels, and what had aided him. Perhaps it would even happen before the other Jewel came into Eremius's hands. For now the sorcerer knew only that this invocation wearied him exceedingly and could make the spell uncertain—or vastly more powerful.

"Chyar, Esporn, Boker—"

Over and over again, more than two-score names of power. As he chanted, Eremius thrust the staff and Jewel alternately to the left and to the right. On either side of him a space in the air began to glow with emerald fire.

The Spell of the Eyes of Mahr could enthrall a dozen men even at its common power. Enhanced, it would hold the village as motionless as the stones of their huts while the Transformed descended upon them.

"Boker, Idas, Gezass, Ayrgulf—"

Ayrgulf was no Atlantean, but he had a place in the history of the Jewels. History, not legend, named him the first Vanir chief who had possessed the Jewels. More history and much bloody legend told of what befell him, when the Jewels filled him with dreams of power he had no art to command.

History and legend alike would speak otherwise of Eremius the Jewelmaster.

To left and right, the glowing green spheres began to flatten into the oval shapes of immense eyes.

Bora saw the eyes take form as he ran from Ivram's house. As he reached the head of the path downhill, the eyes seemed to stare directly at him.

His legs seemed to have a will of their own, and that will was to turn and flee. It would be so easy—much easier than descending the path to the doomed village and dying when the demon behind the eyes swooped.

But—what would men say of him? What would he think of himself, for that matter?

Bora had never known before so much of the truth about courage. Little of it was freedom from fear. Some of it was mastering your fear. A great part was fearing other men's tongues more than whatever menaced you, and the rest was wishing to sleep soundly at night the rest of your days.

Not that he would have many more days or nights if he went down that hill.

Bora descended the four steps Ivram had carved into the rock at the top of the path. As his feet struck bare ground, he realized that the eyes seemed to be following him. Moreover, they were drawing him on down the hill.

He had not fled because he was being ensorceled not to flee! Like a snake charming a bird, the eyes were drawing him, a helpless prey, toward what awaited at the bottom of the hill.

Feet thumped on the stairs behind him. A pungent powder floated about him. It stung nose and mouth like pepper. Bora's face twisted, he clapped hands over his face, his eyes streamed tears, and he sneezed convulsively.

"Go on sneezing, Bora," came Ivram's voice. "If you need more—"

Bora could not speak, half-strangled as he felt. He went on sneezing until he feared that his nose might leap from his face and roll down the hill. His eyes streamed as they had not since he wept for his grandfather's death.

At last he could command his breath again. He also discovered that he could command his feet, his senses, his will—

"What spell did you put on me, Ivram?" he shouted. The shout set off another fit of coughing.

"Only the counterspell in the Powder of Zayan," Ivram said mildly. "The Spell of the Eyes of Hahr is one of those easily cast on an unsuspecting, unresisting subject. It is just as easily broken by the Powder. Once broken, it cannot be recast on the same subject—"

"I'm grateful, Ivram," Bora said. "More than grateful." In his worst nightmares, he had not imagined that what menaced the village would wield such powers. "But can we help the whole village in time?" He was fidgeting to be off down the hill, half-afraid that the urge to flee would rise again if he waited.

"There is ample Powder. I have been making it since you told me of the demons."

"Then give it to me!"

"Patience, young Bora—"

"Oh, the demons devour patience and you too!

Crimson Springs is dying, priest! Can't your Mitra tell you that much, you—!"

"Bora, never abandon patience. I was about to say, that many in the village may well have been sleeping or had their eyes averted when the Eyes appeared. The spell will not bind them.

"Also, I am going down to the village with you. Two of us casting the Powder—"

"Ivram!" Maryam squalled like a scalded cat. "You're too old to die fighting demons—!"

"Life or death are in Mitra's hands, sweetling. No one is ever too old to pay a debt. Crimson Springs has sheltered us for many years. We owe them something."

"But—your life?"

"Even that."

Bora heard Maryam swallowing. "I should have known better than to argue with you. Am I losing my power to understand men?"

"Not at all, and Mitra willing, you'll have many years to practice it on me. For now, I'd rather you loaded up the mules. Take the shrine, but don't forget clean clothing in your haste."

Now Bora heard a faint sigh. "Ivram, I've fled in more haste, and from places I was happier to leave. I've had a traveling pack ready since Bora warned us."

"Mitra bless you, Maryam, and keep you safe."

After that Bora heard only an eloquent silence. He hastened down the hill, having already heard too much of the farewell for his peace of mind.

Ivram caught up with him halfway down the hill. For the first time Bora saw the man clearly. He carried his staff of office in his right hand and a straight-bladed short sword on his belt. Over his shoulder hung a bag of richly-worked leather, with images of Mitra sewn in semi-precious stones.

"There's enough Powder in this sack to unbind the whole village, if we just have time," Ivram said. "We may. If whoever is casting this spell thinks he has all the time in the world—"

"I once heard Yakoub say that 'if' is a word never to be used in war," Bora said.

"In that much, Yakoub is wise," the priest said. "If this is not war, the gods only know what it is." He lengthened his stride, until for all his youth and strength Bora had to strain to keep pace with him.

The Spell of the Eyes of Hahr took all of Eremius's strength and attention. Unguided, the Transformed milled about short of the village, squabbling over the last scraps of the horse and its rider.

Before those squabbles could turn bloody, their Master took command again. The human guards had already pressed on beyond the village, to cut off the retreat of any not bound by the Eyes. Eremius sent a firm message to them, not to enter the village.

If you do, you are at the mercy of the Transformed, and you know how much of that they possess!

As he finished that message, he heard one of the Transformed howl in rage or pain. Into his mind flooded all it felt—the pain of being struck in the eye by a flung stone. No, by a volley of them, as though a score of men were throwing.

Eremius felt outrage equal to his creation's. There could not *be* so many people in the village so free of the Eyes that they could throw a straw, let alone a stone! He opened his mind wider, likewise the senses of his body.

His hearing gave him the first clue, and the only one he needed. The streets of Crimson Springs were thronged with people, hurrying away from the Transformed or standing and sneezing violently.

Who among these wretched villagers could know the arcane secret of the Powder of Zayan? Who? He almost screamed the word aloud, at the unsympathetic sky.

It mattered little. Clearly the intruder to the valley some days ago had done more than escape. He had warned the maker of the Powder. Crimson Springs was defended in a way Eremius had not expected.

That also would matter little. If they thought they could fight the Master of even one Jewel, it would be their last mistake.

Eremius cast his mind among the villagers, counting those bound by the Eyes of Hahr. Enough of those, and he could still sow chaos by sending yet another spell into their minds.

Unnoticed by an Eremius intent on his counting, the strands of Illyana's hair binding the Jewel to his staff began to writhe, then to glow with a ruby light.

Twelve

EMERALD LIGHT CREPT around the edge of the door to Illyana's chamber. The light held no heat, but Conan could not rid himself of the notion that he stood with his back to a blazing furnace.

That was still better by far than seeing such magic with his own eyes. He would have refused to do so, even had not Illyana and Raihna both warned him that it was no sight for eyes unaccustomed to sorcery.

"If this seems to be doubting your courage—" Illyana had begun.

"You're not doubting my courage. You're doubting that I'm the biggest fool in Turan. Go do your best with the magic. I'll do my best to keep anyone from ramming a sword through your—" Conan sketched a gesture that made Illyana blush.

The door rattled. Conan took a cautious step away from it. As he did, the innkeeper stamped up the stairs, puffing and red-faced.

"Has your lady witch set my house afire, besides

everything else?" the man muttered. He looked as if no answer would surprise him.

"Not that I know," Raihna said. She had clothed herself in trousers and tunic. The landlord's eyes said this was no improvement over her previous attire.

"Has the cursed spell *worked*?"

"I don't know that either."

"Mitra and Erlik deliver us! Do you know *anything* about what's going on in there?"

"As much as you do."

"Or as little," Conan added.

The innkeeper looked ready to kill everyone in sight, including himself. His hands clutched at the remnants of his hair. His bald spot and the rest of his face shone with sweat.

"Well, *I* know that there's a mob on the way, to burn this inn if your lady witch doesn't!"

Conan and Raihna cursed together. Even Dessa added a few rough jests about some people's manhood.

"If your servants had the courage of lice, no one would have known of our work until it was done," Raihna snapped. "As it is, I'll be cursed if I let my mistress work in vain."

Her hand darted toward her sword but Conan halted her draw. "No reason to harm this man. He did warn us."

"That won't save us if the mob gathers before we can flee," the swordswoman replied.

"No, but our friend can do more." Conan turned to the innkeeper. "I much doubt this inn has no hiding places or secret ways out. Keep the mob out until Illyana's done, let us use the secret way, and we'll make it seem you were our prisoner. If they think you're afraid of us—"

"They'll know the gods' own truth!" the man blurted. "I don't know why I'm doing this. Really I don't."

"Either you're too brave to betray guests or too cowardly to want your throat slit," Raihna said. "I care little. Now go downstairs and do your work while we finish ours!"

"Yes, and have some food sent up," Conan added. "Cold meat, bread, cheese—travelers' fare."

"I'll do my best," the innkeeper said, with a shrug. "If the cooks haven't all run off as well!"

From inside the house a child screamed like a mad thing. Bora tried the door and found it locked.

"To me! Zakar, try your axe!"

The village woodcutter was one of the first men Bora had freed with the Powder. His head was clear and his body at his command. He came running, swinging an axe as if he would cleave not just the door but the house.

A few strokes shattered the door. Bora and Zakar dashed inside. Bora snatched up the abandoned child, to find it a girl unhurt but witless with fear. As he ran to the door, he saw a basket of bread and smoked goat meat, also left behind in the family's panic.

"Zakar, take that as well. The gods only know where we'll next eat."

"Not in this world, likely enough," Zakar replied, shouldering his axe. "But I won't go alone, because my friend here will eat first. I don't care if we face every demon in creation. There's no demon can do much harm with his skull split!"

Bora could only hope Zakar was right. Something was holding back the demons from the village, giving its people a reprieve. Most of them were now free of the spells and fleeing west. Could they flee far enough before the demons were unleashed again? Bora knew how fast the demons could cover ground.

Outside, Bora looked for someone to care for the child. It was a long search, for the village was now all but deserted. Those who remained were more likely to be held by fear than by magic, and against that the Powder had no strength.

At last two girls a trifle younger than Caraya appeared, leading an aged man between them. "Here," Bora said without ceremony. The little girl began squalling again as she was handed over, but Bora took no heed.

"Your own home's not far now," Zakar said. "We could be there and back before anyone missed you."

"Ivram said he freed them at once." Everything in Bora cried out to be Rhafi's son and not the village's leader, just for a little while. "What he did will have to be enough."

"The gods keep me from—what in Mitra's name is *that*?"

A cloud of dust danced at the far end of the street, where the village gave way to orchards. Out of the dust loped a stooped figure, a monstrous caricature of a man. In the green light its thick limbs shimmered.

One of those arms snatched at a branch. Thick as Bora's arm, the branch snapped like a twig. A second branch armed the demon's other hand. Brandishing both clubs, it broke into a shambling run.

Zakar met it halfway down the street. One club flew into the air, chopped in half by the axe. The second swung. It crashed into Zakar's ribs as his axe came down on the demon's head.

Came down, and bounced off. Not without effect—the demon staggered, and Bora saw blood run. But without slaying—or saving Zakar. One clawed hand drove into his belly and ripped upward. He barely had time to scream before the demon's fangs were in his throat.

The demon threw the dying woodcutter down and looked about for fresh prey. For a moment Bora would gladly have sold his whole family for a spell of invisibility.

Then heavy footsteps thudded behind him. A robed arm flung a small clay vial down the street. It landed at the demon's feet, shattering and spraying the Powder of Zayan.

"I don't know if it will work against whatever spells bind those—creations," Ivram muttered. "A good pair of heels might work better."

"But—there must be—"

"Only the gods can help them now," Ivram said. "Your kin are safe. The village needs you as a live leader, not a dead memory!"

"As you wish," Bora said. He recognized in his own voice the same note he'd heard in the priest's. They both spoke lest chattering teeth otherwise betray their fear. The demon was kneeling, snuffling at the Powder on the ground, as they turned and ran for the other end of the village.

With a sharp *ping*, the strands of Illyana's hair parted. The Jewel arched down from the head of Eremius's staff.

Never in all his years of sorcery had Eremius cast a spell so quickly. The Invisible Hand gripped the Jewel halfway to the ground and lowered it the rest of the way as lightly as a feather.

To slow his heart and breathing, Eremius told himself that the Jewel would not have shattered in a fall from such a height. The message accomplished nothing. Heart and lungs knew that it was a lie. He had contrived a narrow escape from disaster as well as defeat.

He reached for the Jewel, to rebind it with strands of his own hair. His fingers seemed to strike invisible glass a hand's breadth on all sides of the Jewel. He prodded the barrier with his staff, and felt the same sensation.

As he considered his next counter to Illyana's spells, his staff suddenly flew from his hand. Before he could regain his grip, it plummeted down to the Jewel, *into* it, and into the earth beneath the Jewel!

Eremius was still gaping when the ground erupted with a crash and roar of shattering stone. Dust and rock chips stung as his staff flew into the air, part of a geyser of stone and earth. Eremius lunged for the staff, plucked it out of the air, and hastily backed away from the Jewel.

The Jewel itself now seemed to dissolve into a pool of emerald light, flowing like some thick liquid in an invisible bowl. A disagreeably high-pitched whine rose from it. Eremius cringed, as he would have at an insect trapped in his ear.

Then he sighed, stepped back, and began to test the fitness of his staff for use. As it passed one test after another, his confidence began to return.

With the staff alone, he could still command the Transformed well enough to doom Crimson Springs. He could not command the Jewel, for Illyana had bound his Jewel and hers into a spell of mutual opposition. She also could not command her Jewel, and had no more power against him than he against her.

Did that matter to her? Had she sought to destroy his

Jewel, even at the risk of her own? She had always seemed as ambitious as himself to possess both the Jewels. Was she now ready to abandon supreme power for a modest prize? Being known as she who destroyed the Jewels of Kurag would certainly bring little, compared to what might come from possessing them both!

Enough. The Transformed awaited his commands. Eremius composed himself and began forming a picture of the village in his mind.

The door of Illyana's chamber quivered, then fell off its hinges. Conan and Raihna leaped back. Raihna nearly knocked the innkeeper back down the stairs he had just mounted.

The innkeeper looked at the ruined door, rolled his eyes to the ceiling, then handed Raihna a basket.

"Mostly bread and cheese. The cooks not only fled, they took most of the larder with them!" The innkeeper sat down and buried his head in his hands.

Illyana staggered out of her chamber and nearly fell into Conan's arms. After a moment she took a deep breath, then knelt and tore the cover off the basket. Without bothering to don any garments, she began wolfing bread and cheese.

Conan waited until she stopped for breath, then handed her a cup of wine. It vanished in two gulps, followed by the rest of the basket's contents. At last Illyana sat up, looked ruefully at the empty basket, then stood.

"I'm sorry, but—Cimmerian, what are you laughing at?"

"You're the first sorceress I've ever seen who'd admit to being hungry!"

A brief smile was the only reply. Raihna went to

gather Illyana's clothes, while Conan handed the empty basket to the innkeeper.

"Again? I suppose I can expect to be paid by the time King Yildiz's grandson ascends the—"

A furious pounding on the street door broke into the man's speech. The innkeeper rose and handed the basket to Conan.

"Time to go down and play my part. Ah well, if I can no longer keep an inn, there are always temple pageants needing actors! Best make haste, though. I heard some outside say that Lord Achmai had reached town. If he takes a hand, I will not make an enemy—"

"Achmai?"

"So they said. He's a great name in these parts. I've heard—"

"I've heard all the tales told of him, and more besides," Conan snapped. "Now—is there a place on the roof where I can overlook the town without being seen?"

"Yes. But what—?"

"Show me."

"If this is against Lord—"

"It's for all of us! Now choose. Show me to the roof, keep the rest of your promises, and take your chances with Achmai. Or be stubborn, fear him more than me, and die here."

The innkeeper looked at Conan's drawn sword, measured his chances of escaping it, and judged wisely.

"Down the hall and to the right. I'll show you."

From downstairs, the pounding redoubled, and curses joined it.

Bora's own rasping breath drowned out the struggles of those around him to climb the hill. He was younger and stronger than most, but tonight he had run five times as far as any.

Any, that is, except the demons, and they knew not human limits. Most of them, at least—the demons could be slain, hurt, or made cautious. Otherwise, they seemed as insensate as an avalanche or an earthquake.

Stopping to look downhill, Bora saw most of the laggards had somebody helping them. Thank Mitra, the Powder had done its work well. The people of Crimson Springs might be homeless, but they were still a village, not a mob ready to fight each other for the smallest chance of safety.

Bora waited until most of the laggards had passed him. Then he walked downhill, to meet the half-dozen strongest youths and men who'd formed themselves into a rearguard. To his surprise, Ivram was among them.

"I thought you were long gone," Bora nearly shouted.

"You thought an old fat man like me could outstrip a youth with winged feet like yours? Truly, Bora, your wits are deserting you."

"He came back down to join us," Kemal said. "We spoke as you doubtless will, but he would not listen."

"No, so best save your breath for climbing the hill again," Ivram added. "I confess I had hopes of taking one more look at a demon. The more we know—"

"He hoped to make one senseless with the last of the Powder, so we could carry it to Fort Zheman!" one of the men shouted. "Ivram, have you gone mad?"

"I don't think so. But—would anyone but a madman have imagined those demons, before—?"

"For the Master!"

Four robed shapes plunged down the hill toward

Bora and the rearguard. Their human speech and their robes told him that they were not demons. The swords gleaming in their hands showed them to be dangerous foes.

Bora's hands danced. A stone leaped into the pouch of his sling. The sling whined into invisibility, then hurled the stone at the men. Darkness and haste baffled Bora's eye and arm. He heard the stone clatter futilely on the hillside.

Then the four swordsmen were among the rearguard, slashing furiously at men who had only one sword for all seven of them. The man who had complained of Ivram's plans was the first to fall, face and neck gaping and bloody. As he fell, he rolled under the feet of a second swordsman. His arms twined around the man's legs and his teeth sank into a booted calf. The swordsman howled, a howl cut off abruptly as a club in Kemal's hands smashed his skull.

A second swordsman died before the others realized they faced no easy prey. Tough hillmen with nothing to lose were not a contemptible foe at two to one odds.

The third swordsman's flight took him twenty paces before three villagers caught him. All four went down in a writhing, cursing tangle that ended in a choking scream. Two of the villagers rose, supporting the third. The swordsman did not rise.

The fourth swordsman must have thought himself safe, in the last moment before a stone from Bora's sling crushed his skull.

Bora was counting the stones in his pouch when a faint voice spoke his name.

"Bora. Take the rest of the Powder."

"Ivram!"

The priest lay on his back, blood trickling from his

mouth. Bora held his gaze on the man's pale face, away from the gaping wounds in belly and chest.

"Take it. Please. And—rebuild my shrine, when you come back. You will, I know it."

Bora gripped the priest's hand, wishing that he could at least do something for the pain. Perhaps it had not yet struck, but with such a wound, when it did—

As if Bora's thoughts had been written in the air, Ivram smiled. "Do not worry, Bora. We servants of Mitra have our ways."

He began to chant verses in a strange guttural tongue. Halfway through the fourth verse he bit his lip, coughed, and closed his eyes. He contrived a few words of a fifth verse, then his breathing ceased.

Bora knelt beside the priest until Kemal put a hand on his shoulder.

"Come along, Bora. We can't stay here until the demons get hungry."

"I won't leave him here for them!"

"Who said we would do anything of the kind?"

Bora saw now that the other unwounded men had taken off their cloaks. Kemal was taking off his when Bora stopped him. "Wait. I heard a horse on the hill. Did you save Windmaster?"

"I freed him. The rest he did himself. I always *said* that horse had more wits than most men!"

Not to mention more strength and speed than any other mount in the village. "Kemal, we need someone to ride to Fort Zheman. Can it be you?"

"Let me water Windmaster, and I'll be off."

"Mitra—" The words died in Bora's throat. He would not praise Mitra tonight, not when the god had let his good servant Ivram die like a dog.

* * *

Conan crouched behind the chimney of the inn. Enough of the mob now carried torches to show clearly all he needed to see. Too many, perhaps. If he could see, he might also be seen, for all that he'd blacked his skin with soot from the hearth in Illyana's chamber.

Both the mob and Achmai's men were where they had been the last time he looked. Most likely they would not move further—until he made them move.

Time to do just that.

Conan crawled across the roof to the rear of the inn and shouted, "All right! We hold the stables. They won't be in any danger from there!"

As he returned to the front, Conan heard with pleasure a shout from Achmai's ranks.

"Who said that? Sergeants, count your men!"

Conan allowed the counting to be well begun, then shouted, imitating a sergeant's voice, "Ha! I've two missing."

Then, imitating the captain:

"These town pigs have made away with them. Draw swords! That's two insults to Lord Achmai!"

Angry, confused shouting ran along the line of Achmai's men. Conan raised his voice, to imitate a youth.

"Achmai's hired swords want to save their witch friends. Well, take that, you sheep-rapers!"

A roof tile placed ready to hand flew over the heads of the mob, driven by a stout Cimmerian arm. It plummeted into the ranks of Achmai's riders, striking a man from his saddle.

"Fools!" the captain screamed. "We're friends. We want—"

His protests came too late. Stones followed Conan's

tile. A horse reared, tossing his rider from the saddle. Comrades of the fallen men drew their swords and spurred their mounts forward. When they reached the edge of the mob, they began laying about them.

The mob in turn writhed like a nest of serpents and growled like a den of hungry bears. One bold spirit thrust a torch at a swordsman's horse. It threw its rider, who vanished among dozens of hands clutching at him. Conan heard his screams, ending suddenly.

The fight between Achmai's men and the mob had drawn enough blood now. It would take the leaders on either side longer to stop it than it would take Conan and his people to flee Haruk.

Conan ran to the rear of the inn, uncaring of being seen. "Ride!" he shouted at the stable door. It squealed open, and Raihna led the others toward the street.

Illyana came last. As she reached the gate, curses and shouts told Conan that the street was not wholly deserted. Illyana waved, then put her head down and her spurs in.

Conan leaped from the roof of the inn to the roof of the woodshed and landed rolling. He let himself roll, straight off the woodshed on to straw bales. His horse was already free; he flew into the saddle without touching the stirrups.

He had the horse up to a canter and his sword drawn as he passed the gate. To the people in the street, it must have seemed that the blackfaced Cimmerian was a demon conjured up by the witch. They might hate witchcraft, but they loved their lives more. They scattered, screaming.

Conan took a street opposite to the one Illyana had used and did not slow below a gallop until he was out of town. It was as well, for he had not gone unseen by men with their wits about them. Torches and fires showed half a dozen men riding hard after him.

Conan sheathed his sword and unslung his bow. Darkness did not make for the best practice. He still crippled three horses and emptied one saddle before his pursuers saw the wisdom of letting him go.

Conan slung his bow, counted his arrows, then dismounted to let his horse blow and drink. His own drink was the last of the innkeeper's wine. When the leather bottle was empty, he threw it away, mounted again, and trotted away across country.

Eremius raised his staff. The silver head bore gouges and scars from its passage through rocks and earth, but its powers seemed undiminished.

From his other wrist the Jewel glowed, its fire subdued by the dawn light but steady as ever. Once again he considered whether Illyana sought harm to his Jewel, even at cost to her own? That was a question he would surely ask, when the time came to wring from her all her knowledge.

This morning, it was only important that his Jewel was intact. Now he could regain some part of his victory. Not all, because too many of the villagers yet lived. But enough to give new heart to his human servants and even the Transformed, if their minds could grasp what they were about to see.

Eremius rested the head of his staff on the Jewel. Fire blazed forth, stretched out, then gathered itself into a ball and flew across the village. It flew onward, up the hill beyond the village and over its crest.

"Long live the Master!"

Human shouts mingled with the raw-throated howls

of the Transformed. The crest of the hill shuddered, heaved itself upward, then burst apart into a hundred flying boulders, each the size of a hut.

The end of that thrice-cursed priest's shrine!

If the man lived, he would have an end nearly as hard as Illyana's. He and the youth who helped him cast the Powder and free the villagers!

Eremius would recognize them if he saw them again, too. He had torn their faces out of the prisoners' minds before letting the Transformed tear their bodies. Slowly, too, with both minds and bodies. The Transformed had not learned to love the agony of their prey, but they could be taught.

Meanwhile—

Staff and Jewel met again. Once, twice, thrice balls of emerald fire leaped forth. They formed a triangle encompassing the village, then settled to the roofs of three houses.

Where they settled, flames spewed from the solid stone. Eremius lifted staff and Jewel a final time, and purple smoke rose above the flames.

Stonefire was smokeless by nature. Eremius wanted to paint Crimson Spring's fate across the sky, for all to see.

Maryam lifted her eyes from Ivram's dead face to the eastern sky. Those eyes were red but dry. Whatever weeping she had done, it was finished before Bora came.

"A child," she said in a rasping voice.

"Who?" Bora knew his own voice was barely a croak. Sleep had begun to seem a thing told of in legends but never done by mortal men.

"The demons' master. A vicious child, who can't

win, so he smashes the toys."

"Just—just so he can't smash us," Bora muttered. He swayed.

Two strong arms came around him, steadying him, then lowering him to the ground. "Sit, Bora. I can do well enough by a guest, as little as I have."

He heard as from a vast distance the clink of metal on metal and the gurgle of liquid pouring. A cup of wine seemed to float out of the air before his face. He smelled herbs in the wine.

"Only a posset. Drink."

"I can't sleep. The people—"

"You must sleep. We need you with your wits about you." One hand too strong to resist gripped Bora's head, the other held the cup to his lips. Sweet wine and pungent herbs overpowered his senses, then his will. He drank.

Sleep took him long before the cup was empty.

Conan reached the meeting place as dawn gave way to day. Raihna was asleep, Dessa and Massouf had found the strength for another quarrel, and only Illyana greeted him.

She seemed to have regained all her strength and lost ten years of age. Her step as she came downhill was as light as that of her dancer's image, and her smile as friendly.

"Well done, Conan, if you will accept my praise. That was such good work that even a sorceress can recognize it."

In spite of himself, Conan smiled. "I thank you, Illyana. Have you any new knowledge of our friend Eremius?"

"Only that he once more commands his Jewel, as I

do mine. That is not altogether bad. Some part of—of what I sensed last night—told me his Jewel had been in danger."

"Wouldn't smashing Eremius's Jewel be winning the battle?"

"At too great a price. The Jewels are among the supreme creations of all magic. To grind them to powder as if they were pebbles, to lose all that might be learned by using them wisely together—I would feel unclean if I had a hand in it."

Conan would not trust his tongue. He already felt unclean, from too long in the company of too much magic. Now he felt a sharp pang of suspicion. Perhaps the Jewels could teach much, to one fit to learn. Likely enough, though, it would be what their creators or discoverers *wanted* learned.

Something of Conan's thoughts must have shown on his face. Illyana feigned doubt.

"Also, it is said that destroying one Jewel without destroying the other makes the survivor far more dangerous. No one can command it."

"A fine mess of 'it is saids' the Jewels carry with them! Didn't you learn a little *truth* while you studied with Eremius?"

Illyana's face turned pale and she seemed about to choke. Conan remembered Raihna's advice and started to apologize.

"No," Illyana said. "You have the right to ask, a right I grant to few. I also have the duty to answer. I learned as much as I could, but Eremius gave me little help. What he wished me to learn was—other matters."

She shook herself like a wet dog, and the nightmares seemed to pass. "Where do we go now, Conan?"

"Fort Zheman, and swiftly."

"A garrison may show us scant hospitality, unless we use Mishrak's name."

"Time we did that anyway. We're close to country where we need mountain horses. Besides, we owe it to Dessa to leave her among enough men to keep her happy!"

At Illyana's laugh, Raihna stretched catlike and began to waken.

Thirteen

THE WESTERING SUN glowed a hand's breadth above the horizon. Fingers of blue shadow gripped the commander's garden in Fort Zheman. Beside one of his predecessor's rose bushes, Captain Shamil turned to face Yakoub.

"There has to be more than you're telling me, my young friend," Shamil growled.

Yakoub spread his hands in a gesture of dismay that was not altogether feigned. Was this fool about to seek wisdom at a most inconvenient time?

"Why should I lie to you? Even if I did, is not a fair woman in your bed worth much?"

"*If* she's as fair as you say. I remind you that I haven't yet seen the woman, even clothed."

A whiplash of anger cracked in Yakoub's voice. "Must I need to remind you of how long you've served us? Of how this would seem to Mughra Khan? Of how easy it would be for him to learn?"

The reply was not what Yakoub expected. It was a dour smile, spread hands and a shrug.

158

"I have forgotten none of these things. There is something *you* may have forgotten. My under-captain Khezal is not of our party. If I were removed, he would command Fort Zheman."

"Who cares what a well-born lapdog like that may do or leave undone?"

"Khezal's less of the lapdog and more of the wolf than you think. The men know it, too. They'd follow him where he led, even if it was against us."

If I could only be sure he was telling the truth!

Khezal seemed no more than a nobleman's foppish son doing a term on the frontier before returning to a more comfortable post close to court. Having such a man commanding Fort Zheman would be no small victory. Under him the fort would surely fall to Master Eremius's servants.

Then the whole province would be ablaze with rebellion or fleeing in fear. The greater the menace, the larger the army sent to deal with it. The larger the army, the more men under Lord Houma's command. The more men, the more power in Lord Houma's hands on the day he chose to act. If Shamil told the truth, however, Khezal would lead Fort Zheman well enough, besides being no part of Lord Houma's faction. Yakoub pretended to contemplate a creamy yellow rose with a deep russet heart while he weighed risks. He remembered his father's words, "Remember that decision in war is always a gamble. The difference between the wise captain and the foolish one is knowing how much you're gambling."

Yakoub chose to be a wise captain. He could not gamble away power over Fort Zheman.

"I won't command or beg. I'll just offer my help in keeping Raihna's guardians away. Once she knows they're looking the other way, she'll be hot for your bed."

"Now you begin to talk sense. What kind of help? If you're trying to make me think you can fight off a whole merchant family—"

"Am I a fool? Have I seemed to think you one?"

"Better if I didn't answer that, I think."

Yakoub sighed. The fear of failure was giving way to weariness at dealing with such as Shamil. Caraya was so different, so clean in heart and mind and body. It was impossible not to love her.

It was impossible, also, not to wonder. When victory crowned Houma's banners, he could offer her more than she could have ever dreamed of. Would she forgive what he had done, to reach the place where he could offer it?

Yakoub shook off the forebodings. "Well, I don't think you a fool, and the gods grant I am none either. I can make free with my purse. That should keep the lady's guards looking the other way for a night and silent afterward. Can you have some of your men ready to hand, in case my gold does not do all that it should?"

"If you'll pay them."

"That's within reason."

The price they finally negotiated was not. Yakoub considered that if matters went on in this way, Lord Houma might face taking the throne as the only alternative to being imprisoned for debt!

To be sure, Shamil's price had to be considered in the light of what the men would face. Yakoub did not expect many of the men to survive the Cimmerian's sword. This did not matter, as long as the Cimmerian himself did not survive either.

With Conan dead and Raihna the plaything of the garrison, Illyana would be easy prey. To gain the Jewel of Kurag and deliver it to Eremius would be at least imaginable for one swift of blade, foot, and wit. Even if Yakoub could not himself snatch the Jewel and earn Eremius's reward, victory would be far closer.

The shadow fingers gripped almost the whole courtyard when Yakoub left the garden. He turned toward his quarters under a darkening sky and a rising wind. By the time he pulled the shutters of his room, he could hear it whining above. On the keep, the banner of Turan stood stiff and black against the flaming hues of sunset.

"All's well," came Raihna's voice from behind Conan.

The Cimmerian finished his turn more slowly than he had begun it. "Don't slip up behind anyone else here, Raihna. They might finish their turn with sword in hand, ready to push through your guts."

"The men wouldn't be such fools."

"The veterans, no. The others, I don't know. Not the kind to listen to tales of demons on the march without seeing enemies everywhere. And even the veterans lost friends in those outposts that vanished."

"I'll take care." She stood on tiptoe and kissed Conan in a way that might have looked chaste from a distance. It set the Cimmerian's blood seething. With a will of their own, his arms went around her.

Self-command returned. "Come, my lady's sister," he said with a grin. "We must not make anyone suspicious."

"Indeed, no. The family's pride—it would not countenance a caravan guardsman's suit."

"I shall not always be what I am, Raihna," Conan said, still grinning.

"That's as certain as anything can be," Raihna

replied. She gently pushed him away, with hands not altogether steady in spite of the smile on her face.

Both knew that being welcomed at the fort without having to mention the name of Mishrak was either unexpected good fortune or a subtle trap. Until they knew, they were all determined to play out their masquerade as long as possible. If they could play it out for their entire sojurn at Fort Zheman, it might even confuse those who had set any trap, until they sprang it too late.

With the garrison under strength, this wing of the barracks was nearly deserted. Conan and Raihna met no one on their way to her room. From the stairway floated the sound of crude revelry, as the soldiers' drinking hall on the ground floor began its evening's work.

Conan threw the bolts on Illyana's room and likewise that of Dessa and Massouf. Then he shifted one of his knives from boot to belt.

"I'm going down for a cup of wine or two. It's what I'd be expected to do. I may also learn more about the demons."

"Learn more about where to find mountain horses, if you can. I'd rather buy them somewhere else than the fort. It's easier to silence tongues with gold."

"You have your wits about you, Raihna."

"Alas, he praises only my wits. Yet I have heard not one word of complaint about—"

"I wouldn't dare complain about the other matters, woman. You'd leave me fit only for that work Mishrak promised me, in the Vendhyan harems!"

He slapped her on the rump and gave her a kiss without the least flavor of chastity. She returned it in the same manner, then unbolted her door and slipped inside.

The barracks roof rose higher than the walls of the fort. That it held no sentries was a pleasant surprise to Yakoub. Either the garrison was even more slack than he had expected, or Shamil had removed the sentries to ease his own way to Raihna.

Yakoub would be the victor, in either case.

Black clothing and a soot-blackened face made Yakoub one with the night as he crouched at the edge of the roof. Setting the hook took little time; unrolling the knotted rope took less. From his belt he hung the tools he hoped he would not need. They had been made for him and others like him by a master thief, as payment for a gold-paved road out of Agh-rapur.

Entering the chambers of a sorcerer could be a chancy undertaking. Always in legend and often in truth, they used their arts to defend themselves and their possessions in ways difficult to imagine and impossible for common men to defeat. Sometimes the defenses gave intruders a horrible death.

Just as surely, sorcerers had this in common with ordinary men: they could grow forgetful or careless. If tonight Yakoub could at least learn what Illyana might have left undone . . .

And if she has left so much undone that you may snatch the Jewel tonight?

Then Captain Shamil and his men need not look for reward or protection.

Hope lifted Yakoub for a moment. He fought it down. He would not climb down that rope with a head full of dreams. That would only end with him shat-

tered on the stone of the courtyard, with the flies
fighting for space on his eyelids.

Conan joined the soldiers with the resolve to drink
little and listen much. The wine was better than his
resolve and the tales he heard were equal to either.

Rumors of demons swarmed like flies on a
dungheap, and some tales went beyond rumor. There
could be no doubting green lights in the sky and a
pillar of smoke where there was neither forest nor
volcano.

Conan drew out of his fellow drinkers the times of
both. The hour of the green lights was the same as
Illyana's battle against her old Master's demon-
conjuring.

No patrols had gone out from the fort, to seek what
lay behind these portents. The greater part of the
recruits seemed relieved, not to be facing demoncraft
without the aid of stone walls.

Conan was tempted to tell them how little the walls
would aid them, if half of what Illyana said was true.
He recognized the temptation as a child of the wine
and held his tongue.

The veterans seemed less content with the decision
about patrols. They also seemed to blame it more on
Shamil than on Khezal. That the veterans should trust
an elegant lordling of the same stamp as Lord
Houma's son was curious. It was also a matter on
which Conan could think of no questions subtle
enough to be safe.

It was then that he knew he had drunk enough. Best
to seek his bed and a trifle of sleep, if Raihna was not to
watch all night!

Besides, the veterans were outnumbered two to one
by the recruits. Fort Zheman would stand or fall on

what the recruits could do or be led into. Conan resolved to give whoever led them as much help as he would accept, emptied his cup in a final toast to King Yildiz, and marched out.

Conan took no pleasure in being awakened by a barnyard din in the hall. It seemed that he had barely closed his eyes. He dashed water in his face as the din swelled. He was fully clothed save for boots and sword. Snatching his blade from under the blankets, he flung the door open.

As he did, Raihna's door crashed open. Captain Shamil seemed to fly through it, sword in hand but otherwise helpless. Had Conan not caught him by the sleeve as he shot past, Shamil would have bashed his head into the opposite wall.

"Unhand me, you Cimmerian dog!" the man snarled. "I have somewhat to settle with your mistress's oh-so-chaste sister!"

Conan frowned. "Perhaps I should have let you knock yourself against the wall. Then you wouldn't be speaking in riddles."

"You know what I mean!" the captain shouted, loud enough to raise echoes. "Or are you a eunuch without knowledge of when a woman will open her bed to a *man*?"

Conan was not too drunk to know a question best left unanswered. Also, he would have had to outshout Raihna had he wished to speak.

"He is no eunuch, and I can—give you the names of a half-score women who know it!"

Conan was glad of Raihna's discretion. He would have been gladder still, had she not been standing in the doorway of her room, wearing only her sword and a look of fury.

"He is no eunuch, any more than I am a toy for such as you!" she went on. "Be off, Captain. Be off, and I will call this only a misunderstanding and say no more of it. Otherwise—"

"Otherwise *what*, you brazen bitch? Your Cimmerian ape may be no eunuch, but I am no witling. I know that you play the chaste woman only when he may bear tales. Let me settle with him, and you will not call this night ill-spent."

Conan had his sword drawn before the captain's speech was half-uttered. The Cimmerian crouched, parrying with flat against edge while drawing his dagger. The subtleties of Raihna's two-blade style were beyond him; he simply thrust his dagger upward into Shamil's arm. A howl, a momentary loosening of grip, broadsword smiting tulwar like the wrath of six gods —then the captain's sword clanged on the floor and he was holding his bloody forearm.

He was also cursing a great many things and people, not least someone unnamed who had misled him about Raihna's willingness to share a bed. He only stopped cursing when Raihna stepped up behind him and rested the point of her sword on the back of his neck.

"As the lady said, it seems there's been a misunderstanding," Conan said soothingly. "No harm to her and little to you. If we leave it—"

Four soldiers pounded up the stairs. Had they been elephants, they could not have given Conan more warning or been clumsier in their attack. He gave ground, letting them crowd together around their captain. Their efforts to both fight Conan and aid the man left Raihna with time to dart into her chamber.

She returned wearing loinguard and mail shirt over arming doublet, with dagger added to sword. Conan laughed. "I thought you would fight as you were. You might have distracted these donkey's sons."

"Slashes in my skin might have distracted *me*!" Raihna replied, tossing her head. Then she lunged at the nearest man, driving him away from both captain and comrades.

Conan noted that she seemed to be fighting to defeat without killing. He had hoped she would do this, for killing these fools would be no victory. They might be the only four soldiers loyal enough to their captain or sufficiently well-bribed to come to his aid. If they died, though, their comrades would all be called on to avenge them. Not all of Illyana's spells together could stand off the whole garrison of Fort Zheman.

Conan chose a piece of wall to guard his back, stood before it, and raised his sword. "Ho, children of Fort Zheman. Who wants to be the first to become a man by facing me?"

The shutter swung open and Yakoub peered over the windowsill. Illyana's room lay exposed to his gaze.

So did Illyana. She wore no bedgown, and the blankets had slipped down to her waist. The curves of her breasts were subtle but enticing. They cried out for the hands of a man to roam over them.

Between those breasts shone a great emerald. For a moment, Yakoub wondered at her wearing such a jewel to bed. Then the breath left him in a single gasp as he realized what he beheld. The Jewel of Kurag lay within his grasp, as defenseless as its mistress.

Seemingly as defenseless. Yakoub reminded himself of sorcerous defenses, to quell a rising sense of triumph. He climbed over the windowsill and crouched in the shadowed corner. Illyana did not stir.

From the hall outside rose the uproar spawned by

Captain Shamil's visit to Raihna. If that did not wake
Illyana, no sound Yakoub intended to make would do
so. He rose to his feet and stalked toward the bed.

Five paces from the bed, a fly seemed to creep into
his ear. He shook his head angrily, resisting the urge to
slap it. The buzzing grew louder, then faded into
silence.

Yakoub looked at the woman on the bed and shook
his head. He had been deceived about her wealth. That
was no emerald on a gold chain gently rising and
falling with her breasts. It was a mere piece of carved
glass, cleverly mimicking an emerald to the careless
eye. Its chain was only brass, no richer than the
pommel of a common sword.

Such a woman would hardly pay well for a night of
pleasure. Nor indeed would she have need to. The tales
of her being fat and ugly were even less truth than the
tales of her wealth. She was past youth, but not past
fairness, even beauty. She would hardly be buying
men for her bed. Rather would she have them seeking
to buy her for theirs!

Best leave now, and seek her again knowing what
she was and how slender his hopes were. As slender as
the long fingers of the hands that rested lightly on the
edge of the blanket, or the fine hair that flowed across
the pillow.

The desire to leave with dignity filled Yakoub. He
drew a silver ring from a finger of his left hand and
placed it next to the green glass. It rolled down
between the woman's breasts, to rest on her belly just
above the navel. The curves of that belly were also
subtle and exquisite.

Boldly, Yakoub rested one hand on the curves of
belly. Bending over, he kissed both nipples. They filled

his mouth with sweetness, as if they were smeared with honey.

Illyana sighed in her sleep, and for a moment one hand crept across her belly to rest on his. Yakoub knew no fear. Had he seen his death approaching in that instant, he would not have moved from its path.

Another sigh, and the hand rose. Yakoub withdrew five paces, half-expecting to hear the fly again. He heard nothing. In silence he retraced his steps to the window, gripped the rope, and began to climb.

Between them, Conan and Raihna dealt with Shamil's four loyal friends or fellow plotters in as many minutes. All were disarmed and only one wounded.

By then some dozen or more additional soldiers had mounted the stairs. Few were fully sober, fewer still eager to close with Conan and Raihna. Some seemed full of zeal for tending the wounded, at a safe distance from the fight. Most contented themselves with standing about, swords raised and ferocious looks on their bearded faces.

"If black looks could kill, we'd vanish like a puddle in the noon sun," Conan taunted them. "If that's all you can muster, what are we fighting about? If you have more in your arsenal, let's see it!"

This brought a couple of the laggards forward, to be disarmed swiftly and painlessly. Conan spared a glance for the doors to his comrades' chambers. Both remained shut and bolted.

Conan hoped Dessa and Massouf would have the wits to stay inside and Illyana to not only stay inside but cast no spells. He would not see honest soldiers enmeshed in magic without good cause. Besides, the smallest smell of magic about the party would lead to more questions than Conan was happy about answering.

The lack of any will to press the fight was becoming plain. Some of the veterans Conan remembered from the evening's drinking appeared, to lead away the wounded and some of those befriending them. As long as they felt their captain's eye on them, however, a few soldiers were determined to make at least the appearance of fighting.

Conan was now prepared to meet and disarm every one of them if it took until dawn. The wine was entirely out of him. Raihna, on the other hand, had worked herself into a fine fighting passion.

"What do we face here, my friend?" she shouted at Conan. "If this is the best Fort Zheman can do, we'll only die from stumbling over their fallen swords!"

Taunted into rage, a man slashed at Raihna. She twisted clear and his rage blinded him to his open flank. Conan's fist took him behind his right ear and he crashed to the floor.

"This will soon pass beyond a jest," Conan said. "I have no quarrel with any of you save your captain and not much with him. He's been led astray—"

"No woman lies to me without paying!" Shamil roared, waving his bandaged arm.

"Who says otherwise?" Conan asked. "But I wonder. Is it Raihna who lied? Or is it someone else?"

Caught off-guard, Shamil let his face show naked confusion for a moment. He could have no notion that he had been overheard, cursing his deceiver. Then the arm waved more furiously.

"The woman lied, and so did this man! They may not be the only ones, but they're here! Avenge the Fort's honor, you fools, if you can't think of mine!"

The veterans, Conan observed, were altogether un-moved by this argument. The recruits were not. Six of them were pushing forward to within sword's reach of the Cimmerian when a voice roared at the foot of the stairs.

"Ho, turn out the guard! Captain to the walls! Turn out the guard! Captain to the walls!"

A leather-lunged veteran mounted the stairs, still shouting. Behind him ran Under-captain Khezal, sword belted on over an embroidered silk chamber robe that left his arms and chest half-bare.

The scars revealed made Conan think anew of the man, for all his silk clothes and scented beard. It was a wonder he still had the use of his arm, or indeed his life. Conan had seen men die of lesser wounds than the one that scarred Khezal's chest and belly.

"What in the name of Erlik's mighty member—?" Shamil began.

"Captain, there's a messenger outside, from Crimson Springs. He says they were attacked by demons last night. Some of the villagers died. Most fled, and are on their way here."

"Demons?" The captain's voice was a frog's croak.

"You'd best go ask him yourself, Captain. I can settle matters here, at least for now."

Duty, rage, wine, and pain seemed to battle for Captain Shamil. Duty at last carried the field. He stumbled off down the stairs, muttering curses until he was out of hearing.

With a few sharp orders, Khezal emptied the hall of all save himself and Conan. Raihna had returned to her room, to finish clothing herself. The others still slept or hid.

"Will you keep the peace from now on?" Khezal asked.

"It wasn't us who—" Conan began.

"I don't care a bucket of mule piss who began what!" the man snapped. "We're facing either demons or people in fear of them. Either is enough work for one night. I'll not thank anyone who gives me more."

"You'll have no trouble from us," Conan said. "By my lady's honor I swear it."

Khezal laughed. "I'm glad you didn't swear by your—maid's—honor. That little brazen's been eyeing everyone in the garrison, from the captain on down. I'd ask you to keep her leashed too, if there was any way to do so with such a woman."

"When the gods teach me one, you'll be the first I tell," Conan said.

As Khezal vanished down the stairs, Raihna emerged from her chamber, fully clothed and more than fully armed.

"Is that all the satisfaction we have, being asked to keep peace we didn't break?" Her face twisted, as if she had bitten a green fig.

"It's all we'll have tonight," Conan said. "Khezal's not what I thought him. He's not on Shamil's side. That's as good as being on ours. Besides, we do indeed have enough work for one night."

Raihna nodded. "I'll go waken Illyana."

"I'm going down to the gate. I want to hear this tale of demons myself, not what somebody says somebody else said they heard!"

Fourteen

CONAN REACHED THE gate as the messenger from Crimson Springs began the retelling of his nightmare tale. The Cimmerian heard Kemal tell everything, from Bora's foray into the valley of the demons to the flight of the villagers.

"They'll need shelter when they come," Kemal added.

This messenger could be scarcely more than eighteen. A man, though. Conan remembered what he had survived by the time he was eighteen. War, slavery, escape, treachery, and battles with a score of opponents, human and otherwise.

"Shelter? Here? What do you think we are, the Royal Palace of Turan?" Captain Shamil's temper seemed little improved. "Even if we were, no pack of smelly hillmen will overrun—"

Kemal glared. The captain raised a hand to the archers on the wall. Conan sidled to the left, ready to fling the messenger clear of the arrows. He would happily have flung Shamil over the walls like a dead goat from a siege engine. Had he and his charges not so direly needed peace with Fort Zheman and all in it—

"Captain, I'd wager we can bring at least the women and children inside," Khezal said. He must have conjured his armor on to his body by magic, for he was now fully dressed for the field. His helmet and mail were silvered, but both showed an admirable array of patches and dents.

"We have room," Khezal continued. "Or at least we will, once we have formed a column to march upcountry. If we guard their women and children, will the men of the village join us? We shall need guides, and all the stout arms we can find."

Conan observed that Khezal said nothing of the garrison being well under strength. His opinion of the man's wisdom and prudence rose further.

"By Mitra and Erlik, I swear to ask." Kemal swallowed. "I cannot swear that all will follow. If Bora lends his voice, however—"

"We don't need to bribe cowards with our own roof and rations!" Shamil shouted. It seemed to Conan that, foiled in his designs against Raihna, the captain sought *someone* to bully.

Conan was equally determined to defeat him. "Are the other villages in the area in flight as well?" he asked Kemal.

"I rode to none, for Bora's orders were to come here at once. I am sure Bora has sent messengers on foot or on lesser horses than Windmaster to all he thinks in danger."

"Mitra! We are to follow the whims of a stripling, who may be mad or a traitor for all I know. Indeed, isn't he the son of the Rhafi who lies in Aghrapur, suspected of—"

"Rhafi is innocent of everything except quarreling with your greedy louts of soldiers!" Kemal shouted. His hand leaped to the hilt of his knife. Shamil's hand rose to signal the archers.

Neither hand completed its motion. Conan gripped both wrists and twisted, until he had the complete attention of both men.

"Are you demons in disguise, or what? If there are demons, we're fools to fight among ourselves. If there are none, *something* besides too much wine is frightening people!"

"Exactly so," Khezal said, like a mother seeking to calm fractious children. A second glance told Conan that the man was balanced and ready to draw his sword, against whoever might need it.

"If all the villages come down, we can pick the best men to march with us. The rest can help garrison the fort, or escort those who travel on to Haruk."

"They'll find scant hospitality in Haruk, after last night's riot," Shamil said. "Scanter here, though, unless we feed them all the rations we'll need for the march." He shrugged. "Do as you wish, Khezal. You speak with my voice. I go to see to my armor and horses."

The captain turned away. Before he could depart, a dulcet voice spoke up.

"Captain, permit me to help you. I know it is not easy to garb oneself with a wounded arm. I have some experience in helping men in such trouble."

It was Dessa, standing between and slightly in front of Illyana and Raihna. Massouf stood behind the women, wearing trousers and a ferocious look. The girl wore an ankle-length robe, but, Conan judged, not a stitch under it. Certainly Shamil could not have been staring at her more intently had she been naked.

Then he smiled. "Thank you—Dessa, is it not? If you will help me arm, I have some wine too fine to jounce about in a saddlebag. We can share it before we march."

"All I can do for you, shall be done." Dessa said. She slipped her arm through Shamil's and they walked off together. Massouf's glare followed them, and the man himself would have done so but for Conan's grip on his arm and Raihna's dagger pointed at his belly.

"You filthy panderers," Massouf hissed, struggling vainly to escape the Cimmerian's iron grip.

"We send Dessa nowhere she does not gladly go," Raihna replied.

Conan nodded. "Use your wits and not your tool, Massouf. The gods made Dessa a free-spirited wench. You won't make her a quiet little wife. There's a woman somewhere fit for that, if you really want her. Spend your time seeking her, not trying to change Dessa."

Massouf shook himself free and stalked off, muttering curses but at least traveling in the opposite direction to Dessa and Shamil. Khezal looked after him.

"I'll have a watch kept on that young man," he said. Conan grinned. Khezal was probably a year or more younger than Massouf, but seemed old enough to be his father. "Best you keep a watch on your own backs, too. At least until Captain Shamil's been so well bedded he'll not be thinking of women for a while."

"Dessa's the one to do that," Raihna said.

"I believe you," Khezal said. "She puts me in mind of a younger Pyla."

"You know Pyla?" Conan exclaimed.

"Did she never speak of the young officer she spent a week with, last year?" Khezal's scarred chest seemed to swell with pride and pleasurable memory.

"No. She's never been one to bed and brag. But if she endured your company for a week—" Conan made a parody of the court bow.

Khezal nodded, his smile fading. He stepped closer to Conan and said, voice pitched barely above a whisper, "In truth—what are you? I'll not say you told us tales without reason, but . . ."

"Raihna?" Conan said.

The swordswoman nodded and drew from between her breasts the coin badge of Mishrak's service. Khezal studied it for a moment, then nodded again, his face still more sober.

"As well you told us tales. Nor will I tell the captain, unless it's life or death. I've heard things of him—no, I'll hold my peace on that, too, unless it's life or death. But I would ask you to give whatever help you can, all three of you. We're scantily supplied with leaders even for the trained men. With the recruits and Mitra knows how many villagers thrown in . . ."

"We'll help," Conan said. "I've served—the owner of that coin—just long enough to want a good fight, sword in hand!"

By night, stonefire could be turned to any color, none, or a hideous travesty of a rainbow. It all depended on the spell.

Eremius chose a spell that would make the stonefire in Winterhome not only colorless but invisible. Until he felt the heat, anyone who wandered close would have no idea what he faced. If he drew back in time and fled, he would flee with his mind reeling with fear and run until his body reeled with exhaustion.

The more fear, the better. Too many villagers had already fled beyond the reach of the Transformed. Only fear would keep them fleeing, until they brought the garrison of Fort Zheman out to destruction. Then the land would be defenseless and the villagers could be rounded up at leisure. Their fear would feed what the Transformed used in place of souls, before their flesh fed the Transformed's hunger.

Eremius held his staff at waist height and swept it in a half-circle, across the whole front of the village. Five times he stopped the movement. Each time, a globule of stonefire leaped from its head, soared across the hillside, and plunged into the village. Each globule glowed briefly, then settled down to invisibly devour all in its path.

By dawn Winterhome would be smoking rubble like Crimson Spring. So would the other three villages denuded of their inhabitants by fear of the Transformed.

Eremius turned and snapped his fingers at his Jewel-bearer. The prisoner had knelt throughout the firecasting, eyes wandering mindlessly. Nor had Eremius called on the power of the Jewel. He had mastered stonefire years before he had touched either of the Jewels of Kurag.

The prisoner now lurched to his feet. Then his eyes rolled up in his head and he began to toss his arms and flap his hands. Like some impossibly clumsy bird, he actually rose a finger's breadth into the air. Eremius raised his staff in front of him and hastily gave ground.

The Jewel-bearer rose higher. Smoke boiled from either edge of the great arm ring. The stench of burning flesh assaulted Eremius. Only iron will kept him from spewing like a woman newly with child.

The Jewel-bearer now floated a man's height above the ground. His mouth gaped so wide that it seemed his jaws could hardly remain in their sockets. His eyes had turned the color of sour milk.

Suddenly his body arched, lungs and chest and mouth together hurled out a single gurgling scream, and the Jewel-ring burned through the arm holding it. It clattered to the rocky ground. Eremius's heart seemed to leap from his breast in the moment before he saw that the Jewel was intact. He knelt and hooked the ring clear of danger with his staff.

Barely had he done this when the Jewel-bearer crashed to the ground. He sprawled as limp as an eel, every bone in his body save for the severed arm seemingly broken. Eremius hastily left off his prodding of the Jewel-ring and once more gave ground.

Only when he saw the man still dead and the Jewel still intact did he approach either. Not for some minutes after that did he venture to pick up the Jewel. Some minutes after *that*, he found courage to call his human servants to attend.

As they scrambled up the hill toward him, he contemplated the Jewel glowing on the ground at his feet. All sorcerers who knew of the Jewels also knew the tales of what they had seemingly done (and whom they had seemingly slain) of their own will.

Eremius was no exception. Until tonight, like most sorcerers, he had also believed the tales were mostly that. Now he wondered. Had Illyana contrived the fate of the Jewel-bearer, he would have sensed her efforts, perhaps defeated them. He had sensed nothing.

What did soldiers do, when they found their swords coming alive in their hands? Eremius doubted that even such as Khadjar would be equal to that question.

By dawn Conan had finished his work. The last pack mule had been loaded with ration bread and salt pork and led to the corral just beyond the north gate.

The Cimmerian broke his fast with wine and a stew

of onions and smoked goat's meat. Time enough to burden his belly with field rations! As he poured a second cup of wine, he considered how little he would have cared for his present work a few years ago.

Cimmerian war bands could live off the land for a month. Conan had despised the men of civilized lands for needing to bring food with them. Khadjar and experience alike had taught him the error of that.

Illyana took shape out of the grayness, so subtly that for a moment Conan wondered if she'd come by magic. At the look on his face, she laughed softly.

"Fear not, Conan. I use no arts where they might put men in fear. I would ask you, though—have you seen anyone wandering about as if mazed in his wits? Besides Captain Shamil?"

"Ha! That's nothing to what he'll be, when Dessa lets him out of bed!" Conan frowned. "Not that I can remember. But I've had other work at hand, and in the dark it's enough to tell man from woman!"

"Ah well. You and Raihna were the only ones I could ask, except perhaps Khezal. Raihna had seen no one."

Conan sensed an explanation forthcoming, if he would give Illyana time to find the words for it. He hoped she would be swift. The column had to be on the road before midmorning, to have the smallest hope of reaching the villagers before the demons did.

"You are right to suspect a plot last night. Someone sought to enter my chamber and steal the Jewel."

"None of us heard any sound."

"You were not expected to. I contrived a spell in the Jewel, to make whoever entered my chamber lose all memory of why he came. He might not have regained all his wits yet. He was confused enough to leave this ring."

She held out a ring of finely-wrought silver, but

Conan had never seen it on the hand of anyone in the fort. He shook his head.

"Why not contrive a spell to kill or stun him?"

"Conan, I think as do you and Raihna. The fewer who know what I truly am, the better. Not even Khezal has been told, has he?"

"No. But I'd not wager a cup of poor wine on his remaining ignorant. That's a very long-headed man we'll have leading us."

"Two long-headed men, Conan. If Khezal allows you to do all you can, as he must if he's no fool."

Conan smiled politely at the flattery, but no more. He sensed things still unspoken, and perhaps best left so. Except that if you went ignorant into battle you might as well cut your throat beforehand and save your enemies the trouble—

"I did work another spell. It was to make the Jewel hold a picture of who sought to steal it. From that picture, I could have recognized the man at a glance."

"That would have meant revealing your powers, but I suppose one less enemy is never a bad thing. Am I to take it that the spell didn't work?"

Illyana colored slightly. "It did not. I thought I was past making such a foolish mistake. I believe I am. Yet the spell was not wrought as I intended. Was it my failure—or the Jewel's own will?"

The dawn sky seemed to darken and the dawn wind grow cold. No gesture of aversion Conan could think of seemed adequate. He emptied his cup at a gulp, poured it full again, and held it out to Illyana. After a moment, she took it. Although she only seemed to sip, when she handed the cup back it was two-thirds empty.

The wine gave more color to Illyana's cheeks. It also seemed to strengthen her own will, to say no more of what might be happening to her Jewel—still less that held by Eremius.

Conan set the wine cup down and rose. If Illyana wished to say no more, it was not a whim. He would honor her judgment that far.

For no sorcerer before her would he have done this. Illyana, though, had her wits about her more than any other sorcerer, besides a true sense of honor.

It was still a cold thought to take to war, that sorcerers might not truly be masters of all the magic they called to their service.

Fifteen

IN THE TWILIGHT behind Bora, a child wailed. Was it the same one he had rescued in the village, after her parents fled in panic? Bora was too weary to care.

Indeed, he was now too weary to flee even if being the new leader of his village had not chained him like an ox to a millstone. It was a burden to put one foot in front of another swiftly enough to stay ahead of the women and children.

To slough off that burden, to sit upon a rock and watch the village file past—he was almost ready to pray for it. Almost. Each time he was ready for that prayer, he thought of the whispers of the villagers. Bora knew he was one of those men who became heroes because they feared whispers behind them more than swords and bows in front.

The twilight crept up from the valley, deepening from blue to purple. Even finding good footing would be hard work before long, Yet they could not stop. With darkness, the demons' master might unleash them again. Even now they could be on the prowl along the villagers' trail, thirsting for blood—

"Hoaaa! Who approaches?"

The shout came from the archer sent ahead to strengthen the scouts. The other archers of the village marched in the rear, where the demons were most likely to attack.

Bora was loading his sling when the reply came, in an unexpectedly familiar voice.

"Kemal here. I'm with soldiers from Fort Zheman. You're safe!"

Anything else Kemal said was lost in the cheers and sobs of the villagers. Bora himself would have danced, had he possessed the strength. He had just wit enough to walk, not run, down the path to Kemal.

His friend sat astride a strange horse. "Where's Windmaster?" was Bora's first question.

"He was too blown to make the return journey. Captain Conan procured him a stall and fodder, and a new mount for me."

Bora saw that his friend was not alone. A massive dark-haired man sat astride a cavalry mount, and behind him a fair-haired woman in male dress, with a warrior's array of weapons openly displayed. Beyond them, the hoof-falls and blowing of horses told of at least part of a troop at hand.

Relief washed over Bora like a warm bath, leaving him light-headed and for a moment wearier still. Then he gathered from somewhere the strength to speak.

"I thank you, Captain Conan."

The big man dismounted with catlike grace and faced Bora. "Save your thanks until we're well clear of this hill. Can your people march another mile to water? Have they left anyone behind on the road? How many armed men do you have?"

"I—"

"Curse you, man! If you're leading them, it's your duty to know these things!"

"Conan, be easy with him," the woman said. "This is his first battle, and against no human foe. You've no call to behave like your chief Khadjar with a drunken recruit!"

Even in the twilight, Bora recognized the looks passing between Conan and the woman as those between bedmates. He blessed the woman for giving him at least a chance not to make a fool of himself. Captain Conan could hardly be more than five or six years older than Bora, and his accent showed him no Turanian. Bora still felt a greater desire to win the approval of this man than he had felt with any other, save his father Rhafi.

"We certainly will march on to water. We have few waterskins and those mostly empty. We also need food. At sunset, all those who left the village last night were still with us. Above forty of our men and some half-score women are armed. Only a dozen or so have bows or good swords."

Conan jerked his head in what Bora hoped was a nod of approval. "Good. Then we won't be having to send patrols up the hills into the demons' jaws, to save your laggards. What of the other villages in your land?"

"What—oh, will they need rescuing?"

"Of course!" The captain bit off something surely impolite.

"Here." The woman handed Bora a waterskin. The water was cool with evaporation and pungent with unknown herbs. Bora felt the dust in his mouth dissolve and the fog blow from his head.

"Bless you, my lady."

"I am hardly a lady. Calling me Raihna the Bossonian will be enough. My Cimmerian friend is plain-spoken but right. We need to know the fate of the other villages."

Water or herbs or both seemed to be filling Bora with new strength, with tiny thunderbolts striking each limb in turn. "I sent messengers to all the villages I thought within reach. Three returned, three did not."

"What of the demons?" The way the man said the word, he seemed to know that they were something quite different.

"They burned our village with their magic. We saw the smoke. They did not pursue us. That proves little about the other villages, though. We would have been on the road many hours before they were."

"If they believed your messengers at all, before it was too late," Conan said. His lips curled in a smile that to Bora seemed better suited to the face of a demon.

Then the smile warmed. "Bora, you've done well. I'll say so, and I'll say it where I'll be heard."

"Will you speak for my father Rhafi, against those who accused him of rebellion? Our carpenter Yakoub went to Aghrapur to speak also, but he has not yet returned."

"What did your father do? Or was it something he left undone?"

Bora retold the tale briefly. The Cimmerian listened, with the air of someone smelling a midden-pit. Then he looked at the Bossonian woman. She seemed to be smelling the same pit.

"Our friend Captain Shamil has a real art of charming people," she said. "Bora, can you ride?"

He wanted to say "Of course." Prudence changed his words to, "If the horse is gentle enough."

"I think you will find Morning Dew's gait pleasing. Mount and ride among your people, urging them onward. Captain Conan and I will post our men here until you have passed, then join your rearguard."

"Why can't you join them now?" Bora knew he was nearly whining, but could not help himself.

Conan stared hard at him. Perhaps it was meant to be only a curious look, but the Cimmerian's eyes were an unearthly shade of ice-blue. Bora had never imagined, let alone seen, eyes of such a shade. Their regard made him feel about ten years old, standing before his father ready for a whipping.

"Simple enough, Bora," the captain said at last. "There's scarcely room on this trail for your people, let alone them *and* my troop. Would you rather have them taking to the fields in the dark, or trampled by our horses?"

"Forgive me, Captain. As you said, it is my first battle. I still don't know why the gods chose me, but—"

"If the gods want to answer our questions, they'll do it in their own good time. Meanwhile, Raihna's offered you a horse. Are you fit to ride?"

Bora stretched and twisted. All his limbs pained him, but each had enough life to make riding a possibility if not a pleasure.

"If I am not, we shall learn soon enough." He reached for the reins the Bossonian woman held out to him.

As Bora's fingers touched the leather, he stopped as if conjured into stone. Borne by the night wind and perhaps more, a nightmare chorus of screams tore at his ears.

Screams, from the throats of men, women and children in mortal agony. Screams—and the howls of the demons.

Bora bit his lip until he tasted blood, to keep from screaming himself.

Conan and Raihna might also have been statues guarding the gates of a temple. When they finally spoke, however, their words held a calm courage that seemed to flow out of them like water and wash away Bora's fear.

These folk could be put to death. They could not be put in fear. Bora started to thank the gods for sending them. Conan had to shake him to gain his ear.

"I said, the demons must have overtaken a band of your neighbors! Either they were closer than we thought, or *someone* is—sending—the sounds of that battle to us. Raihna has a—friend—who can learn which."

"With the help of the gods, yes. I'm sorry, Bora, but I'll have to ask for my horse back."

Without further words or touching the stirrups, Raihna was in the saddle. In another moment she had turned her mount and was trotting off downhill.

"Bora," Conan said. "Get your people off this trail. All except the rearguard. My men are coming up. Move, by Erlik's beard!"

Bora was already striding back uphill. He would have hung by his fingers from the top of a cliff, if it offered the smallest chance of shutting out those screams.

Two of the Transformed were quarreling over a man from Well of Peace. Over the body of a man, rather. No one could live with his bowels laid open and a leg sundered from his trunk.

One of the Transformed brandished the leg like a club. It cracked hard against his opponent's shoulder. The other Transformed howled more in rage than in pain and sought some other part of the victim to use as his own weapon.

A guard ran up to the Transformed, thrusting at them with his spear. Eremius could not hear his words, but saw his mouth working as he doubtless tried to make them hear reason. He looked down at the Jewel, lying on the ground at his feet. Only with the aid of the Jewel could he hope to save that fool of a guard.

In the next moment, the guard's fate passed beyond even a sorcerer's power to alter. The lunge of a taloned hand sent the spear flying. The guard halted, eyes now as wide as his mouth. The second lunge reduced those eyes and the face around them to bloody ruin. The guard had time for only one scream before the other Transformed rent open his chest and began feeding on the heart and lungs laid bare by shattered ribs.

Eremius shrugged. His guards were not so numerous that he could cast them away like worn-out sandals. Neither were they so few that he needed to keep such utter witlings among their ranks. Anyone who had not learned by now to stand clear of the Transformed while they fed needed no spells to render him mindless. He had never possessed a mind to begin with!

The two quarreling Transformed now seemed loyal comrades as they devoured the guard. When they turned back to their previous victim, they seemed almost satiated. All around them, other Transformed were reaching the same state.

Nor was Eremius surprised. The Transformed had fed on most of the men, women, and children of Well of Peace. It was hard to imagine that any had not fed full.

With their bellies packed to repletion, the Transformed were like any great flesh-eater. Their one thought was sleep. Eremius watched them drifting away from the field of carnage in twos and threes, to seek comfortable sleeping places. When he was not watching them, his eyes were on the Jewel at his feet.

He was unsure of the safest course to follow with it, other than to wear it as little as possible and use it still less. Tonight he had used it only to send the sounds of Well of Peace dying across the miles to all those who might hear and be frightened. Then he had laid it down, ring and all, and kept close watch upon it without so much as *thinking* of using it.

Slowly dawn laid bare the little valley, splashed halfway up either side with blood and littered with reeking fragments. The carrion birds circled high overhead, black against the pallid sky, then plunged. Their cries swiftly drowned out the full-bellied snores of the Transformed.

When the red valley had turned black with the scavengers, Eremius sought his own sleeping place. His last act was to cautiously pick up the Jewel, ring and all, and drop it into a silk pouch. The spells cast by the runes on that pouch should at least give him time to snatch it from his belt and fling it away!

Eremius did not know which will, other than his, was now at work in his Jewel. He would have given his chance of vengeance against Illyana to know.

Sixteen

CONAN UNSLUNG HIS bow and nocked an arrow from the quiver on his back. For his target he chose a vulture feeding on some unidentifiable scraps of carrion. The smears of blood on the vulture's sable breast showed that it had long been feeding here.

Shot from a Turanian horsebow drawn by massive Cimmerian arms, the arrow transfixed the vulture. It squawked, flopped briefly, and died. A few of its mates turned to contemplate its fate, then resumed feeding. Others lacked even the will to notice. They sat as motionless as the blood-spattered stones, too gorged even to croak.

Conan turned away, resisting the urge to empty his quiver. Even the gods could now do no more than avenge the people of the sadly misnamed village, Well of Peace. When the time came for men to avenge them, there would be better targets than vultures for Conan's arrows.

From behind a boulder came the sounds of Bora spewing. Hard upon his silence came booted feet crunching upon the gravel.

Khezal emerged from behind the boulder. "Your lady Illyana says that this was demon work. Has she—arts—to learn this?"

Conan would rather not have answered that question. With a man of Khezal's shrewdness, a lie would be even worse. The death of Well of Peace had taken the matter out of his hands.

"It takes no art to see who must have done this," Conan said, sweeping his arm over the valley. "All the tigers of Vendhya together couldn't have done it. But to answer you—yes, she has certain arts."

"I confess myself hardly surprised," Khezal said. "Well, we shall place the lady in the middle of the column. There can be no safety, but there may be less danger. Also, Raihna can guard Illyana's back when she isn't guarding her own."

"Did Dessa leave your captain still hungry for a woman? Or is he only short of wits?"

Khezal's answer was a silent shrug. Then he said, "If my father still lived, I might long since have arranged matters better at Fort Zheman. With no resources save my own . . ." He shrugged again.

"Who was your father?"

"Lord Ahlbros."

"Ah."

Ahlbros had been one of the Seventeen Attendants, and in the eyes of many the shrewdest of them. As soldier, diplomat, and provincial governor, he had served Turan long and well. Had he lived a few years longer, he might have discerned the menace of the Cult of Doom and left Conan with no battles to fight against it.

"Your father left a mighty name," Conan said.

"But you are on the road to making one yourself, I judge."

"If I live through tonight, perhaps. And if I do, I will owe much to High Captain Mekreti. In his days as a soldier, my father was Mekreti's favorite pupil."

Conan nodded, his opinion of Khezal rising still higher. Mekreti had been to his generation of Turanian soldiers what Khadjar was to this one, the teacher, mentor, and model for all. Had he not fallen in battle against the Hyrkanians, he would doubtless have commanded the whole army of Turan. Anyone whose father had passed on to him Mekreti's teachings had been well taught indeed.

They looked once more at the scene of carnage, then Conan walked behind the boulder to slap Bora on the shoulder. He found him companioned by a man of Conan's own age, whom the Cimmerian had seen about the fort last night.

"Bora—?"

"My name is Yakoub," the young man said. "How may I serve you, Captain?"

"If Bora is finished—"

"At least until my next meal," Bora said, with a travesty of a smile. "And that next meal may be a long time away."

"Well, then. Bora, return to those of your people who march with the soldiers. Everyone who's not fit to face the demons in a pitched battle, send back to guard the women and children."

"No one will admit that they are other than fit, Conan. Not even the women. Besides, are not some of the Fort's recruits also to be sent back?"

"Turanian soldiers go where they are ordered!" Khezal snapped.

"Yes, but if he is not a fool, their captain will order the weak ones out of the battle. Is that not so?"

Khezal looked upward, as if imploring the gods for patience. Then he cast a less friendly look at Bora, which suddenly dissolved into a grin.

"Trained to arms, you would be a formidable foe. You have an eye for an opponent's weak spots. Yes, the recruits will be going back. But there are too many women and children for my men alone. Each village will need to send some of its fighters with their kin, and some forward with us."

He gripped Bora by both shoulders. "Come, my young friend. If you dispute with me, you will only give Captain Shamil the chance to make mischief and leave your friends and kin weakly defended. Is that your wish?"

"Gods, no!"

"Then it is settled."

"What of me, noble Captains?" Yakoub said.

"Yakoub, if it will not shame you—please go with the women and children," Bora said. "I—my family lives yet. With you watching over them . . ."

"I understand. It does not please me, but I understand." Yakoub shrugged and turned away.

Conan's eyes followed him. Did his ears lie, or had Yakoub only pretended reluctance to seek safety? Also, Conan now remembered seeing Yakoub wandering about Fort Zheman at dawn after the attempt on Illyana's Jewel. Wandering about, as if astray in his wits.

His wits, or perhaps his memory?

Conan saw no way to answer that, not without revealing more than he could hope to learn. Seen by daylight, however, he noticed that Yakoub showed signs of soot or grease in the creases of his neck and behind his ears.

Men who blacked their faces often found the blacking slow to wash off.

More intriguing still was Yakoub's profile. It was a youthful rendering of High Captain Khadjar's, complete even to the shape of the nose and the cleft chin. Coincidence, or a blood tie? And if a blood tie, how close—if Yakoub was as he seemed, about the age that Khadjar's dead bastard son would have been—

A horseman rode up. "Captain Khezal, we have met the people of Six Trees. Their armed fighters wish to join us." He looked at the ground and seemed reluctant to speak further.

"Captain Shamil resists this, of course?" Khezal said.

"Yes, Captain."

"Well, it seems we have duties too, Captain Conan. Shall we go down and do them?"

Conan followed Khezal. Yakoub was a mystery but not a menace. He could wait. Captain Shamir and his follies were no mystery but a dire menace. They could not.

Yakoub would gladly have run like a fox, to escape the eyes of that Cimmerian wolf. By the utmost effort of will, he held his feet to a brisk walk until he was out of Conan's sight.

Then he ran most of the way back to the improvised camp of the villagers and dog-trotted the rest. On passing the sentries, he went straight to Bora's family.

"I greet you, Mother Merisa."

"Where is Bora?"

"He will march with the soldiers. All those not fit to fight are returning to Fort—"

"*Aiyeee*! Is it not enough that the gods have taken my Arima and may take my husband? Will they tempt Bora to his doom also? What will become of us without him?"

Merisa clutched the two youngest children to her as she wailed. She did not weep, however, and in a minute or so was silent, if pale. Yakoub was about to ask where Caraya was, when he saw her returning from the spring with a dripping waterskin.

"Yakoub!" Burdened as she was, she seemed to fly over the ground. Merisa had to snatch the waterskin to safety as Caraya flew into Yakoub's arms.

When they could speak again, they found Merisa regarding them with a mixture of fondness and indignation. Yakoub's heart leaped. Now, if Rhafi would be as kindly disposed toward his suit, when he was free—

"Yakoub, where is Bora?"

"Your brother is so determined to prove himself to the soldiers who took away his father that he will march with them tonight," Merisa said.

Yakoub nodded. "We tossed pebbles, to see who would go and who would not. Bora won the toss." He prayed this lie would not be found out. If the gods ever allowed him to wed Caraya, he would never again tell her a lie.

"A good thing, then, that I went for the water," Caraya said practically. "If the younglings can go to the jakes, we'll be ready to march."

Yakoub kissed Caraya again and blessed the gods. They had sent good blood to both Rhafi and Merisa, and they had bred it into their children. Saving such a man was a gift to the land. Marrying his daughter was a gift to himself.

* * *

Eremius raised both staff and Jewel-ring to halt the mounted scout. The man reined in so violently that his mount went back on its haunches. Forefeet pawing the air, the horse screamed shrilly. The messenger sawed desperately at the reins, his face showing the same panic as his mount.

The sorcerer spat. "Is that how you manage a horse? If that is your best, then your mount is only fit to feed the Transformed and you hardly better."

The scout went pale and clutched at the horse's neck, burying his face in its ill-kept mane. The release of the reins seemed to calm the frantic beast. It gave one final whinny, then stood docilely, blowing heavily, head down and foam dripping from its muzzle.

Eremius held the staff under the scout's nose. "I would be grateful if you would tell me what you saw. I do not remember sending you and your comrades out merely to exercise your horses."

"I—ah, Master. The soldiers come on. Soldiers and the fighters of the village."

"How many?"

"Many. More than I could count."

"More than you *cared* to count?"

"I—Master, no, no—!"

The Jewel blazed to life, flooding the hillside with emerald light dazzling to any eyes not shielded by sorcery. With a scream, the scout clapped both hands over his eyes. The movement unbalanced him, and he toppled from the saddle, to thump down at Eremius's feet.

Eremius contemplated the writhing man and listened to his cries and wails. The man seemed sure he was blinded for life.

Capturing a few horses in the village and saving

them from the Transformed now seemed a small victory. The horses could move farther and faster than the Transformed, save when Eremius was using the Jewel to command his creations. The Jewel seemed less self-willed of late, but save when rage overwhelmed him, Eremius continued to be prudent in using it.

As always, however, the human servants he could command with only a single Jewel lacked the resourcefulness, courage, and quick wits needed for scouting. They were better than using the Jewel promiscuously, wearying the Transformed, or marching in ignorance. No more could be said for them.

Eremius allowed the Jewel's light to die and raised the scout to his feet. "How many, again? More than a thousand?"

"Less."

"Where?"

"Coming up the Salt Valley."

Eremius tried to learn more, but the man was clearly too frightened of blindness to have his wits about him. "By my will, let your sight—*return!*"

The man lowered his hands, realized that he could see, and knelt to kiss the hem of Eremius's robe. The sorcerer took a modest pleasure in such subservience. He would a thousand times rather have had Illyana kneeling there, but a wise man took those pleasures that came to him.

At last he allowed the man to rise and lead his horse away. Forming a picture of the countryside in his mind, Eremius considered briefly where to send the Transformed. Victory would not really be enough. The utter destruction of everyone marching against him would be better.

Could he achieve that destruction? The Transformed were neither invulnerable nor invincible. Enough soldiers could stand them off. Still worse might happen, if Illyana (or the Jewels themselves, but he would not think of that) struck back.

The Transformed had to be able to attack together, and retreat together. That meant attacking from one side of the valley—

Bora was kneeling to fill his water bottle at a stream when he heard voices. He plugged the bottle and crept closer, until he recognized the voices.

A moment later, he recognized a conversation surely not meant for his ears. An argument, rather, with Lady Illyana, Shamil, and Khezal arrayed against one another.

"My lady, if you're sure the demons are coming, why don't you use your magic against them?" Shamil was saying.

"I am not complete master of all the arts that would be needed." As if it had been written across the twilight sky, Bora understood that the lady was telling less than she knew.

"You mean you don't have any arts worth more than pissing on the demons, if there are any!" Shamil growled. "All we'd have is a lot of shrieking and dancing that'd scare the men." He contemplated Illyana in a manner Bora recognized even in the fading light. "Of course, if you were to dance naked, it wouldn't matter what else you did."

Bora hoped that Illyana really did have the power to transform Captain Shamil into a pig. From the look on her face, she wished the same. Khezal sought to play peacemaker.

"Captain, if Lady Illyana needs privacy, she needn't stay in the middle of the column. I can take a troop back a ways, to guard her while she works. Or Captain Conan can take some of the villagers—"

Shamil spat an obscenity. "The villagers would run screaming if Lady Illyana sneezed. And I won't spare any of our men. What do you think this is, the Royal Lancers? We'll set sentries and build watchfires as usual, and that's the end of it. You do anything more without my orders, and you go back to Fort Zheman under arrest."

"As you command, Captain."

Shamil and his second in command walked away, stiff-backed and in opposite directions. Bora was about to creep away, when he heard more people approaching. He lay still, while Conan and Raihna emerged into the glow of the fire. The woman wore short trousers, like a sailor's, that left her splendid legs half-bare. The Cimmerian wore nothing above the waist, in spite of the chill upland air. Illyana, Bora realized, had tears in her eyes. Her voice shook as she gripped Conan by one hand and Raihna by the other.

"Is there *nothing* we can do about Captain Shamil?"

"Watch our backs and hope the demons will come soon to keep him busy," Conan said. "Anything else is mutiny. Bad enough if we do it, twice as bad if Khezal does it. We split the men, and we're handing the demons' master victory all trussed up and spiced!"

"You listen too much to lawbound men like Khadjar and not enough to—"

"Enough!" The one word from Conan silenced Illyana. After a moment, she nodded.

"Forgive me. I—have you never felt helpless in the face of danger?"

"More often than you, my lady, and I'd wager more

helpless too. Mutiny is still mutiny."

"Granted. Now, if I can have my bedding—?"

"Not your tent?" Raihna asked.

"I think not. Tonight a tent is more likely a trap than a protection."

"I'll pass that on to anyone who'll listen," Conan said.

The talk turned away from matters Bora felt he needed to know. Staying low, he crossed the stream, then trotted back to the camp of the villagers.

Bora now led only the men of Crimson Springs, and Gelek of Six Trees had done everything necessary by way of posting sentries and the like. With a clear conscience if an uneasy mind, Bora wrapped himself in his blankets and sought the softest rocks he could find.

Sleep would not come, though, until he swore a solemn oath. If Captain Shamir's folly slew the men he led, and the gods spared the man, Bora would not.

Unless, of course, the Cimmerian reached Shamil first.

Seventeen

CONAN HAD SLEPT little and lightly. Now he inspected the sentries under a star-specked sky. Somewhat to his surprise and much to his pleasure, he found them alert. Perhaps Khezal's discipline counted for more than the laxness of Captain Shamil. Or did the ghosts of comrades dead in vanished outposts whisper caution?

Toward the end of his inspection, Conan met Khezal on the same errand. The young officer laughed, but uneasily; Illyana's warning was in both their minds. Even without it, Conan had the sense of invisible eyes watching him from deep within the surrounding hills.

"Let us stay together, Captain," Khezal said. "If you inspect the men with me, none will doubt your authority. Except Shamil. He would doubt the difference between men and women!"

"I'll wager your friend Dessa taught him better!"

"She's hardly a friend of mine."

"I've never seen a woman look at an enemy the way she looks at—"

"Captains!" came a whisper from beyond the camp-fire. "We've seen something moving on the crest of that hill." Conan saw a soldier, pointing with his drawn sword into the night.

Conan stepped away from the fire and stared into the darkness until his eyes pierced it. The sky held no moon, but as many stars as he had ever seen. On the crest of a hill to the south of the camp, something was indeed obscuring the stars. More than one, indeed, and all of them moving.

The Cimmerian drew his sword. Khezal sought to stop him. "Conan, we may need you—"

"You do indeed need me, to scout that hill. There's no demon yet conjured who can outfight a Cimmerian. Or outrun him, if it comes to that."

He left no more time for argument, but stalked away into the darkness.

Eremius sat cross-legged atop a boulder on the far side of the valley from his Transformed. With the Spell of Unveiling, he could see them crouching, ready to swoop upon the soldiers like hawks upon quail. He also saw one man already climbing the hill toward the Transformed, as if eager to embrace his doom.

Eremius would do nothing to deny the man his last pleasure.

Looking toward the head of the valley, he sought a glimpse of the human fighters sent there. He saw nothing. Had the men lost their way, gone too far, or merely found places to hide in until they saw the Transformed attacking? It would do little harm if the humans stumbled on the villagers—at least little harm to Eremius's cause. What it would do to the villagers was another matter.

It would still be better if the men could take the

soldiers in the rear, as Eremius planned. With the Transformed on one side and the humans in their rear, the soldiers would feel themselves mightily beset.

With Eremius's spells on the other side, they might well feel themselves surrounded. Oh, they would have one road open, one that led into a waterless wilderness of hills. They would learn this only too late, and at the same time they would also learn that the Transformed were on their trail.

Eremius contemplated the coming hours with a pleasure almost as great as he could have gained from contemplating a suppliant Illyana. If his plan gained the victory it deserved, perhaps he would have no need of a captain for his wars. A few underlings, to spare him the tedious work of training the men, but none to command in battle. He would be equal to that task himself!

Eremius scrambled down from the boulder and stepped behind it, then drew the Jewel from its pouch. It would be best if he began the necessary spells now. They gave off a trifle of light, though, and for a little while longer the soldiers would not have a horde of demons to draw their attention.

The staff resting against the boulder quivered, straightened, then floated into its master's hand. Three passes of the silvered head over the Jewel, and Eremius stood in a circle of emerald light as wide as he was tall.

He thrust the staff into the ground and began to chant softly.

Conan mounted the slope standing upright. Haste was needed. Also, it was for once desirable that he be seen by the enemy, perhaps to draw them into attacking too soon. He trusted Bora's judgment that the demons did not know archery.

Halfway up the hill, Conan scrambled to the top of a large flat boulder that let him see in all directions. The crest of the hill now seemed empty of movement. He would not have sworn that all the rocks on that crest had been there at sunset, but none moved.

Lighted torches did move in the camp. Conan saw two men joining the nearest sentry post, then two more. Had Khezal awakened his captain over this reinforcing of the sentry posts, or was he leaving the man to dreams of Dessa?

The hills on the north side of the valley were lower than those on Conan's. The Cimmerian could look down upon the crests of several. On one, he saw a faint glow, more like a dying campfire than anything else. He watched it, waiting for it to fade.

Instead it grew brighter. Nor had Conan ever seen coals glowing with the emerald hue of the Jewels of Kurag.

Conan realized he had made a mistake, climbing the hill alone. With a companion, he could have sent a silent warning to the camp, that the magic of the Jewels was about to be unleashed. Alone, he could only alert both sides at once.

"Camp ho! Magic at work on the crest of the white hill! This is Conan the Cimmerian!" He turned toward the crest of his own hill. "You heard me, you spawn of magic and camel dung! Come down and let's see if you have the courage to fight a man who's ready for you!"

Torches danced in the camp as men began to run. A hum of voices rose, like bees from a disturbed hive. Before Conan heard any reply, he saw the crest of his hill sprout dark shapes. For the space of a single deep breath they remained motionless.

Then they spread their arms, howled like lost souls,

and plunged downhill toward Conan. A carrion reek rode the night breeze before them.

Nature had given the Cimmerian the art of being able to move backward nearly as fast as he could move forward. Since he had learned that retreating was not always the act of a coward, it had saved his life several times.

Tonight it did so again. Before the onrush of the demons was well begun, Conan had reached the boulder. He leaped over it and landed on the downhill side. The two foremost demons ran past the boulder, one on either side. Conan slashed at one's legs, with a strength that would have amputated any human leg.

The demon howled, stumbled, clutched at a gaping wound, but did not fall. Instead it came at Conan from the front. In the same moment the Cimmerian sensed the other demon coming at him from behind.

He leaped clear, felt his feet slip on loose stone, and turned the fall into a roll. He came up in the perfect position for two quick slashes. One took the second demon in the groin, the other disabled the first one's other leg. Once again Conan would have expected one or both to go down, but drew only howls of agony.

The demon struck in the groin clapped one taloned hand to its wound. The other lashed out at Conan as he closed, with terrible speed and strength. Conan twisted so that the talons only cut the air. His twisting lent extra force to his riposte. The demon's arm should have flown from its shoulder; instead it only sagged limp and torn.

Seeing that arm from close at hand, Conan ceased to be surprised at the slight damage he was doing. The arm was armored thickly in overlapping scales. His sword had hewn flesh, but barely touched bone or sinew. As for blood, only now was it flowing into the wound.

Fear swept through the Cimmerian like a gust of winter wind. It was not fear of the demon itself. Hideously transformed though its flesh might be, no flesh could stand up against a well-wielded sword. Archery, too, should have its effect, if the archers' hands were steady and their eyes clear.

Conan feared the magic that had conjured these creatures into being. It stank of ancient evil, for all that Illyana also used it. *Must* use it tonight, if the soldiers and villagers were not to die screaming under talons and teeth.

The demon wounded in the groin now hurried off down the hill, crouching low but moving at the pace of a man walking briskly. The demon with the two disabled legs had finally toppled to the ground. It lay hissing and growling at Conan's feet. Clearly it was past fighting for tonight, and too many demons in rude health had already passed between Conan and the camp.

He gave the fallen demon one last look, and his stomach writhed as he saw the shape of its groin and chest. Whatever this demon was now, it had been born into the world a woman.

Conan disliked torturing enemies as much as he disliked killing women. As he passed his sword over the fallen she-demon, he knew it would take an iron will for him to give Eremius an easy death.

From downhill, the howls of the demons now mingled with the voices of soldiers, shouting the alarm, crying out in fear, or screaming as teeth and talons rent their flesh. Conan looked to either side, then plunged downhill like a boulder unleashed in a land-slide.

Bora had heard any number of soldiers' tales and survived the demons' attack on Crimson Springs. He had still never imagined that a battle was so *loud*.

The war cries and death cries of both men and demons, the clash of weapons, the hiss of arrows from those few archers who had unlimbered their bows and found targets—all smote his ears savagely and endless-ly. He forced both the sounds and the sights of the battle out of his awareness, turning all his attention to rallying the men of Crimson Springs.

Only a few needed rallying. This handful had ex-hausted their courage in the first battle and were now empty wineskins. They might have fled, had they not encountered Iskop the Smith.

"You puling jackal-spawn!" he roared. "Choose now! The demons or me!" He flourished a hammer in either hand.

One man tried to brush past Iskop. He misjudged the length of the smith's arm. A hammer lunged, catching him on the side of the head. He threw up his arms and fell as if pole-axed.

The rest of the would-be fugitives chose the demons as the lesser danger.

"My thanks, Iskop!" Bora shouted.

Then there was no time for speech, as the demons closed all along the lines of the villagers. Arrows thrummed, axes and swords rose and fell, spears leaped and thrust. A handful of the demons fell. More had flesh torn and pierced, but came on. Far too many bore no wound at all when they reached the line of the villagers.

The men of Crimson Springs still held their ground.

Some died, but few as easy victims, and more of the demons suffered. When three or four men faced one demon, they might all take wounds. Sooner or later one would slash or thrust hard enough to pierce even the scaly armor.

Bora ran back and forth behind the line, sling in hand. As clear targets offered themselves, he launched stones. Quickly he exhausted his supply of picked stones and was reduced to scrabbling on the ground for more. Few of these flew truly. He shifted his aim to the demons coming downhill behind the ones fighting the villagers. They were a target that even the most misshapen, ill-balanced stone could scarcely miss.

Once while he sought fresh stones Bora wondered why he did not feel fear clawing at his mind. In the battle at the village, only the Powder of Zayan had lifted the burden of fear. Now he and his people seemed to be fighting the demons with no more fear than if they had been misshapen men.

A quick look behind him told Bora that if he felt no fear, it was not for lack of someone's efforts. On the north side of the valley, a man-high wall of green fire danced along the crests. Sometimes long tongues licked downward, almost reaching the camp.

The flames were dazzling and terrible, but were they doing what their master intended? To Bora, it seemed that they were filling the men around him with an iron will to stand and fight. Better the demons who could be slain than the fire that could not!

Three demons flung themselves in a wedge at the men of Six Trees. The line sagged, bent, came apart. Headman Gelek ran to rally his men. A demon leaped completely over the head of the men in front of Gelek. It landed before him, as he thrust with his spear. A taloned hand snapped the spear like a straw. A second raked across Gelek's face. His scream turned Bora's bowels to water.

Its victim disarmed and blinded, the demon gripped him with both hands. Gelek rose into the air, and there he was pulled apart like a rag doll. Stopping only to gnaw on a piece of dangling flesh, the demon flung the body into the ranks of the villagers.

Gelek's death was beyond enduring, for many of those who witnessed it. They broke and ran screaming, throwing away weapons and boots.

Bora felt his own courage beginning to fray. Desperately he sought to calm himself by seeking another stone and a target for it.

Again Iskop the Smith saved the villagers. "On the left, there! Pull back. Pull back, I say, or the bastards'll be behind you. Oh, Mitra!"

Still cursing, Iskop flung himself into the ranks of the demons. Their armor of scales served well enough against swords and spears, not ill against arrows. Smitten on the head by hammers wielded by a man who could lift a half-grown ox, the demons were as helpless as rabbits.

Iskop smote four of them to the ground before he went down himself. Bora and an archer killed two more out of those tearing at Iskop's body. By then the men of Crimson Springs no longer presented a naked flank to the foe.

The demons still came on. They were fewer, though. At their rear, Bora now saw a towering figure, taller and broader than any demon. A bloody sword danced in his hand, and he roared curses in half a score of tongues and invoked thrice that many gods or what Bora hoped were gods.

"Hold! Hold, people, and we have them! Mitra, Erlik, defend your folk!" Bora cried. He knew he was screaming and did not care. He only cared that the Cimmerian was driving at least some of the demons straight into the arms of the villagers.

The gods willing, it would be the demons' turn to feel doomed and terror-stricken.

Conan knew that he must be making a splendid show in the eyes of the villagers. The mighty warrior, driving the demons before him!

The mighty warrior knew better. Few of those demons had taken serious hurts. Too many remained not only alive but fighting. If enough passed through the lines to reach Illyana, all would know how little the demons had been hurt. Also what magic their master could bring to bear, where his servants failed!

Conan's legs drove him forward. He hurled himself through the demons without stopping to strike a blow. A wild cut here and there was all he allowed himself. Even the preternatural swiftness of the demons did not allow them to strike back.

As Conan passed the ranks of Crimson Springs, he saw Bora unleash his sling. The stone flew like an arrow from a master archer's bow. A demon clutched at its knee, howling and limping.

"Go on, go on!" Conan shouted, by way of encouragement. He had seldom seen a boy becoming a man more splendidly than Bora son of Rhafi.

Conan heard no reply. Stopping only to cut at the head of a demon sitting alone, he reached the little rise where Illyana stood.

Had stood, rather. Now she knelt, one hand supporting herself, fingers splayed across the rock. The other hand clutched at her bare breast, as though the heart within pained her.

Two paces in front of her, the Jewel glowed in its

ring. Glowed, and to Conan's eyes seemed to *quiver* faintly.

"Illyana!"

"No, Conan! Do not approach her! I tried, and look at me!"

Raihna came over the rise, sword in one hand, the other hand dangling at her side. Conan looked, and saw that the dangling hand was clenched into a fist, with the muscles jumping and twisting like mice under a blanket. Sweat poured off Raihna's face, and when she spoke again Conan heard the agony in her voice.

"I tried to approach her," Raihna repeated. "I thrust a hand too close. It was like dipping it in molten metal. Is it—do I yet *have* a hand?"

"It's not burned or wounded, that I can see," Conan said. "What did Illyana mean by casting such a spell, the fool?"

"She—oh, Conan. It is not her spell that commands here now. It is the Jewel itself—perhaps both of them together!"

What Conan might have said to that remained forever unknown. The demons he had outrun reached the foot of the rise and swarmed up it. At the same moment, so did Captain Shamil and a half-score of his veterans, seeking to cut off the demons.

Demons and men alike died in uncounted numbers in the time needed to gulp a cup of wine. Conan shouted to Raihna to guard her mistress and plunged down into the fight. He was not in time to keep one demon from gutting Shamil. The captain screamed but kept flailing with his sword, until a second demon twisted his head clean off his shoulders.

Conan caught the first demon as it bent over Shamil, to feed on his trailing guts. Even beneath the scale armor, the spine gave way to a Cimmerian sword-stroke. The demon slumped on top of its prey as its comrade dashed up the rise.

Conan knew that he would be too late to save Raihna from having to meet the demon one-handed. Prudently, Raihna did not try. She leaped back, losing only most of her tunic and some skin from her left breast. The demon lunged again, and this time Raihna feinted with her sword to draw its gaze, then kicked it hard in the thigh.

Its clutching talons scored Raihna's boot deeply. A trifle closer, and it would have gained a death-grip on her leg. Raihna had made no mistake, however. Off balance, the demon staggered and fell, within a pace of Illyana.

It never reached the ground. A child's height above the ground, an invisible hand caught it. A spasm wracked the demon's body, as if every muscle and sinew was being twisted and stretched at once. It screamed, then flew through the air, landing among its comrades just as they overcame the last of Shamil's men. Conan turned to face the demons, suspecting this might be his last fight.

Instead the demons turned and ran. They ran back through the gap in the line before anyone could think to close it and cut them off. Bora sent a final stone after them, but hit nothing.

Wiping sweat and blood from his eyes, Conan gazed about the valley. Everywhere the Jewel-fire or camp-fires let him see clearly, the demons were retreating. They were not running, save when they needed to evade enemies. They were retreating, some limping, others supporting comrades who could not walk, for the most part in good order.

Conan turned his eyes back to Illyana. She now lay

curled up like a child, eyes closed. After a moment he held out his hand for Raihna's tunic. He knelt beside the sorceress and cautiously thrust a hand toward her. A faint tingle ran from the tips of his fingers to his shoulder, but that was all.

He thrust the hand farther. The same tingle was his reward. He gripped Illyana's hair with one hand, lifted her head, and pushed the tunic in under it.

Then he had to hold Raihna, while she wept on his shoulder. It was not until life returned to her hand and Khezal's voice sounded from the bottom of the rise that she realized she was half-naked and her mistress wholly so.

"Best think of some clothing, yes?" she said.

"Unless you're hurt—" He fingered the red talon-weal on her left breast. She smiled and pushed his hand away.

"Not hurt at all. Quite fit for whatever your hands do, when we're alone." She swallowed. "As long as my mistress is not hurt. If you can find some clothing while I see to her—"

"Conan, there's a time for fondling wenches and a time for taking counsel!" Khezal shouted.

"Coming, Captain," the Cimmerian replied.

Eremius allowed the Jewel-fire to burn on the hillside until the Transformed were safely clear of the valley. He needed to see the battle out to the end. Had the soldiers the will to pursue, they might put the Transformed in some danger. They might also worsen their own defeat, letting the Transformed turn on small bands of pursuers.

Magic could have pierced any darkness, but such magic meant drawing still more on the Jewel. This seemed unwise. Indeed, Eremius could not avoid wondering if his quest to reunite the Jewels was a fool's undertaking. Their will apart was becoming worrisome. Their will together—

No. He was the master of Jewel-magic. He might not make slaves of the Jewels, but surely he would not allow them to make slaves of him!

Nor did his own fate bear contemplation, if by abandoning his quest to reunite the Jewels he allowed Illyana success in hers. Consummating his desire for her, and avenging her theft of the Jewel, were goals he could abandon without feeling that his life was at an end. It was otherwise, with Illyana's desire for vengeance on him.

The last of the Transformed fled over the crest of the far side of the valley. Eremius cast his mind among them and rejoiced at what he learned.

Fewer than a score of the Transformed were slain. Thrice that many had greater or lesser hurts, but nothing that could not be healed in a few days. They had taken no captives to strengthen their ranks, but they had slain several times their own strength.

He had not won the sort of victory that ends a war at a stroke, but he had made a good beginning to the campaign. With this, Eremius was prepared to be content for one night.

He willed the Jewel-fire to blaze higher yet for a moment, then allowed it to die. Then he set about calling the Jewel to him. He had not quite mastered the art of casting a mighty spell in the form of a polite request to a greater than he. Indeed, it was not an art he had ever expected to need!

He still contrived well enough. The Jewel rode peacefully in his pouch as he hurried down the far side of his hill. He sensed no magic on his trail, but human foes were another matter. If that towering Cimmerian who rode with Illyana were to stalk him, even the Jewel might not be enough!

Yakoub cast his gaze to the right and the left. As cat-eyed as Bora, he could still make out no other enemies flanking the man he faced.

Either the man was a fool who had strayed apart from his comrades or he was the bait in a trap. Yakoub much doubted it was the second. From all he knew of the demon-master's human servants, they lacked the wits for such subtleties.

Yakoub lowered himself over the edge of the little cliff until he hung by his fingers, then dropped. His feet slid on the gravel. The man whirled at the sound, but too late. Yakoub clamped a hand over his mouth and drove the knife up under his guard and his ribs. His heels drummed frantically on the stones for a moment, then he went limp.

The man did have comrades, close enough to hear his fate if not to prevent it. They shouted, and one rose into view. The shouts alerted the other sentries around the villagers' camp. Feet thudded on stony ground and arrows hissed in high arcs, to fall as the gods willed.

Yakoub crouched in such shelter as the cliff offered. He feared the demon-master's men little, the wild shooting of "friendly" archers rather more.

Screams hinted of arrows finding their marks. Scurrying feet interspersed with shouts told Yakoub plainly that the demon-master's men were fleeing. He remained below the cliff until the guards reached him.

The old sergeant in command looked at the body, then grunted approvingly. "Good work, knife against sword."

"It would have been better, if I hadn't had to kill him so soon. That may have warned the rest."

"Maybe. Maybe his friends would've got in close, too. Then half the recruits and all the hillfolk would've been wetting themselves and screaming their heads off. No way to fight a battle. You saved us that. Sure you don't want to take King Yildiz's coin?"

"Not when I'm betrothed."

"Ah well. A wife's an old soldier's comfort and a young soldier's ruin."

They walked back to the camp together, under a sky bleached gray in the east with hints of dawn. Once parted from the sergeant, Yakoub made his way straight through the sleeping villagers to where Bora's family lay.

Like most of the villagers, they were too exhausted to have awakened during the brief fight. Caraya lay on her side, one arm flung over her two younger brothers. Yakoub knelt beside her, and he neither knew nor cared to what gods he prayed when he asked that she be kept safe.

Prayers or not, she was likely to be safer than he was, at least for some days. The Transformed had not swept all before them, that was certain. Otherwise fleeing soldiers would long since have awakened the camp. As they were, Eremius's human witlings could not stop the march of a column of ants. The villagers would have a safe journey to Fort Zheman.

Yakoub, son of Khadjar, on the other hand, would be marching in the opposite direction. If he survived the march, he would then have to persuade Eremius that he was the man to lead the human fighters and turn them into soldiers.

In silence, he allowed himself another prayer, that

Eremius might be easier to persuade than the normal run of sorcerers. Then he kissed Caraya, forcing himself not to take her in his arms. With eyes stinging from more than the dawn breeze, he rose and turned his face toward the mountains.

It took the rest of the night to put the camp in order, count the dead, care for the wounded, and scout the surrounding hills. Only when all the scouts brought back the same report, of a land empty of demons if not of their traces, did Khezal call his council of war.

"I'd say we won a victory, if we hadn't lost three to their one," he said. "Perhaps they carried off more dead and hurt, perhaps not. Also, I'd wager that was a retreat ordered by whoever gives those monsters orders, not being driven off."

"You see clearly, Captain," Illyana said. She was paler than Conan cared to see, and from time to time a spasm would shake her body. Her voice was steady as she continued. "The orders were given, because of the fight we gave the Transformed. Had the full powers of our enemy been unleashed, we could not have done so well."

"Then we have you to thank for a fair number of lives, if you set bounds on the master of the Transformed."

Illyana shuddered. "Forgive me, Captain, but I cannot accept that praise. I did what I could, and I know I had some effect. Yet I could not use all the strength of my Jewel. We owe our lives in great part to the fact that neither could Eremius."

Khezal looked at the ground as if he expected monsters to erupt from it at any moment. Then he stared hard at Illyana. "I feel I am being told other than the truth. That is not well done."

"There are matters you and your soldiers could not understand without—" Raihna began. Conan laid a hand heavily upon her shoulder and Khezal glared. Between them she fell silent.

"Captain, *I* do not know as much as I might in a day or two," Illyana said. "When I know it, or learn that I shall not know it, then will be the time for us to speak frankly. I shall hold nothing back. By the Seven Shrines and the bones of Pulaq I swear it."

"A cursed lot of good your hesitation will do us if the Transformed attack again!"

"They will not, if we return to Fort Zheman."

"Retreat with our tails between our legs! Who's the captain here, Lady Illyana? I don't remember seeing *your* commission from King Yildiz—"

"You may remember seeing one from a certain Lord Mishrak," Conan growled. "Or did some buffet on the head last night take your memory?"

The silence gave Conan time to reach for his sword, time to fear he might need to draw it. Then all Khezal's breath left him in a gusty sigh.

"Don't tell anyone, but I've been thinking of returning to the Fort also. There are too cursed many villagers to guard in the open field. Behind walls, at least those monsters will have to climb to come at us!"

Eighteen

THE TOWER OF Fort Zheman had thrust itself above the horizon, when Bora rode up on Windmaster.

Raihna patted the gray's neck. "A fine steed. I am glad he is in fettle again. Also that he still has a master worthy of him."

All were silent for a moment. Kemal had survived the battle, but with wounds that took his life before dawn. He had some measure of good fortune; he was senseless and felt no pain.

"Thank you, Raihna," Bora said. "But I did not ride up here to seek praise for Windmaster. I seek Yakoub. He seems to have vanished."

Conan and Raihna exchanged looks that did not include Illyana. This was no matter for her, they had both agreed. Moreover, she was in the saddle at all by sheer force of will. The less she was troubled without cause, the better. "I thought you did not much care for him," Conan said.

"I did not and I do not," Bora replied. "My sister Caraya thinks otherwise."

"You're the head of the family, until your father is freed," Conan said. "I thought that gave you the right to say yea or nay to anyone's courting your sister."

Bora laughed harshly. "You do not know Caraya. She can smite as heavily with her tongue as Mistress Raihna can with her blades." He frowned. "Also, Yakoub has labored to secure my father's release. He has not yet succeeded, but who knows if this is his fault?"

"You have a great sense of justice in you, Bora," Raihna said. "The gods love such."

"Best pray the gods keep you alive long enough to practice that justice," Conan said. "And spare a prayer or two for Yakoub as well. He may have left the villagers once the demon master's scouts were driven off, hoping to join the soldiers. If he met some of those scouts on the road—well, I am sure the scouts are fewer, but I'd not wager on your sister marrying Yakoub."

"Yes, and that means *you* do not ride about alone, either," Raihna said. "We have some cheese and bread, if you have not eaten."

Bora devoured half a cheese, then took his place in the column behind Raihna. Conan mused on the mystery of Yakoub. Could he really be what his face hinted, Khadjar's bastard son? If so, one mystery lay behind his being alive, another behind what he was doing. Best if honest folk like Bora and Caraya kept well clear of either mystery, particularly with a father already arrested as a suspected rebel.

Best also to say nothing of that to Bora. And best of all for Conan not to think too much on the matter himself. If the mystery was deep enough for High

Captain Khadjar to be part of it—

Very surely, best to think of other matters, such as how to make some of the Powder of Zayan and how to contrive a night with Raihna.

Again Yakoub lowered himself down a small cliff. This time he landed silently, on firm ground, behind those he sought. He also left his knife and sword sheathed and held out his empty hands.

"Hssst! Servants of the master."

Had he stabbed them, the two scouts could not have whirled faster. Both drew their swords, but did not advance. Instead they stood in silence, gape-jawed and dull-eyed.

The silence went on so long that Yakoub half-expected to see the sun touching the western horizon. At last one of the men spoke. His words were slurred and indistinct, as though he spoke with a mouthful of nutmeats.

"We serve the master. You do not."

"I wish to serve him."

This brought on another long silence. Yakoub began to consider whether decent fighting men could be made out of such dullards. Perhaps they were only tired, or some had more wits than others?

"Show us a sign," one said at last.

What they would take as a sign, Yakoub could only guess. It hardly mattered, as he had only one thing that might serve. He opened the secret pouch in his belt and held out the ring with his father's seal.

The scout who had spoken took the ring, with such fumbling hands that Yakoub half-expected him to drop it. At last he returned it to Yakoub.

"We do not know this sign."

"Your master will know it."

"Our master is not here."

"Is there some reason I cannot go to him?"

"We would have to lead you."

"Is that forbidden?" Yakoub knew that to shout at these wretches would gain little and might lose much. He still felt his patience being rubbed thin.

The two scouts looked at each other. At last they shook their heads together, like two puppets with the same master.

"It is not forbidden."

"Then I ask you, in the name of the master's victory, to take me to him."

Yet another long silence followed. This time it ended without words. The two scouts grunted and together turned away eastward, beckoning Yakoub to follow.

Khezal pushed himself back from the table and began to pace up and down the chamber. Outside, the villagers camped in Fort Zheman had begun to lose their fear and find their tongues. Women quarreled over a place in the line for water, children shrieked in delight or wailed for their parents, dogs barked and howled.

"Thank the gods we were able to keep what livestock they brought outside," Khezal said. He strode to the window and slammed the shutter. "They may not survive the coming of the de—the Transformed. But this is a fort I have to defend, not the Royal Menagerie!

"I'll have to send them on to Haruk when I've called in all the outpost garrisons. There won't be room and we'd be courting fevers and fluxes. The gods have spared us that, so far."

"What does Mughra Khan say to all this?" Illyana asked. "Not that I complain, you understand. You are a gift from the gods, compared to Captain Shamil."

Khezal's face twisted. "I have looked into Shamil's letters. He was so deep in the toils of those who plot with Lord Houma, the gods themselves could not have pulled him out! The Transformed gave him a more honorable end than he deserved.

"As for Mughra Khan, anything he says will be said after I have done what I know is needed. I have sent the messengers to the outposts this very afternoon. A messenger to Mughra Khan will follow tomorrow."

Conan laughed. "I'd wager you'll one day command an army, Khezal. If not, then Turan's wasting a good man."

"I could do with less praise and more weapons fit to stand against magic," Khezal said. "But the Powder of Zayan will be better than nothing. How long will Lady Illyana need, to make enough of it?"

"I will need two days, to enspell sufficient bowls for mixing the Powder," Illyana said. "Once the bowls are fit, I must then mix the first bowlful and test it. If that proves fit, I can leave matters in other hands for a month or more. I would urge Maryam, the niece of Ivram, as the best hands."

"So you cast the spells on the cooking pots, not on the food?" Khezal said.

"Well put. The spell of the Powder is little-known, otherwise we would have much less peril from evil magic. Also, to place it upon the bowls will call less heavily upon the Jewel."

"What if it doesn't play at all?" Conan put in. The

four in the chamber had no secrets, including the self-will of the Jewels.

"Then Fort Zheman must trust to the valor of its men under the leadership of Captain Khezal," Raihna said.

"Remember what I said about less praise and more weapons?" Khezal shrugged. "How long do you need after the Powder is done, before you march into the mountains?"

"A day for the Jewel to regain its strength, another day for gathering mounts and supplies," Illyana said.

"Tell me what you will need and I will see about gathering it now," Khezal said. "The faster you move, the better your chances of catching Eremius before he returns to his stronghold. If that makes any difference in this kind of war?"

"It does. Thank you, Captain."

"I'm also sending ten picked veterans with you. Yes, I know the smaller the party, the less chance of discovery. Once you reach the mountains, you can order them to stay behind. But Eremius's scouts, bandits, starving villagers, wild animals—you need guarding against all of these."

"We do?" Conan growled.

"You do, and more of it than even a Cimmerian can offer," Khezal said. He rang a bell on the table. From outside the door came a girl's voice.

"Yes, Captain?"

"Wine and four cups. Then go heat me a bath, with enough water for two."

"At your pleasure, Captain."

This time Conan recognized the voice as Dessa's. He looked a question at Khezal. The man grinned.

"I've inherited Shamil's responsibilities. Why shouldn't I inherit a few of his comforts as well?"

Bora shifted the sack of charcoal to his left arm and knocked on the door.

"Maryam, it is Bora. I have the charcoal."

The sound of bare feet gave way to a bolt being drawn. Maryam peered out. She wore only a chamber robe of scarlet silk, belted lightly about her with a gold-tasseled cord. The color went well with her dark skin, Bora noticed. He also noticed how much of that skin was revealed. He knew he should not savor such an immodest display, but found it hard to turn his eyes away.

"Come in, come in. Put the charcoal by the north wall."

Bora nearly stumbled over the dyed fleeces on the floor as he entered. Crimson, indigo, a rich green horribly like the emerald fire of the Jewels, they dazzled the eye but laid traps for unwary feet.

At least he needed no guidance to the north wall. It was piled high with sacks of charcoal and salt, pots of spices and herbs, and stacks of brass bowls. He dropped the charcoal on top of the nearest pile and straightened up, stretching to untwist his muscles.

"How much Powder do they plan to make? This looks like enough to baffle every spell from here to the Iranistani frontier!"

Maryam smiled. "Mistress Illyana keeps her tongue between her teeth, as well she should. Certainly no one will have an easy time, sending magic against Fort Zheman."

She knelt to open a small chest. As she did, her robe dropped away, to expose yet more skin, halfway down the ripe curves of her breasts. Bora twisted again, to look away.

When he looked back, Maryam was holding out two cups of wine. "Shall we drink a toast, to your victory?"

"Best make it to my safe return."

She embraced him, clumsily because she was still holding the wine cups. Her lips nuzzled the side of his neck and caressed his throat.

"So they have the sense to take you with them? The gods be praised!"

"I never thought they were fools, Maryam. That big Cimmerian above all. I'm the best guide they could find, without using magic."

They drank. It seemed to Bora that Maryam was using a trifle of magic of her own, for a single cup seemed to make his head lighter than usual. He noted that she only sipped her wine, and had yet to finish her first cup when he was nearly done with his second.

He would have drunk a third, but she put a hand over the mouth of his cup. "No more, Bora. No more. Young as you are, wine can still do you harm."

She set down her own cup and put her other hand over Bora's mouth. She drew her fingers along his lips and across his cheek, then thrust a hand into the open throat of his shirt.

"Maryam. This is not proper."

At least those were the words that formed themselves in Bora's mind. They seemed to stick in his throat, so that only a croak came out. Then he gasped as if he had run miles as Maryam undid the sash of her robe.

As she stood, she shrugged herself out of it. Bora had never imagined that a woman's breasts could be so splendid. Breasts, and all the rest of the dark lushness now revealed.

"Bora," she said, and the word itself was a caress. "Bora, you have never lain with a woman, have you?"

He had no words, but his eyes seemed to speak clearly. Maryam moved to him and pressed herself against him, from shoulder to knee.

"Then you must have a chance, before you ride into the mountains." She continued to press herself against him, while her hands went deftly to work on his clothes.

Presently he had the wits to help her with that work, and at last to follow her to the bed.

Raihna rolled over in the bed as Conan entered. Bare shoulders alone showed above the blankets. He sat on the bed and ran his hand along the curves under the blankets. He knew that Raihna usually slept naked.

His hand ran back up to the edge of the blankets and started to dive under them. Raihna rolled on her back, letting the blankets slide down to her waist. Before Conan could touch what this movement exposed, she caught his hands and held them against her breasts.

"You're all but healed, from that gash at the Red Falcon," Conan said.

"I heal quickly, Conan. I wish the same could be said of Massouf."

"His wound is elsewhere. Has he been whining again?"

"I would not call it that, Conan. He wants to come with us, into the mountains."

"He does?"

"He spoke to both me and Illyana."

"Supposing that he did, what will I hear that you said to him?"

"We will let him come."

"Crom! Where's the Powder?" Conan started to rise.

Raihna shifted her grip, so that he could not do so without some discomfort. She looked at his discomfited expression and laughed.

"Raihna, this is a poor jest. Massouf wants to kill himself."

"So we surmised. Since Dessa jumped lightly into Khezal's bed, he has known she is not for him."

"Then why, by Erlik's yard, can't he find another woman? That little trull isn't the only bedmate in the whole world for a lad like Massouf. He's a fool. It's like my pining away because I can't bed Illyana!"

Something passed over Raihna's face at those words. Jealousy? No, something different, more complicated, and likely to be revealed only in Raihna's own good time. Conan gently disengaged himself from Raihna's grasp and sat down at the foot of the bed.

"You don't love Illyana," Raihna said at last. "Massouf—well, he would not believe what you just said. He loves Dessa too much."

"Conan, Illyana and I—we have never been allowed love. It is our fate. How could we spit in Massouf's face? How, I ask you?" She turned her face to the pillow and wept softly.

Conan cursed under his breath. He could not imagine a world without women, and he would hardly want to live in it anyway. Certainly, though, such a world might be a trifle simpler!

All the sympathy in the world didn't make a man who seemed determined to die a good companion on a dangerous journey. Conan vowed he would do everything in his power to send Massouf back with the soldiers, when they left.

He also vowed that he would do everything in his power to make Raihna remember this night. Gripping her by the shoulders, he turned her over. Her tear-filled eyes widened, but when his lips came down on hers her arms rose. Strong, sword-calloused hands locked behind his neck and drew him to her.

Nineteen

THE MOUNTAIN STREAM plunged from the little cliff, splashed on a flat rock, then flowed into a deep still pool. Where it went after that Conan neither knew nor cared. He knelt by the pool and lifted a cupped hand to his lips.

"Good and clean. Drink up, people, and refill your waterskins too."

"If it is so clean, I think we should bathe as well," Illyana said. She sat down, pulled off her boots, and flexed her long toes with a look of bliss.

"We had no chance to bathe while we marched with the soldiers. Nor will we have any between here and the valley, I fear."

Conan looked beyond the little valley, toward the peaks of the Ibars Mountains. Well to the fore, the Lord of the Winds rose silver-helmeted, its snowcap blazing in the noonday sun.

The Cimmerian sensed no danger lurking close by, but knew that it could not be far away. Precious little they could do about it, either. These mountains could hide enough enemies to overcome them had they still been guarded by a thousand soldiers instead of ten. The sergeant commanding their escort had swiftly realized this, and made no protest against his dismissal two days before. He had made none against their leaving their horses, either. Hill-born himself, he knew a horse in such country gave neither speed nor stealth.

Speed, stealth (all were masters of it save Massouf, and he was learning), the mountains, and Illyana's magic—together these gave them a chance of reaching Eremius and defeating him.

How good that chance was, Conan would not have cared to wager.

"Well enough. Women first, then Bora and Massouf, then me."

The two young men hurried to posts at opposite ends of the pool. Raihna was the first to strip and plunge in. She vanished completely, then rose spluttering and cursing like a drillmaster.

"Gods, this is *cold*!"

Illyana laughed. "Have you forgotten our Bossonian streams? They were not quite Vanir bathhouses, as I remember."

Raihna ducked under again. This time when she came up, she was in reach of Illyana's bare legs. A mighty splash, and water cascaded over Illyana. She yelped and jumped up.

"You—!"

"I had not forgotten, mistress. But I thought you had, so I would remind you."

Illyana uttered what Conan suspected was an impolite description of Raihna in an unknown tongue. Then she stood up and drew off her tunic, her last garment. Clad only in sunlight and the Jewel-ring, she started to bind up her hair with her neck ribbon.

Conan sat sword across his lap, contemplating both women with pleasure but without desire. Apart from being younger, Raihna was definitely the comelier. Yet had Illyana not been obliged to remain a maiden, she would not have had to sleep alone more often than she wished.

Certainly she could have had Massouf for snapping her fingers. He was trying so hard not to stare that it was more evident than if he had been doing so openly. Bora was finding it easier to be a gentleman, or at least an alert sentry. Conan would have wagered a month's pay that the toothsome Maryam had something to do with this.

Illyana finished binding up her hair and started to pull off the Jewel-ring. Conan reached for it, to put it in his belt pouch. Illyana looked down at his left hand and drew back.

"No, Conan. Your other hand. You've cut this one."

"So I have," the Cimmerian said. He held up the bleeding hand. From the look of the cut, it must have been an edged stone, so sharp that he had not felt it. "I'll wash it out and bind it up. I've cut myself worse shaving. It will be healing before we reach the mountains."

"That is not so important. Even were it far deeper, I could heal it with little use of the Jewel. No, the danger is letting blood fall on the Jewel."

"Does it get drunk if that happens, or what?" Conan's light tone hid fear crawling through him. Illyana had spoken in a deadly sober tone.

"One might call it getting drunk. It is certain that when blood falls on it, a Jewel becomes much harder to control. It is *said* that if a blood-smeared Jewel then falls into water, it cannot be controlled at all."

Conan shrugged and reached for the ring with his

right hand, then stuffed it into his pouch. It was in his mind to ask how Illyana proposed to keep the Jewel free of blood while they were battling the Transformed or whatever else Eremius might send against them.

The words never reached his lips. Illyana sat on the edge of the pool, thrusting her long legs over the edge until her feet dabbled in the water. She raised her arms to the sun and threw her head back. Her breasts and belly rose and tautened, as fine and fair as a young girl's.

She held the pose and Conan held desire for a long moment. Then she slipped into the pool, to bob up on the far side, next to Raihna.

Conan rose and began to stride back and forth along the edge of the pool. Another such display by Illyana, and *he* was going to find it a burden to be a gentleman!

As desire left Conan's mind, an idle thought entered it. Suppose the Jewels were indeed living beings, with their own wills? And suppose they offered Illyana magic *and* bedmates, in return for her obedience?

Never mind the Jewels. Suppose Master Eremius had the wits to offer such a bargain?

Conan's thoughts ceased to be idle, and the mountains about him ceased to look peaceful. Uneasily and suspiciously, he pondered whether he had just guessed Illyana's price.

"Now follow me. Run!" Yakoub shouted.

The twelve men obeyed more swiftly than they would have even two days ago. Once more Yakoub knew that until now Eremius's captains had been the one-eyed leading the blind. By himself, he could do only so much to change this.

But if he taught twelve men everything he knew,

then each of them taught it to six more and they to six beyond that—well, inside of two months all of Eremius's men would be decent soldiers. Not the equals of the Golden Spears or other crack units of foot, but as good as most irregulars.

If only he could train them with the bow! But Eremius had passed judgment on that idea.

Yakoub writhed within as he remembered Eremius's words. The sorcerer had been surprised to see Yakoub appearing and offering to train his men. He had even allowed his pleasure to show, when the training started to bear fruit.

Gratitude was beyond him, however. So was what Yakoub considered military wisdom.

"In these mountains, Master, an archer is worth three men without a bow."

"We shall not be in the mountains much longer."

"Even in the plains, an archer has value against horsemen."

"No horsemen will dare close with the Transformed."

"Perhaps. But if you have to retreat, a rearguard of archers—"

"There shall be no retreats when we march again."

"You are—you have high hopes, Master."

"As indeed I should. You have brought me your own skills, which are considerable. You have also brought me news which is still better. The Jewels of Kurag are about to be reunited."

Eremius turned his back, in a manner that told Yakoub the matter was settled. Not wishing to provoke the sorcerer into using magic to frighten him, Yakoub departed.

He had wondered then and he wondered now what

afflicted Eremius. Was it as simple as not wishing to give his human fighters a weapon that could strike down the Transformed from a distance? If so, what did that say about Eremius's trust in the humans, even when he had made them nearly witlings to keep them from rebelling?

Or had Eremius given over thinking like a captain of human soldiers, and become entirely a sorcerer who might soon have the Jewels of Kurag in his power? If half of the tales about the Jewels Eremius told were true, it was no surprise that Eremius had fallen into this trap.

A trap it was, however, and one that Yakoub son of Khadjar must dig him out of!

Yakoub looked back at the running men. Most were pacing themselves as he had taught, rather than exhausting themselves in a swift frenzy. He increased his own pace, to put himself well out in front.

When he had done this, he suddenly whirled, staff raised. Without waiting for him to single out a man, the nearest five all raised their staves to meet him. He darted in, striking shoulders, thighs, and shins in rapid succession.

Doggedly, the men fought back. Yakoub took a thrust to his knee and another close to his groin.

I would do well to wear some padding the next time. These men are indeed learning.

Then a staff cracked him across the shoulders. He whirled and leaped. The other runners had come up behind him.

For a moment fear and rage twisted his face. Those fools could have killed him by accident!

Then he realized that the men who had come up behind were smiling.

"We did as we would have done with a real enemy," one of them said. "We came up behind him while others fought him in front. Is that not what is to be done?"

"Indeed it is." *Not just padding, but a helmet as well.* He clapped the man who had spoken on the shoulder. "You have done well. Now let us finish our run."

Yakoub waited for all the men to pass before he began to run again. For today at least, he would be happier without any of them behind him!

For the days to come, though, he saw much pleasure. He had often heard his father speak of how the gods gave men no greater joy than teaching the arts of the soldier. He had not understood how true this was, until today.

"Conan, will Dessa come to any harm—as she is now?" Massouf still could not bring himself to say "as a tavern girl."

Conan shrugged. The truth would depend on what she was made of. He did not suppose Massouf would enjoy hearing it. The young man had not given up Dessa so completely that he refused to worry about her.

Even for a man not careless of his life, being worried about someone else was a good way to get killed. As he was, Massouf was less than ever someone Conan cared to have at his side in a fight.

"If she lived as well as she did at Achmai's Hold, I doubt that anywhere in Turan will hold many terrors for her." A thought came to him. "I have a friend in Aghrapur by the name of Pyla. She is also a friend to Captain Khezal. If we both urge her to help Dessa find her feet in her new life, I am sure that help will come."

It might need a trifle of silver, because Pyla did little even for friends without asking payment. Besides, launching Dessa properly would not be cheap.

Worth it, though. If Dessa began her career known as a friend of Pyla, she would have few enemies. The rest could be left, as he had said several times, to the girl's natural talents.

Remembering those talents made Conan's blood race. He muttered a polite farewell to Massouf and returned to the pool. The stone where he had been sitting was wet and dark. There was no sign of either woman.

Either they were playing ill-timed jests, or—

Conan was standing on the edge of the pool when Illyana burst from the water. She rose half her height out of it, like a water sprite seeking to fly. Her arms wrapped around Conan's knees and she flung herself backward.

She might as well have tried to upset the Lord of the Winds. When she realized her mistake, Conan had already gripped her by the shoulders. He lifted and she rose, until her long legs were twined around Conan's waist. She lay back in his arms and smiled invitingly. His lips crushed hers.

For a long moment nothing existed for the Cimmerian, save Illyana in his arms, naked, wet, and beginning to writhe in pleasure. Pleasure was not a sufficient word for what he felt. Madness would have been closer.

Even when Illyana untwined her legs and stood, she pressed against Conan. His hands ran down her back, pressing her tighter. He felt her breasts against his chest, as delightfully firm as they had seemed—

"No," Illyana said, or rather gasped. Her voice was husky with desire. She stepped back, forgetting that they were on the edge of the pool. With a splash and a shriek she plunged into the water again, to come up coughing.

Conan helped her out of the pool, careful to grip only her hands. Illyana herself kept a pace away from him as she began to dry herself with her clothes.

"That is not a *no* for all time, the Jewels—the gods willing. It is only for now, that we cannot—" Her voice was still unsteady, and her eyes seemed glazed. The desire was leaving Conan, but he still judged it wise to turn his back until Illyana was dressed.

It was not until Conan had finished his own bathing that he had a chance for words alone with Raihna.

"Are my wits straying, or was your mistress trying to make me desire her?"

"*Trying?*" Raihna's laugh was harsh, both frightened and frightening. "I judged she was succeeding admirably. That's as well. The gods only know what she might have done, if she had thought she was undesirable."

"If she ever thinks that, I hope some man will have a chance to prove how wrong she is!"

"Not you?" Raihna asked, with a twisted grin.

"I think I was safer as a thief in the Tower of the Elephant than I'd be in Illyana's bed. Less pleasure there, but less peril."

Raihna stood close against him, and ran one hand lightly down his back. "But she did make you want a woman?"

Conan did not need the message carved in stone. He returned the embrace.

"Yes. I hope it also made you want a man!"

Raihna's happy cries echoed from the walls of the valley. Nonetheless, Conan could not shake off the memory of Illyana's eyes and voice, still less her mention of the Jewels.

Twenty

THEY REACHED THE Valley of the Demons so early in their last day's march that Conan ordered them back.

"We want a place beyond the reach of Eremius's scouts, to lie up for the day. Everybody should try to sleep."

"Indeed. It may be our last," Massouf said. He sounded rather as if he welcomed the prospect.

Conan's urge to shake some wits into the man rose again. He forced it down. Massouf might want to die, but he had proved himself hardy and careful, not to mention a good hand with the bow and the spear. If he died, he would likely enough take some of the enemy with him.

Bora found them a refuge that Conan himself could not have bettered. It had a spring of clear water, shelter from the sun, and concealment from the enemy. It even offered a safe way of flight, if needed.

"Bora, if you ever join the army, I'll wager you're a captain before you can turn around," Conan said.

"You are not the first to say so, and I thank you all," Bora said soberly. "But I cannot think of that until I know my father is pardoned and safe. Even then, I will be needed for the rebuilding of Crimson Springs."

Conan found himself exchanging looks with the two women. Bora's optimism was easier to hear than Massouf's grim despair. It altered not a whit their slim chances of both winning and surviving to enjoy their victory.

The night mists swirled up from the valley in their natural silver-gray. No magic or at least no Jewel-spells were at work. Conan crawled to the crest and looked at the scree-strewn slope plunging away into the mist.

"If this is the best way down," he whispered, "Erlik spare me seeing the worst!"

"I am not a god, to arrange these mountains to make our task easier," Bora said. "I can only tell you how they *are* arranged."

"Without any thought for us, that's certain," Raihna said.

The banter kept their spirits up, but it took time. Conan signed for silence, then one by one led the party to the crest.

"Can you climb down that?" he whispered to each one. "Can you climb *up* it again, with the Transformed at your heels?"

He did not ask Bora, who could have taught climbing to goats. The others all nodded, save Massouf, who shrugged.

"If you can't climb, we may not be able to carry you," Conan said, in a final effort to wean Massouf from his dark intent.

"If I am not climbing, I can make better practice

with spear and bow," Massouf replied. His eyes dared Conan to press him further.

"Likely enough there will be places we can defend lower down," Bora said. "If the sentries are alert, they will give the alarm before we reach the heart of Eremius's domain."

"Pray that it is not *too* soon," Illyana said. "The necessary spells must be cast with the two Jewels as close as we can contrive."

"You've persuaded us of that," Conan said. "Otherwise why would we be sticking our head into a wasp's nest to count the wasps?"

What they were doing was in fact many times worse than that. It was also utterly necessary. Illyana had said a wearying number of times that she could no longer fight Eremius's magic from a distance. Before the Jewels' will grew in them, it might have been otherwise. Now, however, they had to draw Eremius close. Otherwise she might exhaust her strength and her Jewel with nothing accomplished, leaving them with no magical protection against Eremius.

"Besides, if Eremius unleashes the Transformed, he must use some of his power to command them. I will have no such burden."

"No, you've a band of thick-witted sword-wielders to save you from it!" Conan had growled. "Proof that my wits are thicker than the mist is that I'm here!"

"Thank the gods for that," Illyana said, softly but with unexpected passion.

Even Massouf managed the climb down with little trouble. Conan was sure they had made enough noise to awaken sentries in Stygia, but no one barred their path.

"Could Eremius be resting his men while he heals the Transformed?" Illyana asked.

"Perhaps," was Conan's whispered reply. "I'd wager he's resting them by patrolling a smaller area. Sooner or later, we'll find somebody ready to welcome visitors."

They moved on in silence. No more words were needed, and the mist seemed to eerily distort speech. It was also thick enough to make their bows and Bora's sling far less useful.

Conan no longer despised the bow as a coward's weapon, but it was still not his favorite. He would gladly have given up his sword, however, in return for not having to trust to Illyana's spells. If he could have been altogether certain they would be hers alone, it would have been different. With the Jewels friends or foes in their own right—

"Hssst!" came from Bora, in the lead. "Somebody ahead."

Before Conan could reply, he heard the whirr of the sling winding up, then a hiss, a thump, and a faint clatter.

"That's one—" Bora began.

"Hoyaaaa! Guard! Turn out the guard!" came a scream from the left. Whoever was screaming was frightened nearly witless, but giving the alarm like a soldier.

Conan cursed. It was all very well to speak of drawing the enemy after you, but when you could not *see* each other in this cursed mist—

Half a dozen human fighters stormed out of the mist, spears and swords raised. Conan and Raihna met them head-on, to keep them from Illyana. In the flurry of steel that followed, Conan had no eyes for anyone save those in sword's reach of him. Two men went down before his blade, then suddenly the mist lay empty before him. Silence returned, save for the diminishing hammer of panic-stricken feet.

"I had one," Raihna said. "Bora picked off another with that sling of his. Will you teach me to use it?"

"The gods willing. How is Massouf?"

The young man raised a bloody spear. He looked as if he did not know whether to sing in triumph or spew in horror. At least first-kill fright was better than black despair!

"Let's be on our way back," Conan said.

"The Transformed are not yet unleashed," Illyana said. She had one hand pressing the other arm where the Jewel-ring sat. It let her make some use of the Jewel without revealing herself with its emerald light.

"They will be, when somebody finds these bodies," Conan said. "Come along. Best we don't let ourselves be surrounded."

"That's putting it delicately," Raihna began.

Then the whole world seemed to turn an eye-searing green, of no hue Conan had ever seen or imagined. A moment later the mist vanished, as if a giant mouth had sucked it out of the valley. The light turned the familiar emerald of the Jewels.

As the vanishing mist revealed the valley around Conan's party, it also revealed at least fifty of the Transformed swarming down the north side.

"Eremius comes!" Illyana screamed.

"Set to devour Eremius!" growled Conan, unslinging his bow. "Stop talking and start shooting, woman. We've a chance to improve the odds!"

Raihna was already unleashing arrows. The range was long even for her stout Bossonian bow, but the target was hard to miss. Every arrow from her bow, then from Conan's, then from Illyana's and Massouf's, struck Transformed flesh.

Struck, but did not pierce. At this range the scales of the Transformed were as good as the finest mail. Conan saw human fighters running downhill on the flanks of the Transformed and shifted to them. He killed four of them before their courage broke. By then he was nearly out of arrows.

The Transformed reached level ground. With arrows jutting from them, the Transformed looked even more monstrous than before. Jewel-light seared Conan's eyes again, as Illyana slung her bow, flung back her sleeves, and began wielding her magic.

When he could see clearly again, the Transformed had ceased their advance. Instead they huddled together, glaring in all directions. Some snatched arrows from their hides, others bit their taloned hands and whimpered like starving dogs.

"I have turned the fear back against them," Illyana cried exultantly. "I did not think to do this!"

"Well, start thinking what comes next!" Conan shouted. "Make them run around in circles until they're all too dizzy to fight, for all I care!"

Raihna sent her last two arrows into the motionless target. One struck a Transformed in the eye. His dying scream made Conan's flesh leap on his bones. Not *all* the fear was returning to the Transformed!

The light diminished, until it flowed from a single source, glimmering like a giant bonfire behind the Transformed. It seemed that the Master of the Jewel had indeed come forth.

"Back, and they will follow!" Illyana cried.

Conan turned to see her fleeing with a doe's grace

and swiftness, breasting the slope with ease. Was the Jewel giving her strength and speed, and if so at what price?

Meanwhile, the Transformed were rallying and starting across the valley, in no particular order but at a good pace. Even the wounded ones moved as fast as a man could walk.

Their carrion reek marched ahead of them. So did a hideous cacophony of hisses, growls, whimpers, clawed feet on stones, even belches and gulpings.

Conan had seen more than his share of unclean magic in his life, but the Transformed were a whole new order of nightmare. Once more he knew he might not easily find it in him to give Eremius a clean death.

Then he had to think about his own death and how to prevent it. His comrades were all on their way up the slope. Two of the Transformed hurled themselves forward. Perhaps they hoped to overtake Bora or Massouf.

Instead, they faced Conan. He hewed at a hand, slashing deep into the webbing between the fingers. Whirling, he slashed the second Transformed across the face, taking its sight. A thrust between the ribs with his dagger reached vital organs.

Conan had to leap backward to avoid the grip of the first Transformed. With sword and dagger at the guard, he watched it stop and stand over its fallen comrade. Then it knelt beside the fallen, trying to stanch the blood from the belly wound and the ruined face.

So the Transformed were not lower than the beasts. Conan thought no better of Master Eremius, but he vowed to give the Transformed warriors' deaths whenever possible.

Conan retreated again. He had nearly overtaken his comrades before the Transformed started mounting the slope. Bora was casting back and forth like a dog for a trail. "I smell a cave around here somewhere."

"If you smell it, perhaps the Transformed are already at home," Conan said. "I doubt if they will welcome us to dinner."

"No. For dinner, perhaps," Massouf said. He was limping but held his spear jauntily on one shoulder.

"There it is!" Bora shouted. He pointed uphill to the right. Conan had just time to see a dark mouth, before the Transformed broke into a run.

Light from both Jewels at once seared Conan's eyes. Dimly, he saw Massouf seemingly turned to a statue of jade. Even his eyes glowed green, as though he had become a creature of the Jewel.

Had he in truth become one? Were the Jewels reaching out for others besides their wearers?

Those uneasy thoughts had barely left Conan's mind when Massouf stripped off his quiver and bow, tossing them to Conan. The Cimmerian caught them as Massouf charged downhill toward the Transformed.

"Crom!"

The Transformed were giving way before Massouf's charge. They hissed and cringed and cried as if Massouf had been a whole army.

Massouf actually contrived to spit one of the Transformed like a chicken, before they regained their courage. A moment of clawing and trampling, and Massouf was gone.

From first to last, he had not made a sound.

Conan stormed up the slope, to where Illyana stood before the cave mouth. Raihna was already piling stones to narrow it.

"Conan!" the hill boy cried. "There will be room inside for me to use my sling. If you will stand to either—"

"Did you kill Massouf?" Conan roared.

Illyana had been drawing off her boots. Now she flinched and stood barefoot, a boot in either hand.

"Did you? Answer me, woman!"

"Conan, I did not command him. I heard no command from the Jewels. I can only say that under the spell cast, the Transformed might be more easily frightened."

"Massouf couldn't have known that!"

"I may have told him without remembering it. Or—"

"Or the Jewels might have told him," Conan finished for her.

Illyana shook her head, as if beset by stinging insects. Suddenly she flung herself into Conan's arms.

"I beg you, Conan. Believe me, that I meant Massouf no harm. He came here seeking death and found it."

That at least was the truth, and for the moment Conan was ready to be content with it. Not that he had any choice, either. The Transformed were halfway up the hill, some still gnawing fragments of Massouf.

Illyana contemplated them, all her unease of a moment before gone. "Good. We have them closing swiftly. If we can hold until they have closed just a trifle more—"

"And how long will that be?" Conan asked.

Illyana stripped off her tunic and waved it like a flag. "Look, Eremius. Look and dream, but know that you will die before you touch!"

"*How long?*"

"I do not know," Illyana said. Then she ran toward the cave, with Conan at her heels.

Twenty-one

CONAN LOWERED A rock the size of a newborn calf onto the pile in the cave mouth. Then he stepped back, dusting off his hands and looking into the cave for any more loose stones.

He had all the light he could wish, pouring from Illyana's Jewel. Unclothed save for the Jewel, the sorceress stood forty paces inside the cave, chanting in an unknown tongue. The world beyond her duel with Eremius might have ceased to exist.

Conan saw no more stones worth adding to their barricade. He was about to tell Raihna when a stone went *wheeet* between them. Conan whirled, glaring at Bora.

The boy was reloading his sling and grinning. "As I said, there is room to send a stone between you."

"Warn us the next time, you young—"

"Captain, I might not be able to warn you. What if you and Raihna are close-grappled with the Transformed? Best you trust me to hit them and not you."

Conan couldn't help laughing. The boy was right, of course. And anyone who could grin like that, in what might indeed be his last minutes of life—

"Bora, perhaps you shouldn't join the army after all. In five years, *you* would be giving *me* orders!"

"They would never make a hillman—" Bora began soberly. Raihna's shout interrupted him.

"Here they come!"

Conan sprang to his post by the barricade. Eremius had taken longer than they expected to form up his creations for battle. What Illyana had done with that time, Conan did not know. He and Raihna had narrowed the cave mouth so that only two or three of the Transformed could attack at once. He had also placed a few throwing stones ready to hand.

The Transformed stormed up the hill in two ragged lines. At Raihna's signal Bora sent a stone hurtling low through the cave mouth. It struck a Transformed in the chest, without so much as knocking him down. Conan flung a fist-sized stone. He aimed for eyes and struck a forehead. Again the Transformed did not even fall. It howled in rage and pain and seemed to climb faster.

"I think we have the pick of the Transformed coming up," Conan said.

"The pick of Bossonia and Cimmeria stand here," Raihna replied. She tossed her head. The Jewel-light shimmered on her hair as it flowed about her shoulders. Then she tossed her sword and caught it by the hilt.

A Transformed flung a stone. It drove chips and dust from the barricade into Conan's face. As he blinked, Bora replied. The slingstone struck a Transformed in the knee, hard enough to leave it limping.

Then the spearhead of the attack reached the defenders. Conan and Raihna had practiced together since the return to Fort Zheman. Now Conan's training in the rude school of surviving and Raihna's training from Master Barathres merged as easily as their bodies did in love.

Conan feinted high to draw the attention of a Transformed upward. His sword crashed into a scaly arm. That upraised arm left an armpit exposed. Raihna's dagger leaped upward into the armpit, finding the expected weak spot where the scales were thin to allow free movement.

The Transformed reeled back, holding a crippled arm. A human would have been dead, and this one at least was out of the fight.

Another Transformed gripped the top of the barricade. Conan hewed at the nearest hand, three, four, five cuts, as if chopping firewood with his sword. At the fifth stroke, the hand flopped limply. At the sixth it fell off entirely, landing on Conan's side of the barricade. Reeking blood sprayed into Conan's face, neither looking nor smelling anything like human gore. The Transformed's howls echoed around the cave.

Conan's fight against the climbing Transformed left Raihna to hold the opening single-handed. Two Transformed who came at her jammed in the opening, letting her slash and thrust until they reeled away bloody and daunted. The next enemy was swifter.

Conan turned to find Raihna in the clutches of a Transformed, being drawn toward it. She had blinded it and thrust deep into its chest, without reaching its unnatural life. The talons were already gashing her flesh. The fangs would reach her throat before the creature died.

They had not done so, when Conan's sword came down across the bridge of the creature's nose. Under the scale armor, the bones there were still thin enough to be vulnerable. Shattering under the Cimmerian's sword, they drove splinters into the Transformed's brain. It convulsed, arching backward. Raihna leaped free, kicking out. The Transformed crashed into an approaching comrade. Both went down.

Raihna stripped off her tunic, used it to roughly wipe her oozing wounds, then tossed it aside. Bare to the waist, she raised her weapons again.

"You won't distract them that way," Conan said, laughing. "You might distract Bora, though."

Bora certainly seemed not to mind fighting in the presence of two splendid and nearly unclothed women. His eye for targets was still keener than his eye for the women. As the Transformed knocked down by the latest kill struggled to its feet, a stone caught it in the eye. The stone was sharp and reached the brain. The Transformed fell, kicked wildly, but did not rise. Other Transformed held back until the kicking ceased.

"That's five down or out against your scratches and tunic," Conan said. "How many left?"

"Oh, not more than forty or so."

"Then we should be finished by breakfast."

"Yes, but whose breakfast?"

With howls and scrabbling feet, the Transformed came on again.

Eremius suspected that his face was streaming sweat, as if he had been in a steam bath. He knew that pain racked his joints so that it needed real effort to stand.

Nearly all his magic was pouring into the duel with Illyana. The little he could spare for the Transformed was barely enough to keep them attacking without turning on one another. Those who took wounds or lost their courage had to do without his help.

This should not be. It could not be, unless Illyana had become greater than he. That was impossible. She did not have it in her to become so.

Eremius turned against Illyana even the little magic he was sparing to ease the pain in his joints. He almost cried out, like a man on the rack. He eased his pain with the thought that this addition of strength might be enough to let him try piercing the veil around Illyana's Jewel.

He tried and failed.

Only after he abandoned the effort, when he could barely stand, did he realize that the failure had told him what he wanted to know. Illyana's Jewel was utterly in harmony with her, defending both her and itself against him. How had she achieved this harmony?

Eremius thought he knew the answer. When he allowed himself to contemplate it, he knew fear as well, for the first time in many years.

Both Conan and Raihna were bleeding from a dozen minor wounds. Their muscles twitched and ached, their breaths rasped, and neither of them had enough intact clothing to garb a tavern dancer.

They fought on, because the Transformed did so. Illyana chanted and the Jewel-light danced and flickered. Bora's sling flung stone after stone, always swiftly, often with effect.

It was still mostly Conan's fight and Raihna's. Neither any longer kept count of the Transformed maimed or slain. Neither kept count of the times they had saved the other's life.

These matters were of small importance, compared with the oncoming Transformed. There had to be an end of them, to be sure, but would that end come before Conan and Raihna reached the end of their strength?

Already Raihna's dagger was blunted from thrusting through scales, and her sword was kinked. Conan's sword showed as many nicks as if he had been chopping wood with it. They might soon lose the power to harm the Transformed even if they still possessed the strength.

It seemed to Conan that the Transformed were somewhat thinner on the ground. It also seemed that the intervals between attacks were growing longer. It was not impossible that the tide of battle was flowing their way.

Would it flow fast enough? They could still lose everything, if the Transformed broke through in sufficient strength to slay Illyana.

Another Transformed—no, two of them—charged the opening. Conan dashed the sweat from his eyes. Matters were not well, when he could hardly count the number of his opponents!

The Transformed facing Conan bore several wounds and an arrow, relics of previous exchanges. It stumbled against the barricade, flinging all its more-than-human weight against the stones. One of them shifted, then another.

With a rattle and a crash, the barricade subsided in a cloud of dust. The second Transformed leaped through the dust. Raihna met him with a desperate lunge. Her sword bent almost double. Conan hewed at the Transformed's neck, but it had the speed to elude him. It leaped between the two defenders, shrugged off a stone from Bora's sling, and lunged at Illyana.

The talons were only an arm's length from the sorceress when she leaped up and back. Conan would have sworn that she *floated* into the air. He did not doubt what he saw leaping from the Jewel—emerald fire, a spearthrust of eye-searing light.

It struck the Transformed. One claw raked Illyana's shoulder, without drawing blood. Then the flesh was boiling off the Transformed's bones, like stew in an untended pot. A wave of indescribable stench swept over Conan, making him blink and reel. When he saw clearly again, only smoking bones on the cave floor remained of the Transformed.

Illyana stood, fingering a shoulder that Conan knew should have been gaping nearly to the bone. The smooth flesh was unmarred. Unbidden and unwelcome, the thought of how he had held that flesh close to him entered his mind.

As if she shared the thought, Illyana smiled.

"I should not have been able to do that. The Jewels—" Whatever she might have wanted to say about the Jewels went unuttered. Instead her face turned grim. "I do not know how often I can do that. I can certainly do it often enough to let you and Raihna attack."

"With what?" the swordswoman exclaimed, holding out her crippled weapons.

Illyana seemed uncaring. "Eremius has drawn closer and the Transformed are weaker. If you attack now, with Bora and me guarding your backs, you may slay Eremius. The second Jewel will come to us. Victory will be ours."

Conan wanted to shake the sorceress. "We'll win no victory with blades too dull to cut butter!"

For the first time, Illyana seemed to notice the weapons in her friends' hands. Her eyes clouded for a moment. Then she rested a hand on Conan's sword, stretching out the other with fingers spread so it touched both Raihna's sword and dagger.

Conan fought the urge to snatch his blade out of Illyana's hands. Sorcery had been too close for too long already. To fight with an ensorceled blade—

Illyana chanted, and Raihna's sword straightened. The nicks vanished from the edge of Conan's sword. A point returned to her dagger. Bright sharp edges gleamed on all of them.

"Crom!"

The Cimmerian god was not one to answer prayers or hear them with patience. For once in his life Conan almost regretted this.

Conan raised his sword, testing the balance and sighting along the magically-restored edge. It seemed as good as new, Ensorceled or not, it was also the only weapon at hand.

He still felt nearly as much fear of Illyana as of the Transformed when he led Raihna out of the cave.

Eremius struggled to understand what had come to pass in the cave. Illyana lived and the Transformed had died in a way that even the power of her Jewel should not have allowed.

He abandoned the struggle when the Cimmerian burst from the cave. Understanding he did not need, when life itself was in peril. Withdrawing his power from the duel against Illyana, he sought to shield, then rally the Transformed.

For a moment he thought he had succeeded. Emerald fire blazed along the thin line of the Transformed. Two were not swift enough to leap clear; the flesh flew from their bones amid howls.

The other Transformed recoiled at those howls. They did not recoil far. They saw that the fire held their enemies away from them, and began to regain their courage. Eremius cast his thoughts at them furiously, forming them into a solid mass, then urging them forward.

They were approaching the line of fire when Illyana appeared at the mouth of the cave. Eremius's thoughts leaped from battle to her awesome beauty, every bit of it revealed to him.

A moment later, he saw his doom revealed as well. Illyana raised a hand, and the line of fire vanished. She gripped Bora's arm with the other hand, then let him wind up with his sling.

Only one stone flew, but the Transformed howled as if each saw a stone flying straight at it. Their solid line broke up. The Cimmerian and the swordswoman plunged into the fleeing remnants.

At first they had to fight a way. Then the Transformed realized that their foes would attack only those in their path. To leave the path of humans who seemed invincible was a simple matter, a few steps, then a few steps more, each step taken more swiftly.

Not all of the Transformed fled like dead leaves before a gale, but few enough fought. The Cimmerian and the Bossonian came down the hill like avenging gods.

Eremius tore the ring from his arm. He still would not dare the spells that offered the last chance with the Jewel so close to his flesh. He cast it to the ground. The gold rang on the stones, and the ringing seemed to go on, filling his ears like the tones of a mighty gong.

The sorcerer clapped his hands to his ears. Shutting out the sound, he tried to array his thoughts once more, for the last spells.

If he succeeded, no more would be needed.

If he failed, no more would be possible.

* * *

Conan had never run so fast in his life, at least after a long battle. Hillman though he was, he feared his legs would betray him. To stumble now would be worse than fatal, it would be humiliating.

At last he felt level ground under his feet. Ahead he saw Eremius, Jewel-ring at his feet and hands clasped over his ears. What the sorcerer heard that Conan did not, the Cimmerian neither knew nor cared.

He only knew that in another score of paces, he could snatch up the Jewel-ring.

Conan had covered half the distance when the Jewel-ring leaped into the air. It did not glow, not with the dazzling emerald fire of before. It did something far worse.

It sang.

It sang with a sad, plaintive note in a voice that uttered no words but somehow held enormous power to paint pictures in Conan's mind. Conan saw a deep-bosomed Cimmerian wench and himself grappled in love before a blazing fire. He saw a snug hut, with children playing before that same fire. He saw dark-haired boys, their features stamped with his own, learning the art of the hunt and the blade from their father. He saw himself with grizzled hair, passing judgments in village disputes.

All that he had turned his back on, the Jewel seemed to say, could be his. He need only turn his back on Eremius.

Conan slowed his pace. He had turned his back on Cimmeria with open eyes, but now those eyes were threatening to blur with sorrow for what he had lost. He knew this was no natural sorrow, but the power of it was sweeping away the last of his knowledge.

Another presence hammered its way into Conan's mind. Illyana's Jewel was crying out a song of triumph.

Equally dazzling pictures entered his mind—riding at the head of an army through a city of towering buildings with gilded roofs, under a sky of northern blue. White clouds shone, flowers showered down upon him, clinging to the mane of his steed, the cheers and chants of the crowd drowned out the babble of the Cimmerian village meeting.

As if slamming a door in the face of intruders, Conan willed both Jewels out of his mind. It did not matter which offered what rewards. Both alike seemed to think that he could be bought. Both were wrong, and their masters with them.

Conan needed no urging to overthrow the creator of the Transformed. What he might see fit to do with Illyana could be left until later.

Conan's sword lunged. Its point darted through the ring. The sharp blade leaped toward the sky, where the mist was gathering again. The ring and its Jewel slid down the blade to the hilt.

"Run, people!"

The last thing Conan saw as he himself turned to run, was Eremius slumping to the ground, his face in his hands.

Twenty-two

THEY WERE HALFWAY out of the valley when Illyana stumbled and fell, to all appearances senseless. Conan laid an ear next to her lips and felt her breathing. Then he handed the Jewel-ring to Raihna, who slipped it on her left arm. Sheathing his sword, the Cimmerian lifted the sorceress and continued the climb.

"Let me go on ahead and find an easier path, Captain," Bora said. "You are hillborn like me, but I have not fought hand to hand with the Transformed this night."

"Not yet," Raihna said. "We may well have heard the last of Eremius. About his creations—"

From the swirling mist in the valley came wild cries, inhuman in their quality but clearly from a human throat. Rage, terror, and pain blended horribly in the cries.

Then the howls of the Transformed rose in a nightmare chorus, swallowing the human cries.

"What in Mitra's name was *that*?" Bora gasped.

"As Raihna said, we've heard the last of Master Eremius," Conan said. "I'd wager that was him, making a light supper for some of his Transformed."

Bora shuddered. "Keep your sling loaded and ready," Conan added. "It's the only weapon we have left for striking from a distance."

"It's also the only weapon we have that Illyana didn't ensorcel," Raihna said, almost meditatively. Conan stared at her in dawning surprise.

"That matters to you?"

"After what I've seen these past few days—even Illyana's magic smells other than it once did. And *anything* flowing from the Jewels . . ." She shook her head. "I will think on it, when I have wits to spare."

They scrambled out of the valley in silence. They also moved in darkness, for which Conan was grateful. Darkness and the resurgent mist hid them from the Transformed, and the Jewels slept. They might have been as exhausted as their rescuers, or even their new mistress.

They left the mist behind in the Valley of the Demons. By the time Bora saw the Lord of the Winds towering against the stars, Illyana could walk again. She was also shivering, naked against the night wind.

Bora realized that whatever her magic had done to keep her warm was passing. He stripped off his shirt and handed it to her. She donned it eagerly, then inclined her head as graciously as a queen.

"We are grateful," she said. Conan frowned and seemed about to speak, then seemed to think better of it. Once again they moved on in silence.

The endurance of his companions surprised Bora.

The Cimmerian and Raihna had to be close to the end of their strength. Illyana had battled Eremius, no less formidable an opponent than the Transformed, and could hardly be accustomed to walking barefoot across mountainsides.

At dawn, they were almost in sight of where they left their baggage. They emptied their waterskins, slung them again, and turned on to the last slope.

All at once Conan held up a warning hand.

"Stop. Everyone hide. I'm going on alone." He spoke softly, as if hostile ears might be close.

"We wish to know—" Illyana began.

Again Conan frowned. Then he said with elaborate courtesy, "You shall know the moment I do. Until then, I ask your good will."

Raihna and Conan exchanged glances. Then Raihna put her hand to the small of Illyana's back and gently pushed her toward a stand of scrubby bushes. As Bora followed the women, Conan was already scrambling down the slope by a route that hid him from below. Once more Bora was amazed at how silently so large a man could move.

Bora had barely time to become impatient before Conan returned as silently as he went. The first knowledge Bora had of his return was a soft bird whistle. Then the black-maned head thrust into the bushes.

"Six of those half-witted humans Eremius used as scouts. They're sitting around our baggage. Swords and spears, no bows. They look a bit more alert than most, but no match for us."

"Must we slay more of the Master's servants?" asked Illyana. She sounded almost petulant.

Conan shrugged. "I suppose we could leave them to the army, like the Transformed. But do you want to

walk all the way back to Fort Zheman clothed as you
are?"

"That might not be necessary."

"By Erlik's beard! How—?"

"Do not blaspheme."

If Illyana had spoken in Stygian, Conan could not
have looked blanker. This time it was Raihna who
frowned, then spoke.

"Forgive us, mistress. We think only of your comfort."

"That is honorable. Very well. We give our consent."
Illyana waved a languid hand downhill. "Do your
duty."

Once again Bora had the notion he was listening to a
queen. A queen—or at least a ruler, consisting of a
woman and one of the Jewels.

Not both Jewels. Please, gods, not both.

Bora cudgeled his thoughts into order and began
seeking slingstones under the bushes.

A Cimmerian battle cry seemed to stun half the
men. The rest leaped up. That made them the first to
die, as their attackers struck. Conan hewed down two,
and Raihna the third.

One of the sitting men fell over, ribs crushed and
heart stopped by a slingstone. His comrades now rose,
one to run, the other to thrust at Conan with his spear.
The Cimmerian had to give ground for a moment, then
hacked through the spearshaft with his sword.

The man had enough of the shaft left to raise it like a
fighting staff. He caught Conan's first slash, then tried
to kick the Cimmerian in the knee.

This display of skill and courage neither altered nor
greatly delayed the man's fate. Raihna slipped under
the guard of his improvised staff with her dagger. He

reeled back, thigh pouring blood, and did not look up as Conan's sword descended.

Bora looked for the man who had fled, and saw him already far enough to make a kill chancy. Then he looked around him. Conan would doubtless have noted any sentries, who indeed could not have been very alert. A second pair of eyes never harmed the chances of victory, as Conan's Captain Khadjar said.

Had Bora seen Master Eremius walking up the hill, he could hardly have been more surprised.

"Yakoub!"

The Cimmerian whirled. Bora pointed. The Cimmerian's sword leaped up.

"Good morning, Captain Conan," Yakoub said. He sounded as calm as if they were meeting to visit a tavern. Then he looked at the bodies of his men. For a moment the calm broke and his face showed naked grief.

"I did not teach them enough," was all Yakoub said. Then he drew his own sword. "I can still avenge them."

"Small chance of that," Conan said. After a moment he sheathed his own sword. "Yakoub, I'd rather not face your father with your blood on my hands. I have no more quarrel with you."

"If you meant that, you wouldn't have killed my men."

"*Your* men?" the Cimmerian snorted. "Master Eremius's tame dogs? What do you owe them?"

"My death or yours," Yakoub said.

"That dung-spawned—" Bora began. He reached for his sling. A moment later he knew that speaking had been a mistake. A muscular Bossonian arm took him across the throat from behind. Raihna's free hand snatched the sling from his grip.

Freed suddenly, he whirled to face the swords-woman. "You—! Whose side are you on?"

"I'm against your dishonoring Conan. Yakoub—"

"Yakoub dishonored my sister! He dishonored my family!"

"Are you willing to fight him hand to hand?"

Bora measured Yakoub's suppleness, the grace of movement, the easy grip on the sword. "No. He'd cut me to pieces."

"Then stand back and let Conan settle matters. Yakoub is the bastard son of High Captain Khadjar. His being out here may mean that Conan's command-er is a traitor. Conan's honor is caught up in this too. If Yakoub won't run, he has to be killed in a fair fight."

"And if Conan is killed—?"

"Then I'll face Yakoub. Either swear to keep your sling on your belt, or I'll slice it apart with my dagger now."

Bora would have cursed, if he'd known words ade-quate for his rage. At last he spat. "Keep it, you Bossonian trull—!"

The slap aimed at Bora never landed. Conan and Yakoub sprang toward each other, and the dawn light blazed from their uplifted swords.

Afterward Bora confessed that he had thought of using his sling to save Conan, as well as avenging his own family's honor. He could not believe that the Cimmerian would be fit to meet a strong opponent blade to blade, not after the night's fighting.

He did not realize that Conan also knew the limits of his strength. The Cimmerian's leap into sword's reach was his last. For the rest of the fight, he moved as little as possible, weaving an invisible armor of darting steel around himself. Yakoub was fresher and just as swift if lacking the Cimmerian's reach. He might have won, had he been allowed a clear line of attack for a single moment.

The deadly dance of Conan's blade denied him that moment.

At some time in the fight, Illyana came down to watch. After a few moments, she turned away, yawning as if she found this battle to the death no more interesting than swine-mating.

Sitting down, she opened the bags and garbed herself. Bora knew a moment's regret at seeing that fair body at last concealed. Raihna was still next to naked, but her face made Bora doubt whom she thought the enemy, Yakoub or himself.

Bora was as surprised as Yakoub by the ending of the fight. He had expected Conan to stand until Yakoub wearied himself. Instead Conan suddenly left an opening that even Bora could recognize, for Yakoub to launch a deadly stroke.

Neither Bora nor Yakoub recognized Conan's intent. The first either knew of it was when Conan dropped under Yakoub's blade. It still came close to splitting his head; hanks of blood-stiffened black hair flew.

Now Conan was inside Yakoub's guard. Knee rammed into groin, head butted chin, and hand gripped swordarm. Yakoub flew backward, to land disarmed and half-stunned. He rolled, trying to draw a dagger. Conan brought a foot down on his wrist and lowered his sword until its point rested against the other's throat.

"Yakoub, I know you owed a debt to your men. I owe one to your father. Go back to him and urge him to go where he need not pretend you are dead."

"That will mean giving up his Captaincy," Yakoub said. "You ask much of both of us."

"Why not?" Conan asked. Sweat ran down him, in spite of the morning chill. For the first time, Bora noticed that the Cimmerian's left shoulder bore a fresh wound.

Yakoub seemed to be pondering the question. What he would have answered was never to be known. As Conan stepped back, green fire of a familiar hue surrounded Yakoub. His body convulsed, arching into a bow. His mouth opened in a soundless scream and his hands scrabbled in the dirt.

Then he fell back, as limp as if every bone in his body had been crushed to powder. Blood trickled briefly from his gaping mouth, then ceased.

Bora turned, not knowing what he would see but certain it would be something fearful.

Instead he saw Illyana sitting on a blanket, as regally as if it had been a throne. One arm was raised, and the Jewel-ring on it glowed softly.

Conan knew that Illyana had declared war. Illyana and the Jewels, rather. Whatever she did, it was no longer wholly as her own mistress.

He was surprised to feel this much charity toward a sorceress. But a sorceress who was also a battle comrade was something new.

"Raihna, give me the other Jewel," Illyana said, holding out her hand. "It is time to let them unite."

Raihna looked down at her Jewel-ring as if seeing it for the first time. Slowly she drew it off and dangled it from her right hand.

Conan willed his body and his mind to avoid any movement or even thought that might betray him.

What powers the Jewels had given Illyana or themselves, he did not know. He was certain that he would have only one slender chance of defeating the Jewels. Unless Raihna was ready to turn her back on ten years of loyalty to Illyana, and Conan would rather wager on King Yildiz's abdicating the throne to become a priest of Mitra—

Raihna's right arm flashed up, as swiftly as if it were thrusting a dagger into a mortal enemy. The ring flew into the air.

Conan barely contrived to catch it before it struck the ground. Rolling, he rubbed the Jewel across his bleeding shoulder. Then he sprang to his feet and flung the Jewel-ring with all his strength toward the spring.

Neither a sorceress nor the power of the Jewels were as swift as the Cimmerian's arm. The Jewel-ring plummeted into the spring and vanished.

Conan drew his sword. He did not suppose it would be much use against whatever the Jewels might be about to unleash. Somewhere in his thoughts was the notion of dying with it in hand, like a warrior.

Somewhere, also, lay the notion of giving Illyana a cleaner death than the twisted power of the Jewels might intend.

Conan had barely drawn when he suddenly felt as if he had been plunged into frozen honey. Every limb seemed constrained, nearly paralyzed. Cold gnawed at every bit of skin and seemed to pierce through the skin into his vitals. From somewhere near he heard Raihna's strangled cry, as if the honey was flowing into her mouth and nose, cutting off her breath.

It would be so easy to stand here or even lie down. So easy to let Raihna the traitoress perish, and live on, satisfying Illyana's desire and his every night and sometimes every day. Satisfying a queen *and* leading her armies was enough for any man.

Was it not so?

"I know you," Conan growled. "Whatever you are, I know you. You don't know me."

He twisted desperately. One after another, his limbs came free. The cold remained, but now he could move his feet. As if through a frozen marsh, he lurched toward Raihna.

She could move only her eyes, but now they turned toward him. She tried to lift an arm. As her hand came above her waist, her face contorted in pain.

The Jewels might have nothing left but vengeance, but they would have that. Or was it Illyana?

"Bora!" Conan shouted. Or tried to shout. It was as if one of the Transformed was gripping him by the throat. He tore at the air in front of his face, but the grip was stronger than he was after a night's fighting.

Conan felt his neck beginning to twist and strain. He fought harder, and the twisting stopped. He even sucked in one deep breath before the grip tightened further.

How long Conan stood grappling with the invisible, he never knew. He knew only that in one moment he was on the brink of having his windpipe crushed. In the next moment the spring began bubbling and seething, spewing foul steam—and the death grip eased.

Conan still felt as if he was wading through a deep stream against a swift current. Compared with what had gone before, it was easy to overcome it, easier still to reach Raihna. The pain still racked her, but she let herself be drawn after him, one torturous step at a time.

At every moment Conan expected the Jewels to return to their vengeance and complete it. Instead the steam from the spring only rose higher, until no water flowed and the gap in the rock looked near-kin to a volcano.

At last Conan felt his limbs moving with their normal ease. All his wounds were bleeding again as he drew Raihna out of the magic. She fell against him, clad only in sword and Bora's sling.

"Run!" Conan shouted. It was an order to both of them. For Raihna it was also to gain her attention. Her eyes were vacant and her mouth slack. It seemed as if it would not take much for her to collapse and die with her mistress, letting the Jewels have their vengeance after all. Conan swore to unknown powers that he would not let this happen, if he had to carry her all the way to Fort Zheman.

Raihna had a warrior's will to abandon no fight until she was dead. Her first steps were stumbling, as if the ground was hot. The next steps were cautious, as if she could not altogether command her limbs. Then Bora took her other arm and with support on both sides she broke into a clumsy run.

They plunged down the hill to the bottom of the next valley, then began climbing the opposite slope. Conan did not know where they were going, or how long they could keep running. He only knew that he wanted as much distance as possible between him and whatever the Jewels were brewing up. Otherwise they might take their vengeance purely by chance!

Behind Conan, steam hissed and the grind and clash of moving rocks joined it. He did not dare turn around to be sure, but it also seemed that a green glow was spreading across the land.

They reached the crest of the hill with barely a single breath left between them. Conan contrived to stand, holding his comrades upright. He could not have done that and also kept running, not to save himself from all the Transformed at once.

It was then that he finally heard Illyana scream. He had never heard such a sound from a human throat. He had never imagined that a human throat could make such a sound. He did not enjoy knowing that it could.

Then the whole landscape turned green and the ground underfoot heaved.

"Down!"

Conan hurled himself and his comrades down the far slope of the hill. They rolled halfway to the foot, bruising and gouging already battered skins. What little remained of Conan's garments remained behind, as did Raihna's dagger.

Unable at last to rise, they lay and saw a vast cloud of smoke towering into the sky. It swirled and writhed and flashed lightning. Dreadful shapes in gray and green seemed to form themselves in the cloud, then vanish. The sound was as if the whole world was tearing itself apart, and the shaking of the ground made Conan wonder if this hill too was about to dissolve in magic-spawned chaos.

The shuddering of the ground and the thunder in the sky died away. Only the smoke cloud remained, now raining fragments of rock. As Conan sat up and began to count his limbs, a fragment the size of a man's head plummeted down barely ten paces away.

Raihna flinched, then looked down at herself.

"Conan, if you are going to embrace me in this state, let us seek a—a—*ahhhhh!*"

All her breath left her in a long wail. Then she began sobbing with more strength than Conan had thought she had in her.

Bora discreetly withdrew. When Raihna's weeping was done, he returned, wearing only his loincloth and carrying his trousers in his hand.

"Raihna, if you want *some* garb, I'll trade you this for my sling."

Raihna managed a smile. "Thank you, Bora. But I think it would be better cut up into strips and bound around our feet. We have some walking to do."

"Yes, and the sooner we start the better," Conan growled. Another rock crashing to earth nearby gave point to his remarks. "I think my sword has a better edge than my—Crom!"

A bladeless hilt rattled to the ground from Conan's scabbard. Raihna clutched at her own belt, to find both dagger and sword gone.

"The Jewels' magic has a long arm, it would seem," she said at last. "Well, Bora, I was right about your sling being free of magic. Would you care to try it?"

Conan reached into his boot and drew his spare dagger. "Illyana didn't touch this either." He stood. "Now, my friends, *I* am starting for Fort Zheman. I don't propose to stand around here gaping until a rock cracks my skull."

"At your command, Captain," Bora said formally. He offered a hand to Raihna. "My lady?"

The Bossonian woman rose, and together they turned away from the smoke cloud that marked the grave of Lady Illyana, briefly mistress of the Jewels of Kurag.

Twenty-three

"So THERE YOU were, deep in the Ibars Mountains, with one pair of trousers, a dagger, and a sling among the three of you. How did you contrive a way out?" Mishrak sounded more amused than suspicious.

"We found help," Conan said. "Not that they wanted to help us, but we persuaded them."

"Them?"

"Four bandits," Raihna put in. "They were holding a mother and daughter captive. The women were from a village destroyed by the Transformed. They fled the wrong way in the darkness and ran into the bandits."

"They must have been grateful for your help," Mishrak said.

"They helped us too," Conan added. "Bora and I crept close to the camp. Raihna stayed back, then stood up. Clothed as she was not, she made a fine sight. Two of the bandits ran out to win this prize.

"Bora killed one with his sling. I took the other with my dagger. One of the others ran at me but I knocked him down with a stone and Raihna kicked his ribs in.

The mother hit the last one with a stick of firewood. Then she pushed him face down into the campfire, to finish him off."

The delicate faces of Mishrak's guardswomen showed grim satisfaction at that last detail.

"And then?"

"Does it need telling? We took the bandits' clothes and everything else that we could carry and left the mountains. We saw no sign of the Transformed or Eremius's human fighters.

"On the third day we met the soldiers from Fort Zheman. They mounted us and took us back to the fort. We told Captain Khezal the whole tale. You may hear from him any day."

"I already have." The voice under the mask sounded meditative. "You left Fort Zheman rather in haste, did you not? And you took the tavern wench named Dessa with you."

"We heard that Lord Achmai was bringing up his men, to help scour the mountains for the last of the Transformed. Considering what happened at our first meeting with Lord Achmai, we decided it would serve the peace of the realm if we did not meet again."

Mishrak chuckled. "Conan, you almost said that as though you meant it. How is Dessa taking to Aghrapur?"

"She's in Pyla's hands, which are about the best to be found," Conan said. "Beyond that, she's a girl I expect can make her own way almost anywhere."

"More than equal to the task, if you describe her truly. Is it the truth, by the way, that Pyla is buying the Red Falcon?"

"I'd hardly know."

"And if you did you wouldn't tell me, would you, Conan?"

"Well, my lord, I'd have to be persuaded it was your affair. But it's the truth that I don't know. Pyla can keep a secret better than you, when she wants to."

"So I have heard," Mishrak said. "You are no bad hand at telling tales, either. Or rather, leaving tales untold."

Conan's fingers twitched from the urge to draw his sword. "It is not well done, to say that those who have done you good service are lying."

"Then by all means let the truth be told. Did you intend to spare Yakoub?" A laugh rolled from under the mask, at Conan's look. "No, I have no magic to read your thoughts. I only have long practice in reading what is not put into letters, as well as what is. I could hardly serve King Yildiz half so well, did I lack this art.

"But my arts are not our concern now. I only ask—did you intend to spare Yakoub?"

Conan judged that he had little to lose by telling the truth. "I asked him to go back to his father and suggest they flee together."

"You thought High Captain Khadjar was a traitor?"

"His son was. Had Khadjar been innocent, would he have told everyone that his son was dead?"

"True enough. Yet—the son might also have hidden his tracks from his father. Did you think of that?"

Conan knew he was staring like a man newly risen from sleep and did not care. Was Mishrak trying to argue for Khadjar's innocence? If he was not, then Conan's ears were not as they had been, thanks to Illyana's magic.

"I did not."

"Well, let us both consider that possibility. If I need either of you again, I shall summon you. For your good service, my thanks." One gloved hand rose in dismissal.

At such brusqueness, Conan's first urge was to fling his reward money into the pool at Mishrak's feet. Raihna's hand on his arm arrested the gesture, giving wisdom the time to prevail.

Why offend Mishrak, if he was in truth going to seek justice for Khadjar, rather than merely drag him to the executioner? Nor was there much Conan could do about it, if Mishrak was determined otherwise.

Others might have use for Mishrak's gold, even if the Cimmerian did not care to let the blood-price for Yakoub soil his fingers. Dessa, Bora and his family, the Hyrkanians who had guarded so faithfully and so carefully—he could find ways for every last brass of Mishrak's money if he wished.

Conan thrust the heavy bag into his belt pouch and held out his arm to Raihna. "Shall we take our leave, my lady?"

"With the greatest of pleasure, Captain Conan."

They did not ask Mishrak's leave to go, but his guards made no obstacle to their leaving. Conan still did not feel his back safe until they had left not only Mishrak's house but the Saddlemaker's Quarter itself behind them.

Raihna drank from the same well she'd used as she led Conan toward Mishrak's house, what seemed months ago. Then she wiped her mouth with the back of her hand and smiled for the first time since they reached Aghrapur.

"Conan, did I once hear you say you preferred to embrace me unclothed?"

The Cimmerian laughed. "When there's a bed ready to hand, yes."

"Then let us spend some of Mishrak's gold on that bed!"

They spent all of two nights and much of the day between in that bed, and little of that time sleeping. It was still no great surprise to Conan when he awoke at dawn after the second night, to find the bed empty.

It was some days before Conan had time to think of Raihna or indeed any woman. There was gold to be sent to Bora, Dessa, Pyla, Rhafi, and a half-score of others. There was a new sword to be ordered. There was a good deal of laziness to be purged from his company, although the sergeants had done their best.

When all this was in train, he had time to wonder where Raihna might have gone. He also had time to consider what might have become of High Captain Khadjar. In the time Conan had known the man, Khadjar never let more than three days pass without a visit to his men. Now it was close to six days. Was there a way to ask, without betraying the secrets of his journey into the mountains?

Conan had found no answer by the morning of the eighth day. He was at the head of his company as they returned from an all-night ride, when a caravan trotted past. Through the dust, Conan saw a familiar face under a headdress, bringing up the rear of the caravan.

"Raihna!"

"Conan!" She turned her horse to meet him. Conan slowed his men to a walk, then reined in.

"So you're a caravan guard in truth. Where bound?"

"Aquilonia. I still cannot return home to Bossonia,

until there is a price paid in blood or gold. But in Aquilonia, I might earn some of that gold, selling my sword. Also, Illyana's father has kin among the nobility of that realm. Some might feel that Illyana's friend for ten years had some claim on them."

"You'll still need luck."

"Who knows that better than I? If I don't have it, perhaps I can still find a home in Aquilonia. Some widowed merchant must be in need of a wife."

"You? A merchant's wife?" Conan tried to keep his laughter within the bounds of manners. "I won't say that's as against nature as Dessa's being faithful, but—"

"I've had ten years on the road with Illyana, and more of them good than bad. Now—well, I find I want to know where my bones will lie, when it comes time to shed them."

"That's a desire that never troubled me," Conan said. "But the gods know, you deserve it if you want it. A swift and safe journey, and—"

"Oh, Conan!" She slapped her forehead, already caked with road dust. "The sun must have already addled my wits. Have you heard about Houma and Khadjar?"

Conan's horse nearly reared as his grip on the reins tightened. "What—what about them?"

"Houma is no longer one of the Seventeen Attendants. He has resigned because of ill-health and given large donations to the temples."

"Large enough that he'll have to sell some of his estates, I'd wager."

"I don't know. I only heard what the criers said in the streets this morning. But it would surely make sense, to cut the sinews of Houma's son as well as Houma."

Conan thought that Houma's son would need cutting in other and more vital places before he was worth anything. But his company was almost past, and he had yet to hear about Khadjar.

Raihna read the question in his eyes. "This I only heard in the soldiers' taverns, but all were saying the same thing. Khadjar has been promoted to Great Captain of Horse and goes to Aquilonia, to see how they fight upon the Pictish frontier. Some of the soldiers were angry, that the Aquilonians or any other northerners can teach the riders of Turan anything."

"I'd not wager either way." Conan also would not wager either way about the truth of the rumor. Khadjar might have been sent to Aquilonia, but would he reach it alive? If he did, would he survive learning how to fight Picts?

Still, it counted for something that Mishrak wanted men to think Khadjar had been honored and sent on a mission of trust. Perhaps Khadjar really *had* gone to Aquilonia—while Mishrak carefully removed all of his and Houma's allies from power, if not from the world. Perhaps promotion would keep Khadjar loyal hereafter, so that his gifts need not be lost to Turan.

Nothing certain anywhere, but that was no surprise. The world seldom was, at the best of times.

No, one thing was certain.

"Raihna, a bed doesn't feel quite the same without you in it."

"How long do you expect that to last, Cimmerian?"

"Oh, as much as another ten days—"

She aimed a mock-buffet at his head, then bent from her saddle and kissed him with no mockery at all.

"Whatever you seek, may you find it," she said. She put spurs to her mount and whirled away up the road toward her caravan.

Conan sat until Raihna was altogether out of sight. Then he turned his own mount's head the other way and spurred it to a canter. It would never do for the new High Captain of mercenaries to think that Conan the Cimmerian would neglect his men as soon as Khadjar's eye was no longer upon him!

THE BEST IN FANTASY

☐ 53954-0 SPIRAL OF FIRE by Deborah Turner Harris $3.95
  53955-9   Canada $4.95

☐ 53401-8 NEMESIS by Louise Cooper (U.S. only) $3.95

☐ 53382-8 SHADOW GAMES by Glen Cook $3.95
  53381-X   Canada $4.95

☐ 53815-5 CASTING FORTUNE by John M. Ford $3.95
  53826-1   Canada $4.95

☐ 53351-8 HART'S HOPE by Orson Scott Card $3.95
  53352-6   Canada $4.95

☐ 53397-6 MIRAGE by Louise Cooper (U.S. only) $3.95

☐ 53671-1 THE DOOR INTO FIRE by Diane Duane $2.95
  53672-X   Canada $3.50

☐ 54902-3 A GATHERING OF GARGOYLES by Meredith Ann Pierce $2.95
  54903-1   Canada $3.50

☐ 55614-3 JINIAN STAR-EYE by Sheri S. Tepper $2.95
  55615-1   Canada $3.75

Buy them at your local bookstore or use this handy coupon:
Clip and mail this page with your order.

Publishers Book and Audio Mailing Service
P.O. Box 120159, Staten Island, NY 10312-0004

Please send me the book(s) I have checked above. I am enclosing $_____
(please add $1.25 for the first book, and $.25 for each additional book to
cover postage and handling. Send check or money order only — no CODs.)

Name _____

Address _____

City _____ State/Zip _____

Please allow six weeks for delivery. Prices subject to change without notice.